Pride Publishing books by Peter E. Fenton

Single Books
The Woodcarver's Model

The Declan Hunt Mysteries
Mann Hunt

I0565731

The Declan Hunt Mysteries

MANN HUNT

PETER E. FENTON

Mann Hunt
ISBN # 978-1-80250-561-0
©Copyright Peter E. Fenton 2023
Cover Art by Erin Dameron-Hill ©Copyright August 2023
Interior text design by Claire Siemaszkiewicz
Pride Publishing

MANN HUNT

Dedication

This book is dedicated to my Calgary friends who have been so supportive of my artistic endeavours.

Chapter One

Even among the younger generation, at fifty-nine, Ian Mann was considered to be an attractive male. At six feet in height, and a lean one-hundred-and-sixty-five pounds, he exuded an undeniable confidence. His long, well-coiffed sandy-brown hair and manicured nails led certain people to question his sexuality but he didn't care what others thought. In fact, he was devoted to his wife of thirty years. He saw himself as the original metrosexual...but one with an edge. He had something that had always left people uneasy — heterochromia. His left eye was grey-green, his right eye, light blue.

Ian had met his wife, Katherine, when he had been living in London. She'd been an up-and-coming fashion model, he, a promising young photographer. They had fallen in love shortly after meeting during a group photo session, and had been married six weeks later.

In London in the nineties, they had been the couple to be seen with. She was beautiful and he had an irresistible charisma. Life for the couple had been filled with parties, drinking and dinners until the day Ian's father had passed away. It was assumed that someone of Ian's social standing would inherit a country estate, or a baronetcy, at the very least. To everyone's shock, Katherine's in particular, what he had inherited was a small industrial complex in the far reaches of western Canada. London's dream couple, the fodder of the paparazzi, had to pull up stakes and move to Calgary, Alberta.

Katherine and Ian had not suffered financially with their move to Calgary. Land speculation and development had taken over as the primary business of Mann Holdings. In the boom years, when the oil industry was at its peak, Ian's company had made a fortune. When he divested himself of control in the company in 2013, holding onto a few properties for sentimental reasons, he'd made even more. When the oil business had collapsed the following year, and people couldn't give away office space, Ian and Katherine were sitting pretty...and hated by many who were forced to sell much of what they had left at bargain-basement prices to cover their essential costs.

But Ian knew how quickly a person's fortune could diminish over time. Now, all that was left was their Mount Royal home, a financially strapped AAA hockey team Ian owned and a factory building, a building that someone had offered to buy at a meeting earlier in the day. He had declined, even though the money was much needed.

Ian had decided not to say anything to Katherine about the offer. He went into his office and backed up the files from his phone to the cloud. As an extra precaution, he also saved them onto a USB stick. Then he tipped up his desk lamp and tucked the stick beneath the hollow base. Once the lamp was back in place, Ian headed down to the front door with his bag and hollered, "Katherine, I'm heading out in a few minutes." It was Ian's night out with the boys. This week was a special celebration and was being held on a Thursday, the night before the Calgary Stampede opened.

"Be right there, darling," Katherine called out. Even after all these years of living in Calgary, her voice still carried the accent of the city in which she had been raised.

Katherine rounded the corner from the living room. Ian admired her appearance. She was tall and slender, with chestnut-brown eyes. Her auburn hair, normally worn long, was twisted into a loose French roll. She wore a cream-coloured dress, accented perfectly by a gold chain with a diamond pendant and exquisite matching earrings.

"Have a wonderful evening," she said, before bending in to kiss him. "Will you be late?"

Ian replied, "I don't think so. No later than usual. You look like you're heading out."

Katherine checked her earrings in the hall mirror. "Last-minute call from Deirdre. A friend of hers is in town and she decided to host a cocktail party for him."

"I hope he's old and ugly, so you won't be tempted," Ian said.

Katherine smiled. "I wouldn't worry. I'd be more concerned by the fact that Michael's back from college."

Michael was Deirdre and Simon Taylor's twenty-year-old son. A handsome athlete, debate team leader and, if rumours were true, in the running for a Rhodes Scholarship. Ian had joked about Michael being just Katherine's type.

Katherine turned to Ian. "Deirdre was sorry that you couldn't make it tonight, but I told her that your boys' nights out are sacred."

"You are a doll," he said as he leaned in to kiss her. "See you later."

With that, he grabbed the handle of his suitcase and wheeled it out to the garage.

* * * *

Ian loved his boys' nights out and tonight's was the perfect antidote to the unpleasant meeting he'd had earlier in the day. At the party Ian observed his usual rituals, saw the usual people and as always, avoided drinking so he was totally in control. When he looked at his watch, he was surprised at the time. It was late and he had to get home. He changed into his street clothes, bade the rest of the party-goers adieu and trundled his suitcase back to the car. He pressed the button on his key fob to open the trunk and was about to stow away his bag when a voice from the shadows said, "You come here often?"

Ian jumped.

"Jesus, what the fuck are you doing here?" Ian snapped.

"Just being curious, I guess. Just wondered what you got up to in your spare time."

"I don't appreciate being stalked. What do you want?"

"You know what I want!"

"We've talked about this before."

The figure pulled a knife out of his coat pocket.

Ian saw the uncertainty in his assailant's eyes. "I can't do anything about this right now, but tomorrow, I'll call you and give you what you want."

The attacker lowered his knife slightly. Ian talked, soft and slow, saying what he knew his attacker wanted to hear. He finished with, "I promise."

"You'd better be telling the truth," the assailant said as he spit his gum out on the drive and disappeared back into the shadows.

Ian started shaking. *I've got to get home. Katherine will be worried.* His trunk was open and his suitcase was still sitting on the ground. He put his bag in the trunk and drove down the driveway, through the gates as they opened and out onto the main access road.

A figure stepped out of the shadows and flagged him down.

What does he want now? he thought. He lowered his window and said, "I'll deal with this tomorrow."

Then Ian realised that something wasn't quite right.

A voice said, "I don't believe you. Give me the keys."

"What?"

"The car keys. Give me your car keys!" the attacker snapped, reaching in the window and grabbing onto Ian's hair. It was then that Ian saw the gun.

His heart pounded as he pulled the keys out of the ignition and handed them over with a shaky hand.

"Out of the car. Now!"

As soon as he stepped out, Ian was grabbed and dragged towards the back of the car. The trunk lid popped open. The man tore off the emergency trunk lid release tab before saying, "Get in."

"Where are you taking me?"

"Get in and you'll find out."

Ian climbed into the trunk and curled himself into a protective ball as the lid slammed shut. He was in total darkness. His suitcase, which contained all of the objects of the beautiful aspect of his life, pressed painfully into his back. The engine roared and the car reversed, then sped ahead. Every turn, corner, pothole and stop sent him ricocheting around his tight prison cell. As the car bounced on a particularly deep rut, his head hit the hinge of the trunk and blood trickled down his face.

The car came to an abrupt stop and the driver's side door opened, then closed. The trunk lid popped open.

He wasn't sure where he was. It was remote, and in the distance he could hear water running.

"Get out."

Ian's limbs felt heavy and he was having trouble disentangling himself from the suitcase and other items in the trunk.

The man said, "Now, I hope you know I'm serious about this. Are you going to give me what I want?"

Something inside Ian snapped. For once, he wanted things to go his way. He stared directly at his attacker and said, "No, you will not get what you want. And you will pay for this. I'll go to the papers and tell them everything."

Then Ian started to run. He got twenty feet before his left foot caught on a tree root and he fell. He looked back and could see that his assailant was nearly on top of him.

Ian curled his legs beneath him, and with every last ounce of strength, launched himself directly at his attacker, driving his head into the assailant's stomach and knocking the wind out of him. Ian turned around and started to run past his car and along a trail which seemed to head towards a street lamp.

He got no more than fifty feet down the path when the man tackled him from behind. He landed with a crack. Ian looked up into the sky. *So many stars*, he thought. *So many...*

When Ian came to, he felt as if he were floating. His head throbbed and he couldn't see out of his left eye. His brain swam in a sea of confusion. He was naked. None of this made sense. Ian tried to stand up but his legs wouldn't oblige. He was surrounded by water. His brain shouted messages of *danger* and *get to safety*, but his body failed to cooperate. The cold water felt good. It eased the pain. The trees and stars above swirled as he thought, *I used to like swimming*. Then he descended into blackness.

Chapter Two

Declan Hunt glanced down at his coat, frayed at the edges and covered with grime. His toes poked through the ends of his shoes, and as he stumbled along the street, he swerved around the people who walked past him. Occasionally he mumbled an apology. It was around two in the morning and the part of the block he walked down was poorly lit thanks to three burnt-out street lamps.

He leaned up against a lamppost and pulled a cigarette out of his pocket, holding it in his shaking left hand. He tried to light it but the match went out before the cigarette was lit. A large man was moving along the street towards him. He was tall — about six-foot-two — and built like a brick wall.

"Hey, buddy — got a light?" Declan asked.

Brick Wall stopped and looked at him, then pulled out a fancy gold lighter, lit it and held it up to the partially smoked cigarette.

"Thanks."

Brick Wall grunted an acknowledgement then walked farther along the street, entering a building a few doors down.

As soon as the man was out of sight, Declan stubbed out the cigarette and put the butt back into his coat pocket. He didn't normally smoke, and at fifteen bucks a pack, he wasn't going to just throw one away. It might come in handy later.

After a few moments, he headed towards the building where the guy had gone in. It was a two-storey wood-framed structure that looked like an old store that had gone out of business. How this building had escaped the wrecking crew was anybody's guess. On one side of it was a smart little bistro. On the other, a condo was going up. An alleyway separated the old store from the construction site.

How convenient.

Declan hurried around the corner and down the alleyway. The wall of the building was punctuated by a single window, too high to reach. A small dumpster had been pushed up against the wall under the window, right next to a door.

He hoisted himself up, making as little noise as possible, and levered himself high enough to look in.

Inside, Brick Wall was talking to another guy seated at a desk. Declan couldn't see the face of the second man as his back was towards the window. The two of them seemed deep in conversation and the man who was sitting gesticulated wildly with his hands. Brick Wall took him by the shoulder and led him out of view. Declan surveyed the room. It appeared to take up the entire first floor. On a table along the back was a large model of a grand old building. Other than the desk and the table with the model, the space was empty.

Declan leaned a little farther to the left to get a better view. Suddenly the building was moving upward and he was heading down. His body hit the dumpster lid with a sound like a mallet pounding on a giant kettle drum. As the dumpster continued to roll, he blinked to clear his vision, only to see the high-mounted alleyway lights and the face of Brick Wall staring down at him.

"Whadda we got here?" he asked. "A little late to be sightseeing."

Declan rolled himself off the dumpster and hit the pavement. He had intended to run, but before he could get to his feet, Brick Wall had grabbed him by the jacket and hoisted up his one-hundred-and-eighty-five pounds without effort, then slammed him back down on the edge of the steel dumpster. Declan crumpled to the pavement.

"A guy's gotta learn not to poke his nose in another fella's business," Brick Wall said, before sending the toe of his sizeable right shoe crashing into Declan's ribs. Several kicks followed before Declan felt himself being picked up again. He heard the sound of the dumpster lid being opened, then fell into a pile of rotting waste as the lid slammed shut and he was surrounded by darkness.

* * * *

Joan Beckerman unlocked the street-level door of the office, picked up the mail that had come through the slot and began the slow walk up the flight of stairs to the second floor. She wasn't sure which creaked louder — the wooden steps or her sixty-eight-year-old knees. She turned the key in the lock and entered the outer office.

Mrs B, as Joan was known in the office, occupied the only desk in the main reception room, along with a couple of comfortable chairs, a couch and a coffee table with *up-to-date* magazines to ensure that no one would confuse this with a doctor's office. She loved this space. It was warm and comfortable. Large, mullioned windows let light pour in from the street. The walls were a deep red-brown brick — rare for Calgary where most old structures were wood-framed. And the floors — wide planked wood, worn by the feet of a thousand people over the seventy-year history of this building. It wasn't old by international standards, but here in Calgary, it was a grand old dame.

She dropped the mail on her desk. There were a couple of bills and an envelope, probably containing a payment — she recognised the return address of the elderly man who had hired them to look for his missing brother. They'd found him buried legally in Queen's Park Cemetery.

Before she could deal with any of these matters, coffee had to be made. Without caffeine, her brain didn't function properly.

As she waited for the coffee to finish brewing, Mrs B tidied her desk for the day. She was, undeniably, an organised woman. As the sole employee of Declan Hunt Investigations, aside from Declan, she was responsible for dealing with the clients, maintaining Declan's schedule, billing and whatever else was required to keep the company going. And for that, organisation was the key to success.

The coffee maker gurgled, letting her know that caffeine was mere moments away. She returned to her desk, coffee in hand — black, two sugars — and sorted the contents of the envelopes. The bills went into one pile, the payment from the man in search of his brother in a second stack. The payment also included a note.

Seeing as how you found my brother deceased, and now of no use to me, I see little reason to pay you the full amount demanded. Enclosed you will find a cheque for half your bill.

Mrs B let out a sigh. She had wanted today to go smoothly.

The street door opened, followed by heavy footsteps on the stairs. A man dressed in a long dirty coat entered through the office door. His face was unshaven and grimy. He walked with a limp.

"Good Lord, what the hell happened to you?" Mrs B asked.

Declan paused. "Some people in this city have no respect for the homeless." As Declan straightened his body, he winced and grabbed his side. "Can't take a kick like I used to."

"Did you find Mr Attwal?" she asked.

"Not yet, and I've pretty well run out of leads," he said as he winced again.

She moved towards him. "Here. Let me help you."

Mrs B got him up to his apartment, which occupied the third floor of the building. She helped him take off his coat and shirt. "If it's all right with you, I'll chuck these into the wash," she offered.

"Thanks."

She looked at his strong chest and rippled stomach muscles. While attractive to many, they had no effect on her. The bruising, however… She pursed her lips and inhaled. "Oooo, that's going to hurt tomorrow."

She touched the area. Declan inhaled sharply.

"Oh, come on. I've seen you in worse shape."

"What—no sympathy for the guy who gets beaten up just so *you* can get a paycheque?"

"Stop your whining. Nothing appears to be broken."

"You're a harsh woman, Mrs B."

She walked over to the fridge and took out an ice-pack, which she wrapped in a tea towel and handed to him. "Here. You know what to do."

She went into his bathroom and returned with the first-aid kit.

"Take these," she said, passing him a couple of pills. "Vitamin C might help lessen the bruising which, if I know my beatings, will be spectacular over the next few days. I'll wrap you up to give you some support. But first... You've gotta go shower. You smell like you've spent the night in a dumpster."

"Where do you think they threw me after they did this? It took me an hour to crawl out after I came to."

Declan went into the bathroom and had a shower. By the time he had finished, Mrs B had laid clothes out for him on the bed. She returned with a coffee.

"It has sugar in it. I figured you could use the energy."

He took it from her and had a sip. She stood there, trying to figure out how to break the news to him.

"You're a lifesaver. I don't know what I'd do without you," Declan said, as he eased himself down onto the edge of the bed.

Mrs B paused, then said, "Well, now that you mention it... I guess there's no point in beating around the bush."

"I wouldn't expect you would."

"You remember how I told you my daughter and her friend were going on a three-week trip to South America?"

"Yeah, I think so," Declan replied, taking another sip of his coffee.

"Well, it seems her friend tripped over her cat, and somehow fell out of her window."

Declan choked and hot coffee shot up and out through his nose. "Ow, ow, ow," he cried.

"Luckily she lived on the second floor, so she only broke her leg." Mrs B shook her head.

Declan mopped his face with his towel. Mrs B took it from him and proceeded to use it to clean the floor. As she got up, her legs began to buckle and she steadied herself against a chair.

"Are you okay?"

"I'm fine. Anyway, I got a call from my daughter last night, all in tears because of her vacation. Well, it was — look, she asked me to go with her in her friend's place and I said yes."

She stared at him, waiting for a reaction. "Well, I couldn't let her go on her own, could I?"

"And when does this happen?" Declan asked.

"I leave Sunday."

"Sunday? Like this Sunday? Two days from now Sunday?"

"That would be Sunday. So, you'll need to hire a replacement for me for the time I'll be away."

"Well then" — he seemed to be piecing things together — "would you call a temp agency and see what they can do?"

"You're not going to be using one of those companies. They charge an arm and a leg, and the poor temp only sees a fraction of it. Anyway, I've already placed an ad on one of those job-search websites. They'll send you a list of the top ten candidates with interview times starting on Monday."

"Monday?"

"No need to thank me. I'm only doing my job. Now I'd better leave you to rest."

She left Declan, who was staring out of the window with a hurt expression on his face.

He'll get over it, she thought. *After all, it's only three weeks.*

Chapter Three

Charlie Watts woke up from a crappy, late afternoon nap. It was another crappy sleep in a long line of crappy sleeps he'd had since moving out of his small, under-furnished bachelor apartment and back into his old room in his parent's basement in Brentwood. It might have been fine when he had been taking classes at the nearby University of Calgary, but as a grown man, it just wasn't cutting it.

Since graduating from university with a major in IT-Systems Development and a minor in psychology, Charlie had been working a string of low-paying internships which had led to high praise but no job offers. The IT industry seemed to be a revolving door of interns. Why would they hire someone full-time when they could just cycle through high-tech student drones? At twenty-four, Charlie was beginning to wonder if a full-time, permanent job was the twenty-first-century version of the unicorn.

It had been four weeks since he had returned home—four weeks since his birthday—and his world was shrinking. Aside from his friend Carrie, he had no social life, and he couldn't fully realise his social potential because he hadn't gotten around to telling his parents he was gay.

He'd gotten so desperate to live out his non-existent gay life that, when the plumbing in the downstairs bathroom had started to act up the previous week and his parents had called in a plumber, Charlie had followed up their call with one of his own. He had informed them that his parents were terrified of older men coming into their house—he claimed they had been bound, gagged and robbed by a fifty-year-old cable repairman. The company had assured him that they would send out Mitch, a young, very competent plumber to deal with the issue, and they had also assured him that Mitch was very sensitive and good at dealing with seniors. Charlie's fulsome fantasies of a well-muscled tradesman playing with his pipes were dashed when he was introduced to the plumber, a thirty-year-old woman named Michelle—Mitch, for short.

"Charlie-boy, dinner's ready," his mother yelled from upstairs.

"Fuck," he muttered to himself.

"Now!" his dad yelled even louder. He was obviously no happier about the return of the prodigal son than Charlie was. "And don't forget to wash up."

What am I, five?

He swung by the bathroom with its newly repaired plumbing and washed his hands. As he did, he glanced in the mirror. A kid with a triangular face, wispy blond hair and jade-green eyes stared back at him. The guy in the mirror was cute, if maybe a bit gangly. Wiry, his grandmother had called him. It wasn't that he was without muscle… It was just that little of it had made it north of his waist. The way he saw himself was all thighs and ass with a series of twigs sticking out from his narrow upper trunk. Charlie and the wispy kid in the mirror locked eyes on each other. What did *he* think of the 'real-world Charlie'? Did the mirror-kid find him attractive, or did he just see a geek?

I've got to get out of here and find a job. Now!

* * * *

As soon as Charlie had finished his mother's traditional Friday-night dinner of meatloaf with gravy and canned peas, he pushed himself back from the table. "I'm going to go out for a bit."

"Going to meet up with some of your friends?" his mother asked.

"Yeah — some friends," he replied without enthusiasm, as he began to leave the room.

"Maybe a nice girl?" she added hopefully.

"I'm sure there'll be one there."

As he walked down the hall he heard his father call out, "Don't forget to say goodbye to your gran."

He pivoted on his heel and headed towards the rear of the house. His father always reminded Charlie to visit her before he went out, sounding like he strongly expected one of them not to be around by the end of the day.

Elsie Watts, Charlie's grandmother, looked nowhere near her seventy-eight years. She had brightly dyed red hair, green-flecked hazel eyes and perfectly applied makeup that highlighted her strong cheekbones. She occupied the large back bedroom of the house which had been set up as a bed-sitting room, complete with a comfortable easy chair and a large-screen television. She had moved in a few years earlier after falling and breaking a hip. She was fine now, but Maggie and Ted always fussed over her like she was a combination of a china doll and a needy child. She was one of Charlie's best friends.

"Hi, Gran. How's your day been?" he said, bending down to give her a kiss on the cheek. He moved her TV tray and the remnants of her dinner off to the side and plunked himself on the floor beside her.

"Oh, you know this place — it's been a bucket of laughs."

"Solve the mystery yet?" he asked, indicating the television which was playing a British detective show.

"Third character in did it...as usual. The writers must think we're all a bit dense not to pick up on that."

"And Constable Winslow will always wander off in mid-interrogation to take a phone call," Charlie added, laughing.

"And they always manage to get his shirt off at least once an episode."

"Thank God," Charlie added, without any reservation. He smiled. This was the only place where he felt safe. He had never told Gran that he was gay. She had always sort of known it and, when she had brought it up in conversation, she hadn't seemed to be enquiring, only stating a fact, like that he had blond hair.

"So, I heard you were going out."

Charlie nodded.

"Then stop wasting your valuable time with an old lady, and get moving. Go find your own Constable Winslow. I dare you."

Charlie popped up onto his feet. "Love you, Gran."

He bent down and gave her another kiss on the cheek. He turned to leave when she interrupted.

"Oh, here. I have something for you."

Charlie turned. Her hand was extended towards him. She held up two twenty-dollar bills.

"Gran…" he said, reprovingly.

"Go on. Buy yourself and the constable a pint on me."

"I don't drink anything that expensive."

"Maybe *he* does. Now go."

She shooed him out like a fly, both of them laughing.

* * * *

Charlie wandered down 17th Avenue with his closest friend, Carrie Wallace. They had met in Charlie's second-year Introduction to Social Psychology course and soon become inseparable. Carrie was the only person, other than Gran, who knew for certain that Charlie was gay. She was sympathetic to his frustration with living back at home and had taken him out to try and drown his sorrows.

They had started at the Crown and Anchor Pub with a few pints and bar-hopped their way to the bright red and blue neon sign of the Wild Rose Saloon. They'd snuck in through an exit to the tent set up for the throngs of tourists in for the Calgary Stampede known best for its world-famous rodeo. After several shooters, they were feeling no pain. Carrie clutched Charlie's arm as if she were trying to stop him from floating away.

"I think I gotta call it quits," she said. "When the patio lights get this swirly, it's time to go home."

"Noooo," Charlie sang out. "One more drink. Pleeeeeease," he begged.

"I am way too drunk. Thank God I'm working the evening shit tomorrow."

Charlie burst out laughing. "Haaaaaa—you said shit."

"I did not!"

"You did too! You did, you did, you did."

"Oh shut up," Carrie countered, then gave him a big, sloppy, tongue-filled kiss, which Charlie returned in kind.

"You know what I love about you?" Charlie slurred as he held her.

"Is it my beautiful wavy black hair? My perfect nose? My copper-coloured eyes? How about my luscious lips?"

"All of those, but what I really love is that you tolerate me," Charlie replied. "We're perfect for each other... If only you were a guy."

"Can't help you there, sweet man. Anyway, I'm grabbing an Uber, which I will hopefully not vomit in on the way home. One more of those and I'm banned for life." She thought for a moment. "Can you imagine? I'd have to lower myself to taking cabs like the other puking drunks?" She grabbed his face and kissed it again. "Look what's become of me!"

"You look great to me, my love. Now, you take your magic carpet ride home. I've got one more stop before I return to prison."

They stepped out onto the street and Charlie waited with Carrie until her ride showed up. He walked a few blocks then hailed a cab, giving the driver instructions to get to his last stop of the night.

Ten minutes later, Charlie got out of his cab and stepped into Bar-None. He admired the huge space with its wooden floors, polished over the years by many feet and grit from the streets—wood that was washed cleaner, but not entirely clean, by some poor, nameless staffer, who everybody called the Kid. The name was more of a job title than an epithet—sometimes it was a young, muscled blond, sometimes a young skinny brunette. He was responsible for maintaining some level of cleanliness in order to keep the health board happy. The clients didn't care. Today's Kid, a short, shaved-headed tough, walked by Charlie and headed towards the toilets with a box of urinal cakes and the ubiquitous pail filled with bleach and water. Without looking back, the Kid shouted a general announcement, "Toilets are being washed in a minute. Use 'em now or forever hold your pees." The Kid laughed at his own joke. Two guys at the bar did the math in their heads, then, just to be safe, slid off their stools and headed off to relieve their bladders.

Charlie had only been here a few times before. He found a seat at the bar, recognising the bartender on duty. His name was Mickey. Charlie loved his short black, textured hair with rainbow highlights. He wore an unbuttoned plaid shirt, open to the waist showing off his hairy muscular chest, and tight jeans that left nothing to the imagination.

"Hey, Mickey, how's it going?"

"Pretty good start to the night. The usual for you, Charlie?"

He remembered my name! Oh my God!

"Uh, sure," Charlie replied.

Charlie remained at the bar, casting his gaze around the room, looking for anyone he knew, or someone that he thought he would like to. The men here were old enough to date his father. The thought of that sent chills down his spine.

Charlie's phone chirped. *Probably Carrie checking up on me*, he thought. He glanced at the screen. It showed a new email, but not from Carrie. It was from an employment matching service, one of the tons he'd registered with. He had plugged in his particulars, in as much detail as possible, and the algorithms were supposed to match his skills with suitable jobs on record. He'd finally had a hit. He opened up the email.

Dear Charlie Watts,

It is our pleasure to offer you an interview for the following employment match.

Position: Office and technical manager

Period: Three weeks, commencing immediately

Employer: Declan Hunt Investigations

Please see attachment for full job description.

Charlie got no further before he let loose with a loud, unflattering laugh, and started to choke on his beer. That night's Kid was behind him in a moment, and slapped him on the back. Mickey was there a second later.

"Are you all right, Charlie?" Mickey asked. With Mickey in front, and the Kid slapping him on the back, Charlie realised that this was obviously what he needed to do to get attention in a gay bar.

"I'm okay. The beer just went down the wrong pipe."

"Thanks, Kid," Mickey said, letting the Kid know he could halt his assault on Charlie's back. Then, to Charlie, he said, "Take it easy. It's not last call for another hour."

"It's just that I got a job match!" Charlie blurted out, holding up his phone for Mickey to see. "The first one in... Well, forever..."

"Congratulations," Mickey said, as he glanced at the email. "Well, you certainly landed an interesting company."

"Yeah, right? A private investigator! What the fuck do I know about that?"

"It says there that they want an office manager and tech person. Are you organised?"

"Well… Yeah."

"Do you know about tech stuff?"

"I have my degree in it," Charlie responded, his liquor-soaked brain slowly piecing things together. The alcohol combined with the fact that the most beautiful bartender in the world first, knew his name and, second, was talking to him, made the whole world a very unsettled place at that moment.

"And I happen to know that if you get a chance to meet Declan Hunt," said Mickey, who took Charlie's phone away from him, tapped out something on it then returned it with the image of a man on the screen, "you will not be able to stop yourself from coming in your pants."

Charlie looked at the image on the phone. There was a picture of a man, stripped to the waist. Every fibre of the substantial muscles in his arms and pecs were bulging as he carried a man away from a burning car. The hero's perfect body was covered in a sheen of sweat and—Charlie used his fingers to zoom in on the image. His face was that of someone who had seen a hard life. A scar cut across his left eyebrow, dividing it in two, and his nose, which might have been broken at some time, had a slight bend to the left. Charlie scrolled down the image of his body towards his—*oh my God, he has a hard-on!* He could clearly make it out under his jeans. Charlie focused his eyes on the man's face. He had the look of… *Gran—I think I've found my Constable Winslow.*

Charlie set down his phone and sipped his last drink of the night, then got up from the bar.

Mickey winked and said, "Hey, Charlie. Good luck with the job. I got a good feeling about it."

Charlie winked back and said, "Thanks Mickey."

He made his way out onto the street. Charlie wasn't in any mood to go home, so he made one more stop — The Black Bean Eatery, a twenty-four-hour diner known for its cheap coffee, great pie and for being Calgary's destination break-up joint. More relationships were ended at this restaurant than in Vegas.

Charlie ordered a coffee and slice of key lime pie, then he pulled up the email and opened the job description attachment.

Wanted: Office manager for reputable private investigations firm. General duties include client contact, bookkeeping, filing and running errands. Strong computer knowledge an asset. Must be discreet, have a clean criminal record, follow instructions without question and be able to work under stressful conditions.

Charlie re-read the job description. *Strong computer knowledge an asset...*

His knowledge was beyond strong on the computer side of things.

Discreet, and a clean criminal record...

Check. His life was far too boring to have a criminal record and, as far as discretion went, he'd been keeping a big secret his entire life.

Then there was that image of this Hunt guy that was burned into his brain. Imagine spending every day with him...

What the hell? What do I have to lose? He was going to land this job! It would be a lot more exciting than his last internship working for an oil company cleaning up their databases. He grabbed his phone, opened the email he had received at the bar and hit the 'Accept' icon.

Before he got home, he'd received an interview time — Monday, eleven a.m.

Chapter Four

It was Saturday, July ninth — his mother's birthday. Had she still been alive, Declan would have spent the evening having dinner with her. But she wasn't alive, and he'd woken up fuelled by anger. The night before had been punctuated by one of his recurring nightmares — the one where he'd hidden under his bed as his father had yelled at his mother, "You're the reason he's nothing but a God-damned faggot! You and your mollycoddling. This is your fault."

Declan hadn't been able to focus all day and there'd been no further leads on the Attwal case, so he decided to head down to Bar-None. The place was just the way he liked it — empty, except for Mickey tending bar and a couple of old-timers talking to their best friends — the dregs of beer left at the bottom of their near-empty glasses.

Before Declan could say anything, Mickey had placed a tall double-shot vodka and soda on the bar.

"Thanks, Mickey," Declan said.

"Good to see you, Dec." Mickey was one of only a few to call him that and not be corrected. Ever since he was a kid, Declan had hated that nickname. Dec Hunt had quickly morphed into the juvenile moniker De-cunt, which even more rapidly morphed into Declan's fist connecting with whoever had said it. They'd quickly learned that they could only make that joke once. Mickey always said *Dec* with overtones of friendship and a smile that came across as a visible hug. Declan liked that, and on many days needed it.

The detective took his drink and headed off to his regular corner table where he sipped and watched. He'd been coming here since he was legally allowed to drink. A gay bar rarely carded patrons unless they were obviously underage. Even so, if it was crowded, which it usually was after ten o'clock, they ignored the occasional under-eighteen-year-old. Most of them were street kids just looking for a warm place to hang out, or to make a few bucks from a discreet hook-up in the toilet. They weren't hurting anyone, and gay men looked after each other. No one else did, and that was why Declan was in business—Calgary's only openly gay private investigator. He hoped his mom would be proud of him.

He raised his glass. "Happy Birthday, Mom."

* * * *

Time was a blur. Declan had polished off several drinks. He made his way back to the bar, slightly glassy-eyed.

"Another?" Mickey asked.

"I'm done for the night," Declan slurred.

Mickey rang up the bill and took Declan's credit card, which he tapped. Mickey knew Declan would have a hard time with the buttons, so he usually did it for him, and he never gave himself more than a fifteen-percent tip.

"You're not driving tonight, I hope?" he asked.

"Nope. I'm just a short walk away from where I'm headed."

"Good. Now hand them over." Mickey held out his hand. He had a gentle, mothering smile on his face.

"Right," Declan said, handing Mickey his car keys. "I'll see you tomorrow to pick 'em up." He turned to walk away, then stopped. "Thanks."

"For what?"

"For watching out for me. If only I was your type, I'd —"

"Get outta here, Dec, and have fun."

Declan headed out of the door and made a right up the street. He was drunk and on nights like this there was only one place for him to go — The Greek.

* * * *

The Greek, formally known as The Greek Men's Health Spa and Steam Room, was Calgary's largest gay bathhouse. It had been opened in the late 1960s by Spiros Adamos, a Greek émigré who had escaped the actions of the Greek military junta of 1967.

In Adamos' mind, every city needed to have a men's steam room, and Calgary was no exception. Over the decades, the focus of the steam room had shifted from older European men looking for relaxation to younger gay men looking for anonymous sexual release. It was into this world that Declan entered.

"Hey, Declan, good to see you back."

The guy at the desk seemed happy that Declan had arrived. Declan paid him twenty dollars and headed for the locker room.

The smell of male sweat and body odour attacked his nostrils. This was where he started his search for the night. Declan was shopping for just the right body. He opened up his locker and stripped down to a jock strap. His head was dulled by the alcohol. He scanned the small crowd of men heading back out into the real world. Back to their families, their wives and children and the lies.

He checked out the guys who were just arriving — flushed with excitement as they began their own conquests. Declan was surrounded by men peeling off tight jeans and western shirts, cowboy hats still in place — a sign that the Calgary Stampede had truly begun. Some would walk around in hats, boots and a towel. Some, like him, in just a jock strap. Declan wondered how many of them had actually seen a horse, let alone ridden one. This was bathhouse chic, Calgary-style. Tonight, they would be riding something a lot harder and possibly more dangerous.

Declan headed into the dimly lit hall. He passed one cowboy. The guy looked him up and down, raking his chest hairs with his eyes. This cowboy was the real thing. His legs were bowed out from years of riding horses, not like the Kmart cowboys from the locker room. But Declan wasn't in the mood for western today. He continued his hunt down one hall, pausing to look into every open door.

He knew every turn of the hall maze. A newcomer would often tread the same path over and over again. Not him. He never wasted time. It was like a military mission or a bank robbery — get in, get out. He stopped at the open door to room thirty-two. He looked in. There, stretched out on the narrow bed, lay a short, sinewy guy, maybe twenty-five, with a military haircut and a muscular ass that jutted out like a shelf. The guy probably got in with a Military Active Duty discount. But he had the look Declan needed. He looked like a cop.

Following protocol, Declan stepped into the room and waited. If the guy smiled, or nodded, he was in. If he turned his head away, Declan would continue down the hall. The occupant nodded and Declan closed the door.

This guy liked it rough. He was strong, but no match for Declan's muscles — even after the vodka. They played like a couple of dogs trying to assert dominance. They sniffed each other, licked the other's heavily scented pits, and their tongues probed every orifice. Finally, as the guy began to tire, of the game at least, Declan, normally a bottom, took the dominant position, pushing the guy's head into the thin pillow. On nights like this, Declan needed to be in control.

He slid a condom over his thick cock. He preferred to bareback, but he didn't know where this guy had been. He might eat food that fell onto his own kitchen floor, but he never ate off a stranger's.

He penetrated him quickly. When Declan was in a mood like this, he went in fast and furious, fucking him hard. When he was spent, Declan pulled out, and slapped the guy hard on the ass. He left him on the narrow bed looking like a deflated blow-up doll.

After a spell in the steam room where he fended off a couple of suitors, Declan showered, changed back into his clothes and headed for the exit.

* * * *

Luke Fraser sat in his apartment, a two-bedroom condo in the Beltline district of Calgary. It was a nice building, well kept up and only a five-minute drive from an off-track betting establishment that showed the races.

It was looking like another night alone, which made no sense to him. He was perfect—five-foot ten, and a hundred and ninety pounds of muscle with short strawberry-blond hair, a dimpled chin and dark-blue eyes. He would have been at home on the cover of a high-end fashion magazine. Why was he still single? He just wanted to find himself a partner, someone he could share his life with—a lover and a friend. He'd tried hard, but hadn't had any luck.

It was true—he could be opinionated at times, and maybe that came across as too pushy, but for whatever reason, he was just plain lousy at meeting men in gay bars. The one guy he used to play darts with had dumped him because he said that Luke was too competitive and was a sore loser. There was a guy out there for him, but where?

It was his first full weekend off in months, and he wasn't about to spend it alone. Luke wasn't in the mood for shopping on Grindr. He wanted to see what was on offer in person, so it was off to The Greek.

He parked his car on the street six blocks away, in front of a busy restaurant. He didn't want to take the chance of anyone spotting it near the bathhouse. Luke walked the rest of the way there, always aware of who else was on the street.

As he approached the doors to The Greek, a handsome, dark-haired man careened out of the exit and stumbled into his arms. Their combined momentum caused them to rotate on the spot, like two dancers. For a brief moment, as they spun, they locked eyes on each other and the previously sullen man's face broke into a wide, beautiful smile before he whirled Luke out onto the deserted street where the dance ended.

"I am so sorry," Luke offered.

"Why? It was the best dance I've had all night."

The guy gave Luke a kiss on the cheek, detached himself and continued on his way.

Luke watched him weave his way down the street. There was something about this beautiful, drunken man that sent a small shockwave through his body.

Chapter Five

Declan tumbled out of bed Sunday morning after another restless sleep. He had thought his night at The Greek would have helped, but there'd been more bad dreams. They seemed to be coming more frequently.

Declan decided he could afford to skip his daily workout. He stood in the shower letting the stream of hot water pelt his body. He looked down and saw the deep purple and blue bruises on his torso from Friday night's altercation. Declan admired the guy who'd done this. He knew what he was doing — making a point to be remembered. A lesser man would have just killed him, but killing led to bodies, and bodies led to the police. It was too high a price to pay for people like Brick Wall.

Declan finished his shower, slowly dried off and dressed. Then he made his way down to his desk and sipped a coffee. His cell phone rang and he was tempted to let it go to voicemail until he saw the name of the caller — Attwal.

Saanvi Attwal had approached him several days earlier. Her husband, Palvinder Attwal, had been kidnapped. He was a well-known accountant in Calgary who, unofficially, handled the accounts of some of the less reputable members of Calgary's "business" world.

Obviously, she couldn't go to the police with this matter, and Declan had a reputation for discretion and results.

Declan answered, "Good morning, Mrs Attwal."

"Mr Hunt," she said, as if he had been the one to call her.

"I haven't found him yet. I looked into one possibility Friday night," he said, "but there was no sign of your husband. Have they been in contact with you since we last spoke?"

"They have," she answered coldly. "They called last night before supper. They said that if I didn't turn over all of the files my husband had relating to them, that their relationship with him would be terminated —"

Declan suspected that the business relationship would not be the only thing that was terminated.

" —and that if they found out that I had withheld or copied any files, they would make sure that my whole family would be *disappeared*."

"That's the word they used? Disappeared?"

"Disappeared. That is what the man said."

"And do you know where the files are?" Declan asked.

"On his computer, of course. Did you think he would keep records like that on paper?"

"If they just require the computer files, why don't you just turn over your husband's computer to them?"

"Because *all* of Palvinder's client files are on that computer. Really, Mr Hunt, I'm beginning to doubt that I chose the right man for the job."

Declan hated being treated like a child.

Saanvi continued, "The computer contains accounts of a number of his clients, some of whom are undoubtedly competitors of the men who are holding Palvinder. My husband and his clients would prefer not to have these files turned over to them. It would not be good for…business…or Palvinder."

"I can understand that. Can you access the contents of the computer and remove the other accounts?"

"Do you think I wouldn't have already done that if I could? The computer is protected."

Declan thought for a moment. "Mrs Attwal," he said, "I believe I can get in touch with people who can break into that computer and remove all but the kidnappers' files. Would you be able to get it here to my office?"

From the pause on the line Declan could sense her weighing her options.

"It would be best if I didn't come to your office," she said. "And you shouldn't come here, just in case my house is being watched. I will have the computer brought to you by someone I trust. You will have it in the next few hours."

"Good. Now, how would I recognise the files that belong to the kidnappers?"

There was another pause on the line. "Search for the word 'Monarch'."

She hung up. Now, all that he had to do was find someone who could crack the security on the computer.

He pondered his options and searched through contacts he could trust, but none were suitable for the job. Two hours had passed when Declan heard the ground floor door open then light footsteps coming up the stairs. There was a gentle knock.

When Declan opened the office door, there was a young girl, no more than ten, standing in front of him. She wore a backpack emblazoned with a ladybug. She walked past Declan, over to the couch and removed her pack.

"Mr Hunt?" she asked.

"Yes. That's me."

"Thought so."

She opened up her pack and pulled out a very heavy laptop and power adaptor, which she placed on the coffee table. Then she zipped up her pack, put it back on and left the office, closing the door behind her.

Declan smiled, took the laptop into his office and plugged it in. He looked it over. Declan was not a technical person, but even he could tell that this was no off-the-shelf machine. There were no identifying maker marks on the matte-grey chassis. This was a custom-built job. Military grade.

He opened it and immediately spotted a problem. He picked up the phone and placed a call.

"You got the computer?" Mrs Attwal said as soon as she answered.

"I did, but there's a problem. It requires someone's fingerprint to access it."

"Oh?"

"Do you know anyone, other than your husband, who might have a fingerprint registered on this computer?"

"No. It would only be Palvinder's."

She paused for a moment. "But not to worry. I will deal with it."

Declan asked, "How?"

But it was too late. She had already disconnected.

What the hell is she going to do?

* * * *

Saanvi Attwal waited by the phone. She prided herself on being a strong, take-control person. She reviewed the facts. One—under no circumstances would her husband divulge one of his client's secrets to another. She knew he would never turn over the computer to them. Two—she knew that without him, the computer could not be opened. Three—she knew she could not bear to see anything happen to that silly old fool. Four—she could do nothing to hurt him.

The phone rang. The display said *Unknown number.*

"Hello."

"Well? Do you have the computer files?"

"I…I am working on it. I must speak to my husband. He's the only one who can make this happen. Please. Just for a minute."

There was a long pause. She heard a scraping sound, like something being dragged. Then—

"Saanvi? Is that you?"

"Yes, my silly old man. I have no time. The computer—it requires your fingerprint to open it."

"My dear wife, you have been so strong through this whole ordeal. I will take care of everything. Give the children my love."

The call was disconnected.

* * * *

A large man yanked the phone away from Palvinder Attwal. "Is she going to give us the computer?" he asked.

"No. She is far too smart for that. We both know that if you get it, there is no guarantee that I will see the end of the day — your competitors will see to that." Mr Attwal paused. "Look, I understand — this is all about business. And you are wise enough to know that business goes both ways. You need certain files so you can continue to function, and I need other files to stay alive." Mr Attawl chose his next words carefully. "If you let me go, I will return with all of your files and we can agree that our business relationship is at an end. No harm, no foul as they say."

"They say that, do they? I say you don't leave here until I get what my employer wants." The large man shoved him into a tiny room and began to close the door.

"Wait. There is another solution to this problem," the accountant said, then proceeded to explain what could be done.

His screams echoed off the walls as they took him up on his offer, and took a little something extra for their troubles.

Chapter Six

Charlie told himself that he was ready for his interview. He had showered and shaved, dressed nicely, tamed his unruly hair as best he could and managed to find parking. He checked one more time to ensure that all of his support material was still inside the portfolio case that was securely tucked under his arm as he approached the address...one hour early. Luckily there was a street-level café in the building that housed Hunt's office. He would wait there. It would give him time to calm down and collect his thoughts.

He entered the café — *Les Trois Magots*. A little bell announced his arrival, not that the woman behind the counter would have had any difficulty noticing him. It was a small establishment.

"Good morning," she chirped as Charlie closed the door behind him. The woman was small in stature, had curly ash-blonde hair and soft grey-blue eyes. She had a warm smile and creased face that said *I love you, now sit down and eat.* Her name badge identified her as Gwen. Charlie liked her immediately.

"Hi," Charlie said, as he smiled and headed over to the counter. "A large latte and…" He surveyed the array of baked goods. "One of those…please," he added, pointing to a flaky pastry that showed hints of chocolate concealed inside.

"One large latte, and one *pain au chocolat*. Is that for here, or to go?"

"Here, please."

"Have a seat and I'll bring them right to you."

He made his way to a small table in the corner where he could discreetly see who might be heading in for an interview ahead of him. Like any battle, it was important to know who the enemy was. He placed his portfolio case on the table in front of him so he wouldn't forget it.

Gwen was there in a moment with his order. "I think you'll like this," she said of the pastry. "It's my speciality."

"You make them yourself?"

"You bet. I studied in Paris for six years."

"And you ended up in Calgary?"

"Sometimes life has its own plans for us," she said with a smile, then returned to behind the counter.

Charlie sipped his latte and stared out the window. No one had entered or exited the office of Declan Hunt Investigations. He must be the first interview.

He knocked back the rest of the drink. Coffee was probably not the best idea this morning. He already felt the caffeine doing laps around his circulatory system, and he knew that he'd have to pee—but not now. Not when he had the chance to go. His body would wait until mid-interview, then his knee would start to vibrate…like a five-year-old's. He grabbed the pastry, shoved it into his mouth and bit down.

His teeth didn't slice through it. His molars didn't flatten it like a piece of bread. The pastry actually shattered in his mouth, like a glass Christmas tree ornament hitting the floor. His tastebuds were flooded with a burst of flavour as shards of buttery pastry flew through his mouth, across the table and all down the front of his clean white shirt. Then came the wave of chocolate. "Oh, my God!" Charlie covered his mouth, his eyes darting up to see if Gwen had seen him.

"Are you all right?" she asked.

"This," he said, holding up the pastry, "is the best thing I have ever tasted in my life! I bit into it, and it just…shattered in my mouth. You said you made this?"

"I most certainly did, and you have just given me the greatest gift a baker could receive. Thank you. And for that compliment, I'm giving you another one. And don't you dare complain about the calories."

She brought another pastry over and put it down in front of Charlie.

"This is pure alchemy," he said.

Gwen laughed. "So what brings you to this part of the city? I haven't seen you here before."

"I'm applying for a job. Upstairs."

"Oh," she said with a certain inflection which elicited a "What's wrong?" from Charlie.

"Nothing. Nothing at all." She paused for a moment. "But you look pretty young to have much experience in detective work."

"Oh, I'm just going for an office position. Do you know anything about the company? I mean, is it a good place to work? Did you know the person they're replacing? Do you know why they left?"

"Slow down, and eat." She sat down across from him. "I'm not going to be spreading any gossip about the man upstairs. One thing I've learned in life is that when someone tells you something about another person, they're either trying to sell you something you don't need, or trying to stop you from buying something that *they* want. Just go in there and keep an open mind. Be honest, 'cause if you don't, it'll just catch up to you. I'm a pretty good judge of character and you seem like a good kid, so just be yourself, and don't let Declan scare you."

What Charlie heard from Gwen's speech was "I'm not going to spread rumours" and "Don't let Declan scare you." He started to panic then took a bite of the second *pain au chocolat* and the calm washed over his body again.

"So," Gwen interrupted him, "what time's your interview?"

"Eleven."

"Then you'd better go and take advantage of the washroom, brush yourself off and head up there."

Charlie took her up on the offer. Before he left the washroom he brushed off any crumbs remaining on his shirt, fixed his moppish blond hair as best he could and returned to pay the bill.

After the transaction, Gwen handed him a box. "Here. Give these to Declan. If he says anything, tell him I *ordered* you to bring them up. Use those exact words."

"Will do. And thanks for everything. I think I'm as ready as I'll ever be."

"You'll do well. Poke your nose in when you're done and let me know how it went."

"You got it."

"Oh, one more thing," Gwen added. "You may want to take that," she said, indicating his crumb-covered case on the table.

Charlie left the café, portfolio carefully tucked under his arm, and entered the door marked Declan Hunt Investigations.

At the second-floor landing, there was another door stencilled with the name of the company. Below that was a note stating "Just come in." Charlie checked his phone—10:56 a.m. He silenced it, took a deep breath and opened the door.

It was a bright, uncluttered room, toned with warm woods and brick. It was peaceful—so different from the other offices he'd worked at. His heart rate increased. *I would look so good working here!*

He stepped inside and closed the door behind him. Charlie was all alone. What was the protocol in this situation? Should he call out? Maybe he should clear his throat? He looked around to see if there was an obvious place to direct his throat-clearing when Declan Hunt entered from a side door. He was wearing khakis, brown loafers and a snug-fitting white shirt with his sleeves rolled up to below the elbows. His black hair shone like it had just been washed. His strong jaw was covered in a five o'clock shadow. He looked even more handsome than he had in the photograph—if that was possible.

"You must be Charlie," he said, approaching with his hand extended.

"Yes." Charlie took Declan's hand. He had a firm handshake. Charlie's pulse quickened and, to his horror, he started to get an erection. He used the box from Gwen to cover his growth spurt.

"Is that for me?" Declan asked, pointing to the box, smiling.

"What?" Charlie replied, thinking that he was referring to the bulge in his pants.

"The box…"

"Oh… Yes. The lady who runs the café downstairs asked me to bring them up to you."

"That was no lady. She's the devil in disguise," Declan said as he reached forward to take the box, but Charlie was in no position to give it up that quickly.

"I'll just put it here," Charlie said as he walked to the desk, imagining all sorts of things which would deal with his not-so-little problem — thoughts of influenza, injured puppies, seeing his mother naked. That seemed to help.

"You obviously have lovely neighbours," Charlie said, turning, after shifting his portfolio to cover his mid-line issue.

"She's not so much a neighbour, as my landlord…and my stepmother."

"Your stepmother? Wow, and I thought it was bad enough still being at home with my folks at twenty-four — I'm so sorry. That didn't come out right."

Declan smiled. "Don't worry about it. Sometimes we just never quite grow up the way we thought we would. Now, come on. Let's have a talk in my office."

Charlie followed Declan, all the while staring at his firm buttocks, thinking, *You grew up just fine.*

Once they were seated on opposite sides of Declan's desk, Charlie removed two pieces of paper from the portfolio. "Now, Mr Hunt—"

"Please—call me Declan."

"Of course... Declan." Charlie was having trouble controlling his quavering voice. "Here are letters of reference from my previous employers and —"

Declan interrupted, "Rather than spend time talking about what you did in the past, I'd like to focus on what I'd like you to be doing for me in the future."

"Sure," Charlie said, his rehearsed speech now thoroughly derailed.

"You'll be filling in for my regular assistant, Mrs B, who has taken a three-week leave. Most of the work will be standard office duties, scheduling, invoicing, answering enquiries — that sort of thing, which I don't think you'll have any problems with."

"Okay..."

Declan continued, "Now, about the agency — we sometimes deal with confidential cases that involve clients that, shall we say, work outside the law."

"...All right."

"And, you may already know that we specialise in clientele from the LGBTQ2S+ community."

"Of course," Charlie lied. He had not even thought to look up anything about the company other than how hot the owner was.

"So, I assume that won't be a problem with you, given that you'll be on the front line dealing with the clients?"

Charlie replied, "No. Not at all. I get along really well with... Lesbian, gay, bisexual, trans and...plus...people. I, myself, am...gay, that is. Have been for ages."

Please interrupt me and stop me from making an ass of myself.

Declan smiled. "Good. Now — why do you want to work here?"

Because you're hot.

Anything is better than spending more time in my parents' basement.

Did I mention that you're hot?

All of these thoughts screamed through his brain in the split second before he said, "To be honest, I know I can do the job. It seems like it'll use most of the same skills my last six jobs required and I was good at those, but...I thought maybe, just maybe, for the first time I can do something that really matters to *real* people instead of corporate entities. Even if it lasts only three weeks, I'd be grateful for the opportunity."

Declan sat in silence, staring at him.

Charlie rose to leave.

"Hey, where are you going?" Declan asked. "Don't you want to get to work?"

"What?"

"The job is yours, if you want it."

"Don't you need to check my references?" Charlie asked.

"Gwen called up the moment you left her place and gave you the thumbs up. So did Mickey at Bar-None."

"The bartender?"

"Yeah. I trust that guy with my life which, by the way, he's saved a few times. He texted me Friday night and told me you'd be accepting the offer of an interview."

Charlie shook his head in disbelief. "How did Mickey know? I hadn't made up my mind when I was talking to him."

"He's got this thing... He just senses stuff." Declan came out from behind the desk. "So, can you start right away?"

"Yes! But don't you want to see the other candidates for the job?"

Declan smiled. "I cancelled the other interviews."

"Why?"

"A detective learns to trust his gut — and Mickey's. Now, come on. Let me give you a tour, that is if you're still interested in working with me."

"Sure... I mean yes! I'd love to."

"And you're okay to start right away?"

"Absolutely!"

Declan began to show him around. "You've already seen the main office space. That's your desk over there," Declan said, indicating the one Charlie had placed the pastries on. "By the way, if Gwen's offering anything free for me...just say no. I like to pay my own way, even with Gwen."

"It would be a shame to..."

"They're yours. Go wild. Now here," he said, opening a door behind the desk, "is a kitchenette with a coffee maker, espresso machine, fridge, microwave. And your washroom. The client washroom is through the next door out in the main room," he explained.

Declan opened a pantry unit beside the counter. "Now, in this cupboard are the electronics that apparently run the telephone, computers and security system. The manuals are down there." He pointed to a stack of books, still factory shrink-wrapped. "As you can see, neither Mrs B or I had a clue as to how any of that stuff works, which is why nothing is...working. I figure since you're here and you seem to have experience in that sort of thing, you might as well try to get the tech up and running. Just let me know if there's anything that'll affect me directly. I'll deal with any fall-out from Mrs B when she gets back."

Charlie stared in awe at the high-tech jungle. If there was a seventh heaven, this was the eighth.

"All right, so far?" Declan asked.

"Oh, yeah," Charlie replied, smiling.

"Okay then..." Declan placed his hand on Charlie's back and directed him to his chair.

He rotated Charlie to face the computer. With one hand on Charlie's shoulder, and the other on the computer monitor, Declan said, "This...is the computer. Oh..." He pulled off a Post-It note that was affixed to the monitor. "This...is the password. Mrs B always left it here for security reasons. You know, in case she forgot it..." Declan gave him a pat on the shoulder.

"That's it. Good luck." Declan turned to walk away, then turned back. "Play around and see what you can figure out. I'm an idiot when it comes to how this office works. Mrs B would never tell me anything. I think she thought I'd just fuck it up." He paused. "And she was probably right. I'll be in my office if you need anything. If I'm not there, you can find me in my apartment upstairs, just through the green door behind my desk."

Declan smiled and left the room.

Chapter Seven

Charlie sat for a moment, getting his mental bearings. The first thing was to have a look at the computer, to see what secrets it held. He glanced at the Post-It note with the password. Mrs B had an interesting notion as to what constituted a secure password. Hers consisted of a long string of randomly selected letters, digits and symbols. While this was good in theory, it wasn't practical if the only way to remember the password was by attaching a Post-It to the monitor.

Charlie logged on to the machine and changed the password to one that was more appropriate — *CharliesD0main!*. Mrs B would probably have a fit when she came back, but that would be Declan's problem.

A search of the computer revealed the standard office software. The office email — which he opened with Mrs B's same complex password — proved to be far more interesting. In one folder, labelled *Fan Mail*, Charlie was delighted to find a number of romantic propositions — many with photo attachments. It seemed that Mrs B had taken to sending thank-you notes to all of them, even attaching a signed image file of Declan to some of them.

Holy crap – she was trying to set him up!

Next on the list were the IT manuals in the storage cupboard.

When he returned, arms loaded with sealed manuals, he was greeted by the sight of a young boy standing in front of his desk. The child, dressed in a little suit, his black hair neatly combed, stared back at him. He couldn't have been more than ten years old.

"Mr Hunt?" he asked.

"Uh, no. I'm Mr Watts. May I help you?" Charlie replied, slightly confused.

"I have been asked to deliver this to Mr Hunt," the boy said, holding up a small cardboard box.

"Well, Mr Hunt is busy at the moment. I'm Charlie, his assistant. I can take the box for him."

The young boy looked around, appearing to assess the situation and the quality of the business, before saying, "All right."

The boy handed the box to Charlie, then pulled out a piece of paper, which he also passed to him.

"Print your name where it says 'Print', and sign and date the lines next to it where it says 'Sign and Date'," the boy instructed, pointing to the appropriate spaces on the delivery slip.

Charlie noted that the header of the paper read "Attwal Accounting Services". Charlie filled out the sheet and handed it back to the tiny courier who, in turn, tore off his carbon copy and left the office, but not before turning and giving Charlie a huge smile as he waved goodbye.

Charlie shook his head in amusement and proceeded to open the package.

* * * *

Declan sat at his desk trying to get his laptop to respond. It was like waiting in line at a checkout as the person in front was paying for their groceries with loose change. It was excruciating. Time was standing still.

His phone chirped, signalling an incoming text. It was from Saanvi Attwal.

The key will be delivered to your office this morning.

That woman is fast, he thought. *But what does she mean?*

The answer came in the form of a shrill scream from the reception room.

It only took Declan a few seconds to reach Charlie, who was standing, hands clenched to his chest, eyes bugging out from his head. Declan's first reaction was to laugh. He always found it funny when men screamed like little children. But that look of complete terror on Charlie's face…

"Look at me, Charlie!" Declan called out, hoping his voice would distract Charlie from whatever had scared him. It worked. Charlie's head turned so he was staring directly at Declan.

"Charlie…what is it? What happened?" Declan asked.

"The box," Charlie squeaked out, pointing to something on his desk. "It's an…ear?"

"What?" Declan replied, walking towards him. He was close enough now to see into the plain cardboard shipping box. Inside it lay a bloody, severed human ear. Beside it he saw the shipping receipt from Mrs Attwal.

"What has she done?" said Declan, before he realised. "Wait—this can't be right. An ear won't do me any good. I need the finger."

Charlie continued to stare at him in shock.

Declan picked up the box and shook it. From underneath the ear, the distal portion of a human finger rolled out. He picked it up to examine it. Relieved, he said, "Thank God."

Charlie screamed again.

"Charlie, it'll be all right. I can open the computer now that I've got the finger," he said, holding it up for him to see, as rationally as if he were stating that water was wet.

Charlie dropped into his chair.

Declan said, "You'll be all right. Just give me a minute." He returned to his office.

Declan placed the box on his desk, then moved to the wall on the left. He opened a closet door to reveal a large safe which stood as high as his chest. Fiddling with the combination lock, he opened the heavy steel door. Next to his handgun and a few boxes of ammunition sat Attwal's computer.

He took the finger out of the box and ran it over the fingerprint scanner on the laptop. He hoped the finger was fresh enough. If they'd waited too long to get it to him, the fingerprint could have deformed enough that it would be unrecognisable. A second later, the screen came to life and Declan was able to access the computer desktop.

"Does that sort of thing happen a lot around here? Receiving body parts, I mean."

Declan looked towards the door. Charlie stood there, pale and shaking.

"Come here and sit down," Declan said.

Charlie made his way to the chair farthest from the finger but remained standing behind it. Declan pulled a flask out of his desk drawer and poured some amber liquid into a glass.

"Here," he said, giving it to Charlie.

Charlie took a healthy gulp, then coughed up half of it. "Sorry," he wheezed.

"Puppy," Declan said, smiling as he discreetly placed the finger back in the box. "Now, come here," he said, patting the back of his chair. "Sit."

"I am not a dog," Charlie muttered, as he sat in Declan's chair.

"Good boy." Declan put his hand on Charlie's shoulder. He continued, "I need you to do whatever you have to do to disable the fingerprint reader on this machine. I have to be able to boot it up without Mr Attwal's…help."

Charlie worked at the keyboard for a minute before turning to Declan, smiling. "There. That should do it."

"Should, or will?"

"Definitely *will*."

"You're here for a good reason, Mr Watts."

Declan looked at Charlie and saw that the colour had returned to his face. The shock of the finger incident was starting to wear off.

"I want you to search through the computer and locate the data files," Declan said. "The ones I'm interested in will have the keyword 'Monarch'. Either in the folder or file name. Maybe in the contents. I'll be right back."

Declan picked up the small cardboard box and went to the kitchenette where he put the finger and ear in the freezer on ice. He doubted they would be of any use to Mr Attwal at this point but, just in case…

He returned to find Charlie hunched over the keyboard, typing wildly away. He stood, watching. *Did I ever look that young?* Charlie was only eleven years younger than him.

Declan saw Charlie for the first time in his natural environment, where he felt most at ease. His slender fingers sailed across the keys without hesitation. *He's kinda cute.*

"Declan?"

"What?" Declan was startled to find Charlie staring at him.

"I'm done," he said, his mouth in a lopsided smile as he turned the computer screen towards Declan. "The files were encrypted but whoever did this really didn't know too much about data security. The files are all in a folder labelled 'Monarch'."

"Excellent. Now copy all of the other data folders over to… Where could you copy them that would be safe?"

"I have a secure cloud server available, if that would help?"

Declan didn't even try to understand him. "Sounds good. Transfer all of the folders to your…"

"Cloud server?"

"To your cloud server, then completely wipe them from the laptop. I want no one to be able to find them. 'Monarch' should be the only data folder left."

"Got it."

As Charlie worked, Declan texted Mrs Attwal that the laptop was ready for pick up. In a matter of seconds he received a response.

They will be there to pick up the computer soon. Make sure it has only their files on it!

"That woman doesn't believe in wasting time," he said.

He looked up from his phone as Charlie sat back with a satisfied look on his face.

"All done?" Declan asked.

Charlie nodded.

"Now, since you're in computer mode, can you have a look at my laptop? If it runs any slower, I'm going to have to throw it through a wall."

Chapter Eight

Charlie returned to his desk and got to work on Declan's laptop. When he was working on a computer, he felt in control. Two hours, and a few of Gwen's *pains au chocolat* later, Charlie finished with the computer. He was about to return it when the outer door opened. A man entered. He was short, had slicked-back hair, a greasy moustache and a face only a boxer's mother could love. He stood with his hands in his pockets, his eyes scanning the room.

"May I help you...sir?" Charlie enquired.

"I was told to come here and pick up a computer and the contents of a box that was delivered this morning. When you give me that, I'll give you the location of the target," he said.

A momentary rush of fear passed through Charlie's body, then he reminded himself that it was broad daylight outside, and this wasn't a movie. No one was going to take a machine gun from under their trench coat and fill him full of lead.

"If you would care to take a seat, I'll get Mr Hunt for you. In the meantime, would you care for a coffee or a pastry? I can promise they'll change your life."

A few moments later, Charlie knocked on Declan's door before inching it open. Declan was busy reading a thick dossier, and photographs covered the surface of his desk.

"Hi?" the detective said, turning the two-letter word into a paragraph.

Charlie squeezed himself through the partly opened door, then closed it behind him. "Uh, sorry to disturb you," Charlie said in a hushed tone, "but there's a rather rough-looking man out there asking to retrieve the computer and the package we received this morning. He said something about having the location of the target... Whatever that means..."

Declan smiled. "Excellent. Follow me."

As he moved to the door, Declan grabbed Mr Attwal's laptop. "And get the box out of the freezer."

* * * *

Declan stepped into the reception room and saw one of Calgary's toughest enforcers seated in the waiting room with a small cup of espresso and a plate of Gwen's pastries. As instructed, Charlie retrieved the box from the office freezer.

"Sir," Declan said, with a confused smile. "I see that my assistant has made you comfortable."

"You were right. These are great," the enforcer said, waving the pastry around.

"Oh, if you like, you can pick up more from the shop downstairs when you're done here," Charlie said, helpfully.

"My wife'll love 'em. She'll kill me for bringin' 'em into the house, but they won't last a second once she tries one."

Declan got things back on track. "I believe this is what you came for," he said, handing him the machine. "This is the laptop containing only the files you're interested in with Mr Attwal's other client files removed."

"Good. Now, give me the finger," the enforcer replied.

Declan indicated Charlie should hand the box over to the man, who opened it to check the contents.

"This is only the ear. Where's the finger?"

Declan smiled. "Oh, you just have to shake it around. It likes to hide."

The enforcer shook the box, and the finger bounced out from underneath the ear and onto the floor. Charlie gasped so loud that it startled the other two men.

The enforcer picked the finger up. "Wouldn't want that falling into the wrong hands, now would we?" he said. "Wrong hands. Get it? Finger... Hand?"

Charlie grimaced.

"So," Declan continued, "my man here said that you had some information for me."

"Yeah. You can pick up the body at Abel's Wrecking Yard. You know the place?" he said, all the while tossing the finger into the air and catching it.

"I know the place," Declan replied.

"It'll be in the trunk of a red 1970 Dodge Challenger, midway back in the lot."

"Will it still be alive?" Declan calmly enquired.

"Depends on how long you keep me here talking."

"We'd better go, then. Dead bodies don't pay their bills," Declan said.

The man left, but before closing the door, he said, "Thanks for the tip on the pastries. I'm gonna pick up a box."

The door closed and Charlie sat down before his knees gave way. "That man was playing with a human finger! He was just tossing it like he was flipping a coin."

"He was just trying to scare you," Declan said.

"He succeeded!" Charlie's voice was reaching a near-hysterical pitch.

Declan knelt down, took him by the shoulders and looked him in the eyes. "Charlie, you're all right. He wasn't going to hurt you. I wouldn't let anything happen to you. Do you understand? This is part of what I do here. What *we* do here." He felt Charlie's breathing start to slow down. "You're gonna be okay now."

Charlie nodded his head.

"Good. Now, we have a very important job ahead of us. We have to save a man's life."

"Okay," Charlie said weakly.

"You wouldn't happen to have a car downstairs?"

"Yes."

"Good. We'll have to use yours. Mine's parked at Bar-None."

He rushed Charlie to the door and down the stairs. They exited onto the street and Declan asked, "Which way?"

Charlie quickly walked down a side street and led Declan to a small, light-blue, four-door hatchback.

Declan stared at it. "This isn't a car. It's a Chevette!"

"I'll have you know this car was one of the first four-door models of its kind. It's a classic!"

"Okay, let's see if this dodo can fly." He ran around to the passenger door and waited for Charlie to reach over and manually unlock it.

According to the GPS on Declan's phone, it was a fifteen-minute drive from his office in Kensington to Abel's Wrecking Yard on Beaufort Road. He suspected that Charlie had been trained in defensive driving from an early age because it had been nearly twenty-eight minutes and they still hadn't arrived.

"I can understand why they sent the finger, but why the ear?" Charlie asked. Focusing on driving had apparently calmed Charlie's nerves.

"Maybe it was a warning that they have ears everywhere and that we should keep our mouths shut."

"Good to know."

They pulled into the wrecking yard and Charlie followed Declan as he ran into the office. "I'm Declan Hunt. I'm here about a car."

The old man behind the counter answered, "Yeah, I was told you were comin'. Interested in the bright-red Dodge Challenger, I hear. Good car. Couldn't believe someone'd wanna t' scrap 'er. People nowadays, right? Livin' in a disposable world. Not willin' to—"

"I'd love to see it," Declan interjected.

"Pulled it out into the drive, jus' so you could have a look at 'er. Jus' head straight down the main road, first left. Ya can't miss 'er. Left the keys in the ignition."

Declan raced out the door, and down the drive, yelling back to Charlie to bring his car.

The Challenger was just where the old man had said. Declan opened the driver's door. The detective pulled the keys out of the ignition and ran back to the trunk. He calmly slid the key into the lock, and turned it. The trunk lid opened. Inside lay the body of the accountant Palvinder Attwal.

Charlie pulled up, got out of his car and cautiously approached the Challenger.

The man lay on his right side. He was trussed up so tightly Declan was surprised he could breathe — if he was still breathing. To make things worse, he was gagged and blindfolded. His head was still partially bound in a turban which had staunched the bleeding from the severing of his left ear. His left hand was a ball of blood-soaked rags.

"You'll be all right now, Mr Attwal," Charlie said in a loud voice.

Declan pulled a small knife out of his pocket, and cut the man's restraints, starting with the gag. He was relieved to hear the body suck in air.

"Charlie," Declan said calmly, "I want you to help me lift Mr Attwal out of the trunk."

They extracted the rotund little man from the trunk and helped him into the back seat of Charlie's car. It was at this point that Charlie turned his back on the two and vomited beside the Challenger.

Declan threw him a sympathetic glance then ran back to the office.

"Okay — this is what you're going to do," he said to the man behind the counter. "You're going to call nine-one-one and ask for police and an ambulance. Tell them you have an injured man. You'll stay here until they arrive, then direct them to us. You'll tell the police that you were showing us the car when all of a sudden you heard a noise coming from the trunk."

He could see the old man processing this step by step. Declan had dealt with guys like this before. They knew when it was important to play dumb.

"When they ask, and not before, you'll tell them the car was dropped off early this morning by a guy. He said it was his dad's car. The father gave up driving and didn't want it around anymore. You don't remember much about the guy. He was middle-aged and white. He went home to get the registration papers, but hasn't come back yet. Do you understand?"

The old man just nodded.

"Good. Now make the call."

Declan ran back to the car. He saw Charlie crouching down beside Mr Attwal, talking softly to him. He was giving the injured man small sips of water from a bottle he held in his hand.

"Not too much, Mr Attwal."

After all that, he remembered his name.

Charlie went to the front door and got a cloth out of the glove compartment. He dampened it with the water. "Just lean your head back a bit if you can. I'm going to put a damp cloth on your forehead. It'll help to cool you down a bit."

He's stayed calm through this whole thing.

Declan crouched down. "Mr Attwal—the ambulance and police will be here soon. They'll take care of you," Declan said in a calm voice.

Mr Attwal nodded. "When the police arrive, we must make sure they don't find out the truth. I must protect my family."

"Agreed. We'll make this as simple as possible for the cops and for you. This'll be your story. You were walking home from work. The only thing you remember was that a light-coloured van pulled up beside you and a couple of men wearing masks jumped out and dragged you into the van. They put a hood over your face, but said nothing."

"That's just what happened," Mr Attwal said.

"Good. Then you won't have to lie. From that point on we'll have to be a little more creative. They kept asking you for documents. You had no idea what they meant. They kept calling you... Mr Singh. You told them your name was Palvinder Attwal. They didn't believe you. Do you understand, Mr Attwal?"

"Yes. They called me Mr Singh."

"Good. They kidnapped the wrong guy, but wouldn't believe you. Do you still have your wallet on you?"

"No. They took it."

"In our story, it must have fallen out of your pocket when they grabbed you. Look...I know this is a lot to remember."

"No. I've got it."

"Good. After doing all of these horrible things to you, they got a phone call that you overheard. You heard enough to understand that they had grabbed the wrong guy. One of them said they knew a place where they could dump you and let nature take its course. They threw you in the trunk and the next thing you knew, we were pulling you out."

Throughout this entire exchange, Charlie knelt on the ground, staring at the detective, his mouth slightly open.

"Yes," Mr Attwal said, nodding. "I see where you're going with this."

Declan could make out the sound of a siren in the distance. "It won't be long now, Mr Attwal. And you," Declan said to Charlie, "follow my lead. Offer nothing to the police unless you've heard me say it first."

"Okay," Charlie replied in a quiet voice.

Declan put his hand on Charlie's shoulder. "You're doing beautifully. Just keep listening."

The paramedics arrived as the police stepped out of their cruiser.

"Oh, shit," Declan muttered.

"What?" Charlie asked.

"It's McKeckran." Declan said.

"What the fuck!" the older of the two police officers said. "Why am I not surprised to find you involved in whatever the hell this is?"

Declan smiled. "Just dumb luck, I guess."

"Well, what's your story?"

Declan related the facts, as he'd created them.

"So, just to get this straight, Hunt, you came here to find a car for your boyfriend —" He pointed to Charlie.

"Assistant," Declan corrected.

McKeckran leered. "Sure…your assistant. And in the process you just *happened* to find a body in the trunk. Pretty big coincidence."

Declan said, "My vehicle's out of commission at the moment and his Pinto isn't always reliable."

McKeckran turned away and headed back to his young partner as the paramedics loaded Mr Attwal into the ambulance. The police conversed for a few moments then looked back at Declan and Charlie. McKeckran laughed.

"We'll be in touch," the older cop called to them, then turned and headed back to his cruiser, adding a sibilant "ladies."

Charlie tensed. Declan gripped his upper arm. "Don't," was all he said.

They waited until the ambulance had driven away.

"Who was that asshole?" Charlie demanded.

"One of the reasons I got out of the force," he said, still looking in the direction that the cruiser had headed. "He's an old friend of my father's. Let's get back to the office."

"Are you sure you want to be seen in my *Pinto*?"

"Ah, I just said that for McKeckran's sake. So, you got a name for your car?"

"Wha—? No!"

Declan stared at him.

"Francine," Charlie admitted. "Shut up."

Declan grinned. "I said nothing."

* * * *

Constable Luke Fraser turned to Sergeant Gerry McKeckran as the Chevette passed by and said, "You know that guy?"

"Hunt?" Sergeant McKeckran snorted. "Oh, I know him. He's Sam Hunt's kid."

"Declan Hunt?"

"Yeah. The guy was canned from the force for being a fag."

"I didn't think you could do that," said Fraser, shooting McKeckran a quick sideways glance.

"There's a lot of things you can't do *legally*, but there are ways around everything," he replied, then laughed.

"Yeah. I guess so."

Fraser had only been on the force for six months but, in that short time, he'd learned many things. The most important thing he'd learned was to keep his personal life hidden. That was why he had said nothing when Declan Hunt, a man he recognised as the stranger he'd shared a brief dance with outside of The Greek, drove away from the wrecking yard.

* * * *

It was late in the afternoon when Declan and Charlie got back to the agency.

"My office," Declan demanded as he took the lead. Charlie was sure he'd said or done something wrong.

"Your car keys," Declan said, holding out his hand. Charlie surrendered them. Declan dropped the keys into a dish on his desk. Then he went to a cupboard, pulled out a bottle and two glasses and poured them each a healthy serving of Scotch. He handed one to Charlie.

"You can take an Uber home tonight and back here tomorrow, then you can retrieve your keys. I'll reimburse you in the morning."

"Sure."

Charlie looked at Declan across the desk—his dark wavy hair, the drop-dead-sexy scruff on his face, those piercing blue eyes and the way they bore right into him. *Oh my God, he's staring right at me. We're staring at each other!*

Declan took another sip of his drink. Charlie did the same, but his was more of a gulp than a sip. He choked.

"Easy, there. You don't have to kill it. Make friends with it," Declan said to him, with a slightly crooked smile that made him even more attractive.

"So…your first day at work…" Declan started.

"Yeah…"

"You did an excellent job."

"Oh," Charlie said, surprised. "Thanks."

"No one would have picked you out for a computer guy with no field experience. Congratulations," Declan said, raising his glass.

"Thank you. It was, uh, not what I expected. Is that usually what you do?"

Declan laughed. "Nah. Sometimes things get really crazy. Actually, you've experienced more in your first day than I normally would in a month."

Charlie could feel the Scotch rounding off his rough edges. "So that older cop..." Charlie started, then paused, staring into his glass. "He knew you."

"Yeah."

"He seemed to be a..."

"Total prick?" Declan offered.

Charlie smiled. "Yeah. That's about right."

"McKeckran's always been like that," Declan said. "Always trying to prove what a man he is."

Charlie scowled. "Think he's trying to hide something?"

"Wouldn't be the first guy to cover up who he really is."

They both sipped their drinks before Charlie asked, "So, you used to be a cop?"

"Yeah, but that's not a story for today. I'm not drunk enough for that walk down memory lane."

"Sorry. I didn't mean to..."

"No. Not a problem. Just not right now." Declan knocked back his drink. "I think I'm gonna go take a nap. I didn't get much sleep last night."

"Good idea." Charlie finished his drink. "So, uh...I guess I still have a job?"

"Yeah. You still have a job. Take the rest of the day off." He tossed Charlie the office keys. "Don't forget to lock up when you leave, okay?"

"Sure thing."

Declan opened the door to the stairs leading up to his apartment, then turned to Charlie.

"I watched how you dealt with Mr Attwal. You kept him calm, even though I knew, deep-down, you were scared shitless. That was great work. I think you've got what it takes."

"See you tomorrow." Charlie said. "And don't worry — I'll call an Uber."

Charlie enjoyed the ride home. He was exhausted from the day, and the Scotch was warming him like a hug from the inside. He stared out the window, and thought about his new boss...thoughts he probably shouldn't be having. But seeing Declan in action had made him even sexier.

This job was going to be a lot more interesting than he'd ever thought it could be.

Chapter Nine

Declan was leaving school. He stood for a moment watching Rebecca, his only real friend, walk towards the school bus she took home. He never rode the school bus with the other students. He had to walk the one-hour trip home, even if it was snowing or pouring rain. It was his father's rule. It would toughen him up.

As he stared down the road, off in the distance, he saw his mother's car. She pulled in to the school's curved drive. He saw her through the windshield. She was wearing her large sunglasses. He froze. She stepped out of the car just long enough to yell, "Get in," which he did. Strange – he'd never gotten into the car before in the dozens of times he'd had this dream.

There was no seat belt. Odd...he knew her car had seat belts. Odder still was that he noticed it. Mother and son stared at each other for a moment. She slammed her foot down on the accelerator. The car rocketed forward. His gaze was locked on his mother's face, her lips curled into a snarl like a dog ready to attack.

Then her face relaxed, looking almost beatific — like she had found salvation. He turned forward to see the oncoming concrete wall. His mouth opened in a silent scream.

Declan woke in a cold sweat.

* * * *

Charlie'd had a fitful night's sleep. Nightmares of finding dead bodies in car trunks were mixed with dreams of Declan cradling him in his arms as he carried him away from the crime scene. Charlie's eyes drifted open, and his heart was pounding. He could still smell the scent of Declan's body. He wanted to stay in bed forever, not wishing to abandon this feeling, but he had to get to work.

Charlie got up and quickly masturbated in the shower as he fantasised about Declan. He dried off, got dressed and called an Uber, arriving at the office at eight a.m. He thought he could get used to this life of being chauffeured to and from work but he knew that after this morning, it would be back to Calgary Transit or Francine.

He walked into Gwen's shop. The doorbell chimed as he entered.

"Well, hello there, stranger," Gwen called out.

"I'm sorry I didn't poke my head back in yesterday, but things got a little hairy."

"They have a habit of doing that around Declan. So...can I assume that you being back this morning is a good sign?"

Charlie smiled. "I got the job!"

"Well, good for you. Declan'll be lucky to have you."

"I understand that you put in a good word for me."

"I'm surprised he told you. So…what'll it be this morning?"

"A *pain au chocolat* and a latte, please."

Gwen packaged up the pastry and coffee and handed it to Charlie. "I threw in a bag of cookies for later," she said.

Latte and breakfast in hand, Charlie mounted the stairs to the office and opened the door.

First on his to-do list was to activate the security system, which he'd noticed that Declan had been paying for since it had been connected two years ago. Mrs B had probably been too frightened of accidentally setting it off to complete the installation process. After that, he had to familiarise himself with the bookkeeping.

There was a terrible crash from upstairs. The lights suspended from the ceiling shook.

Charlie raced to Declan's office, then to the door at the bottom of the stairs to his apartment. He hesitated for a moment before opening it. He scanned the office for a weapon as another crash shook the room. Charlie made out an audible "Oof." He looked around and saw a hammer on a side table, picked it up then opened the door quietly and crept up the stairs.

As Charlie reached the third floor, he was greeted by a grunt, followed by a third crash. He leapt into the room, hammer swinging wildly, letting out a terrifying scream.

"Jesus Christ," Declan yelled, dropping his barbell on the floor. "What the hell are you doing?"

Charlie scanned the room, hammer still swinging, ready to defend himself against an attacker. Instead he found himself alone with his boss, who was wearing nothing but trainers, tight shorts and sweat.

Charlie mumbled a quick apology and ran out of the room.

* * * *

Thirty minutes later, Declan entered the main office, dressed in jeans and a tailored paisley shirt. Charlie was typing away at the computer, his face still flushed. His lips were pursed so tightly he appeared to have none. He was taking his anger out on the keys. Declan watched, then broke out laughing.

"Oh...my...God, you should have seen your face. You were absolutely wild-eyed!"

"Of course I was. I thought someone was trying to kill you."

"And if there'd been someone, you would have scared the shit out of them. You terrified *me*!" Declan paused. "I'm sorry. I shouldn't have laughed. Here — let me get you a peace offering. Latte, right?"

Charlie stared at him for a moment. "Extra foam," he said, before getting back to work. As he listened to the espresso machine hiss, Charlie's pulse slowed, but the embarrassment failed to subside.

"Here you go. One latte — extra foam — for the man who tried to save me." Declan patted him on the shoulder. "I really do appreciate what you did. You put your life on the line to help me."

"Well..."

"I'll be in my office if anything else comes up."

Declan turned to go. Charlie said, "Wait. So, the crooks win then? The ones from yesterday. You give them the evidence and they walk free?"

"Well, technically, they were always *free*. It never got to the arrest stage of the process."

"That's just semantics."

"Yeah, I guess so."

"So what if they come back and kill Mr Attwal anyway, just to keep him quiet?"

"We all know that they now have Mr Attwal's only copy of the company's books. He was afraid to make a second copy. Two copies are harder to keep track of than one. He said it — his wife said it. I believe it. There's a weird truth in it. It was only a dumb mistake on Mr Attwal's part that made the thugs panic. Mrs Attwal said they were late in paying him for the third time in a row and he made a threat that he shouldn't have."

Declan walked back to Charlie's desk. "I know these guys. They're brutal, but they won't kill unless they're backed into a corner. Now that Mr Attwal knows it, and since they have their books back, he's no threat."

"So, it's just status quo, criminally speaking?"

Declan crossed his arms. "Look — do I care that I'm giving up information that would get this mobster off a money-laundering charge? Yeah, but that's not our concern here. That's a cop's job, and we're not the police. Their job is to uphold the law. We just try not to break it too much while we're trying to save the life of some mobster's accountant. That's the way I work around here and if you don't understand that, maybe this job's not for you."

Declan returned to his office, and closed the door.

Declan tried to make up for things, and I just criticised him, Charlie thought. *Stupid, stupid me!* He threw back the latte, forgetting that it had just been made, and scalded his throat. He slammed the mug down, knocking it over and spilling the remaining coffee all over the top of the desk.

"Shit shit shit shit," he cried, then fanned his mouth. *I am such an asshole.*

Charlie ran into the kitchenette to get a cloth, then ran back and mopped up the spill. "You are such an idiot."

"I'm not sure what I did, but I'm sorry." A man stood in the doorway of the office. Charlie stared at him, startled.

"I... That wasn't for you — about you. I don't... Can I help you?"

"It looks like I should be asking *you* that question," the stranger said, pointing to Charlie's desk.

"Oh, right. I'm fine."

The stranger smiled. "I'd like to talk to Declan Hunt...if he's free."

"Ahh," Charlie said, his head rotating from looking at the stranger to the door of his angry boss. "Sure. I'll see if he's available. Be right back."

Charlie walked to the door. He composed himself and knocked gently. After a two-count, he opened the door just wide enough to stick his head in. Declan was at his desk, looking at his laptop.

"Excuse me, but there's a gentleman to see you. He looks vaguely familiar," Charlie informed him in a near whisper.

Declan looked back at him and, in a voice of equal volume, whispered back, "What does he want?"

Charlie wasn't prepared for this question, so he signalled *Wait a minute* with an upraised index finger, closed the door and quickly walked back to the stranger. Before he could ask him the purpose of the visit, Declan's door opened.

"Can I help you?" Declan asked. "Oh, it's you. You look different in civvies."

Charlie could see Declan's body language change — his muscles tensed.

"Uniforms do that to a guy," the man replied.

Charlie finally recognised him. He was the younger cop from the wrecking yard.

"Lucas Fraser," he said. "But my friends call me Luke."

"So, Constable Fraser, what can we do for you?" Declan was cool, but professional.

"For starters, you could let me apologise for my partner's behaviour yesterday — to both of you. He's a bit of a —"

"Jerk," Declan interrupted.

"That's one word for it. I could think of several others — asshole, bigot and homophobe might do for starters," Luke offered.

"Well, we agree on something after all," Declan said.

"I just want you to know that we're not all like that."

"Would you like a coffee?" Declan asked.

"Sure," Luke said.

"Charlie, make it two cups."

"Two cups it is," Charlie replied.

"And then join us in my office."

Charlie smiled.

* * * *

Declan took Luke into his office.

"Nice place you've got here," Luke said. "A lot nicer than where I work. Although I probably don't have to tell you that. Things probably haven't changed much since you left the service. District 7, wasn't it?"

"Yeah."

"That fight of yours is legendary."

"I try to forget it."

"We never will—gay cops, that is. When I found out who you were, I wanted to come and apologise in person."

Declan stared at him.

"Most of us are still flying under the radar," Luke continued. "You're kind of an unspoken hero to us."

"That wasn't my intention," the detective said.

"Sometimes I'd like to fight back like you did."

"Why don't you? It might be the only thing that'll bring about change."

"Too scared to lose my job and pension, I guess. You've got bigger balls than any of us—and the pressure of having your old man in a power position in the force. Jesus, I can't begin to imagine Christmas around your family table."

Declan was happy when Charlie came in with the coffees.

"I hope you don't mind, but I also brought cookies." Charlie placed a plate on the desk, then shot Declan a glance. "Gwen made me! You might be good at saying no to her, but I'm new here."

"These look great," Luke said, helping himself to one. "Now, regarding the incident at the wrecking yard—and this is strictly on the QT—failing anything showing up from fingerprints from the car, the case'll be closed. Everyone's happy to believe it's a case of mistaken identity—one that the accountant would sooner forget. It's also possible that someone higher up the chain has a vested interest in keeping things quiet, but that's above my pay grade."

"Do you know how Mr Attwal is doing?" Charlie asked.

"The doctors are going to try and cosmetically restore his ear, as best they can, but there's nothing to be done about the finger."

The office phone rang. Then a second time.

"Oh... I'll get that," Charlie said, scampering out of the office.

There was an awkward pause as Declan and Luke stared at each other for a moment.

Declan started. "So...that partner of yours..."

"Yeah. Not the easiest to work with."

"He has no idea about you?"

"Not a bit, and I'd like to keep it that way. I don't think it'll be hard with McKeckran. The thing about bigots and homophobes, they're not the brightest people out there. For McKeckran to figure it out, I'd have to make an obvious pass at him."

"Or try to kiss him," Declan joked.

"I'm not that desperate. Besides, there are better guys out there to go after," he said, locking eyes with Declan.

Is he flirting? Declan wondered.

Luke shifted in his chair.

"What you're doing—it's a big secret to keep." Declan said. "You up for it?"

"I don't have much of a choice, do I? Unless I want to follow your example. You seem to be doing well for yourself since you left the force."

"*Left* is a polite term for it."

"I was thinking about that. It's funny that Professional Standards never looked into it—the fight, that is."

Declan crossed his arms. "My father had to be good for something."

Luke nodded. "We all just figured that the guy whose chops you busted was too scared of you to press charges."

"Might have been that, too." Declan laughed. "Anyway…things worked out okay for me."

"So, I hear you handle mainly gay clients?" Luke asked.

"Most of the time I help out people who are too afraid to go to the cops. A lot of times they're gay. Sometimes it's parents trying to find a gay kid who's run away and they don't want their neighbours to find out. Most of the time it's pretty routine—collecting evidence for wrongful-dismissal suits, partners dealing with cheating spouses—same as in the straight world."

Luke said, "I'm working on a case like that with McKeckran. Looks like the husband's gone AWOL. The wife filed a missing person's report. McKeckran thinks he's gay and has run off with his boyfriend."

"Based on what?"

"He saw a photo of the guy at the house. Said he looked gay. I asked what made a guy look gay, and he said he could always tell. He claims he has a sixth sense. Obviously, that's not true."

Declan shook his head. "How do you not just lose it?"

"I talk it out," Luke replied.

"With who?"

"With myself, mainly."

"I thought maybe you debriefed with your boyfriend."

"Me? No way." Luke laughed. "I don't think I could put a boyfriend through that. Unless he was a cop, maybe. Civilians and cops don't mix."

"Yeah. It didn't work out well with my folks."

They both sat in silence before Luke broke the deadlock. "Well...I guess I'd better head out and let you get some work done. I just wanted to come and apologise."

Declan rose and shook Luke's hand. "Thanks. I appreciate it. You know, if you ever want to talk about things, I've got a willing ear. No charge."

"I just might take you up on that."

"Good. Here's my number." Declan miraculously pulled a card out of thin air and tossed it to him. "Call me. Any time."

"Thanks," Luke said, then handed Declan his own card. "Don't let that go to waste."

As they went to leave the office, Luke turned to Declan. "We've met before, although you might not remember it."

"Sure. At the wrecking yard."

"Nope. It was out in front of The Greek last Saturday night. We had a dance in the street."

Declan remembered the ghost of a dream...dancing with a good-looking guy... "That was you?"

Luke said, "Jeez, I thought I made a stronger first impression."

* * * *

Charlie sat at his desk, his hand still on the telephone receiver, which he had replaced on the cradle.

Declan and Luke exited the inner office. Declan was smiling.

"You wouldn't happen to be free for lunch tomorrow?" Luke asked.

"Sounds good," Declan replied, then turned to Charlie. "Book me out of the office for tomorrow afternoon."

Charlie nodded.

"See you later, Charlie. It was nice meeting you," Luke said.

Charlie grunted. "Yeah."

"And nice to finally meet you, Declan."

Luke left the office, and Declan stared after him.

"Well, back to work." Declan spun on his heels and headed back to his office with a noticeable bounce in his step.

"Wait," Charlie yelled out a bit too loudly.

Declan turned. "Yes?"

"There was a phone call."

"I heard."

"It was from Mrs Beckerman's daughter."

"Oh?"

"She and Mrs Beckerman were out for a walk yesterday." Charlie's voice began to quaver. "She collapsed."

Declan's face lost all of its colour.

"Her daughter said that it was a heart attack. She's in bad shape but they got her to the hospital and they're taking good care of her. Her daughter said they don't know if she'll make it."

Declan stood in silence for a moment before he passed Luke's business card to Charlie. "Could you call Luke and cancel lunch tomorrow?"

"Sure."

"I'm going to head out for the afternoon. You're in charge 'til I get back," Declan said, patting him on the shoulder.

"Declan? I'm so sorry."

Declan nodded at him and opened the door to leave. He paused before turning back to Charlie. "I might be needing you for a little longer than three weeks."

"Sure. You can count on me. I'm not going anywhere."

"Thanks, I appreciate it." He nodded, then left, closing the door behind him.

Chapter Ten

Declan walked slowly down the stairs. It was hard to believe that he might never see Mrs B again. She had been with him from the beginning. She was a tough old broad—her words, not his, although, inside, he agreed. She'd been his rock when he had opened the business. At one point she had loaned him five hundred dollars when things were tight and he needed repairs on the old van he'd been driving.

He found himself outside on the street, standing in front of Gwen's window. He wasn't sure how long he'd been standing there before Gwen stepped out to see what the problem was. He looked at her for a moment in silence.

"Joan Beckerman had a serious heart attack yesterday."

Gwen put her arms around him and gave him a big hug. "I'm so sorry."

Declan could feel the shock working its way through his body. He didn't know what else to say. What came out was, "I've asked Charlie to stay on."

"That's a good idea."

Declan gave her a kiss on the top of her head and walked away.

* * * *

It was still early in the day for Bar-None. There were only a few regulars sitting in their seats. Mickey stood behind the bar and chatted to the day's Kid. This one was a step above the usual, the bartender thought. The Kid seemed to have opinions that were based on fact. He wanted to do things with his life greater than swabbing urinals and mopping up puke. Mickey doubted he would last. The Kids that stayed on longer had an air of destitution about them.

Light spilled into the bar from the outside world as the door opened and another customer entered. Mickey turned to see Declan. *It's a little early for him to be showing up.* "I was wondering when I'd see you. You didn't pick up your van yesterday."

Declan said nothing, just made his way to his usual table and sat down. He seemed deep in his own thoughts.

Without asking, Mickey dropped off his drink. When he received no reaction, he said, "Tough case?"

Declan looked up at him like he was seeing him for the first time. "Uh...no. Just some personal shit I've gotta work through."

"Sure, Dec," Mickey answered. "If you need me, you know where to find me."

Mickey returned to the bar, picked up his cell phone and placed a call. It was picked up on the second ring. "Good afternoon, Declan Hunt Investigations. Charlie Watts speaking. How may I help you?"

"Hey, Charlie, it's Mickey," the voice said on the phone.

Charlie picked up a pencil and pad of paper. "Mickey. Declan's out right now, can I help you with anything?"

"Declan's why I'm calling. Just a heads-up. He's here at the bar and something's wrong. Not sure what, but I thought you might want to keep your eye on him just to make sure he's okay."

"Yeah, I think I know what's going on. Thanks for letting me know." No sooner had he hung up the phone, than it rang again.

"Good afternoon, Declan Hunt Investigations —"

"Oh, thank God. You're in. We need your help. He's gone."

* * * *

It was six p.m. when the office door opened and Declan entered. Charlie was still at his desk. He stared at Declan, trying to judge his emotional state. He looked a little rough.

"You're still here," Declan said.

"Yeah, I was just taking care of a few things before I headed out..."

"You're a terrible liar. I wasn't planning on throwing myself into the river." Declan headed back towards his office.

"Oh, I wasn't worried," Charlie said. Even Charlie could hear the lie in his voice.

He continued, "Hey — we had a call when you were out. It's a potential new client."

"What's the story?" Declan's eyes seemed to brighten a bit.

"A couple in one of those new condos along 9th Avenue in Inglewood," Charlie said, referring to his notes. "A Marc Robichaud and Cory Menchin — they were tag-teaming me on the call and sounded like a cute gay couple, for what that's worth... They lost one of their dogs."

"A lost dog?"

Charlie consulted his notes again. "They're sure it was kidnapped by one of Marc's exes."

"A missing dog?"

"Its name is Mini-Wheat — it's a wheaten terrier. Anyway Marc is devastated and their other dog, Shredded Wheat — "

Declan's mouth broadened into a smile.

"Don't you start. Anyway, Shredded Wheat won't eat — "

Declan started laughing uncontrollably.

"Look — this is serious. It could mean money coming in. I was just looking at the books, and you're not exactly flush with cash."

"Mini and Shredded Wheat?" Declan squeaked out.

"Just count yourself lucky that you didn't have to deal with these guys. My leg is bruised from pinching it just to try to stop myself from laughing."

"Oh, God. Thank you. It's just what I needed. Mrs B would have peed herself over that. But we have to find a better case than that or we'll both be out of a job."

"I take it that it's a *no* when it comes to looking into Mini-Wheat?"

"May I never have to stoop that low," Declan said before heading toward his office. He stopped and turned back towards Charlie. "Since you're still here...do we have anything you can copy Mr Attwal's non-Monarch client files onto so we can send them over to him? He'll probably be anxious to have them when he gets back to work."

"I've got something at home that'll work. I can courier them over first thing in the morning."

"Perfect. I'll let Mrs Attwal know. I'm going to take a long, hot shower and you're going to get yourself out of here. Your folks'll have the cops out looking for you."

He stepped into his office, then poked his head out again. "And, Charlie... Thank you for being here for me."

Charlie smiled and nodded, then called the dog owners and let them know that Declan's workload wouldn't allow him to take on another case at the moment. He was pleased to hear that the dog had shown up. Their house-cleaner had taken it for a walk.

No sooner had he disconnected when the phone rang again.

Charlie answered. "Good..."—Charlie glanced at the clock on the wall—"evening. Declan Hunt Investigations. How may I help you?"

"My husband's gone missing, and I don't think the police are taking it seriously. He's been missing for five days."

"Mr Hunt is...in conference at the moment. May I take your name and number and have him return your call once he's free?"

There was a prolonged silence on the phone. "Hello," Charlie continued. "Are you still there?"

"My name is Katherine Mann. I...I think it would be best if I came in and met with Mr Hunt in person."

"Certainly," Charlie replied, checking Declan's schedule. "Would...ten tomorrow morning work for you?"

"Thank you."

"Do you know where we're located?"

"Yes. I was given your address."

"Good. We'll see you at ten."

The woman disconnected.

Interesting. She didn't want to discuss things over the phone, and she was referred to Declan. Charlie sat at the computer to see if he could find out who Katherine Mann and her husband were.

Twenty minutes later he had located the information and cribbed together a brief biography of them both. This was movie-of-the-week stuff. Once Charlie had printed the document and proofed it, he added a handwritten note to the top — *For tomorrow's ten a.m. meeting.* He underlined the time for emphasis. He looked at the report to ensure that he'd missed nothing, then, to be extra certain it could not be missed, he highlighted the time in bright pink. He placed it in the very centre of Declan's desk and left for the evening.

* * * *

Declan dried himself off after his shower and threw himself onto the bed. He was exhausted.

His cell phone rang. He looked at the clock. How was it nine p.m.? He must have dozed off. "Hello."

"Hey, it's Luke. Hope I'm not interrupting."

"No. Not at all. I was just lying here in bed."

"Pretty early night. I thought you'd be out at a bar with friends, partying it up."

"Yeah. That's me all right," Declan replied.

"Look, I got a call from Charlie this afternoon. He said you'd had to cancel our lunch. Is everything okay?"

"Yeah, sorry. I had a bit of a rough day. I found out a close friend of mine had a heart attack and might not make it."

"Sorry to hear that," Luke said.

"I'll be all right. It was just a bit of a shock."

"Would you like some company tonight? You know, if you want to talk…"

Declan thought for a moment. "Yeah. That would be nice. Just buzz from downstairs and I'll let you in."

"Be there in thirty."

Declan did a quick tidy on the place, then a quick check of himself. He threw on some jeans and a long-sleeved white linen shirt. The street-door buzzer sounded. He hurried down to the office.

Declan got to Charlie's desk, and buzzed Luke in.

When he opened the door, Luke was standing there, his strawberry-blond hair perfectly coiffed. He wore a tight T-shirt and even tighter jeans, and white cotton trainers on his feet. *God, they must be size thirteen.*

The moment was broken by Luke, who said, "Can I come in?"

"Uh, yeah, of course. Sorry."

Declan took him up to his apartment and they settled on the couch next to his home gym and bed.

"I was sorry to hear about your friend," Luke said.

"Thanks."

They stared at each other.

Luke's breathing seemed to be the only sound in the room. An alarm bell went off inside Declan's head. *There's something about this guy. He's different. If I start something with this one, it's going to be more than a one-night stand at The Greek.*

"I needed to see you. I haven't been able to get you out of my mind," Luke said as he reached up and caressed Declan's chest.

His other hand touched Declan's cheek and stroked the bristly stubble with the back of his index finger, then moved to his soft lips.

Declan parted his lips. Luke smiled and leaned his body into Declan's. His mouth replaced his finger as they started to kiss.

Declan reached behind Luke and grabbed his T-shirt, pulling it up and over his head. Luke unbuttoned Declan's shirt and revealed the bruising on his body. "Oh my God. What happened to you?"

"Some people just don't like me."

"Idiots," Luke said, before sliding down Declan's torso and gently kissing the purple-blue skin.

Luke continued down his body, pausing at Declan's navel, which he teased with his tongue, then farther down, along the narrow trail of hair, before Declan said, "Come with me," and took him to the bed.

Declan stripped off Luke's pants, then, starting at his neck, moved downward, forming a scent map of Luke's muscular body, one he would store away in his mind.

Each part had a different smell—the tang of his armpits differed from that of his pubic hair, which was unlike that of the musky trail that led from his balls to his ass. Every part of him had a unique scent. Even his belly button and, of course, his feet. The smell of a man never failed to arouse him, even more so than the taste of him.

He sucked on Luke's toes, then worked his way back up his body, stopping at his aroused cock which he circled with his tongue until it was rock hard and covered in spit. Declan straddled his body, then rolled until Luke was on top of him. Luke placed his shoulders underneath Declan's raised knees and pushed his legs back until his cock was brushing against Declan's balls.

"Fuck me," Declan said. "Now!"

Luke obeyed. Declan gave himself up to Luke and got what he needed most. Tonight, he needed someone else to take control.

Chapter Eleven

Charlie stood at the counter as Gwen put the finishing touches on his latte. He checked his watch. It was 8:43 a.m.

"You know, you could just save the money and make one of these upstairs," Gwen said.

"Yeah," Charlie replied, "but why work if you can't treat yourself to the little pleasures in life?"

"I like the way you think."

As she rang in the order, Gwen asked, "How's he doing? That was tough news about Joan, especially coming so hard on the heels of the anniversary of his mom's death."

"He never said anything about his mom to me. He seemed okay when I left last night."

"Keep your eye on him. Let me know if there's anything I can do."

"Sure thing." Charlie paid the bill and turned to leave. Through the window, he saw the street door to the office open, and Luke walked out.

What the fuck?

Charlie waited until the cop was out of sight before he left the café and dashed up the stairs to the office. His mind raced with thoughts of what to do. His fantasy life with Declan was vanishing before his eyes.

As Charlie entered the office, Declan walked out of the kitchenette with his morning coffee.

"So…have a *restful* night?" Charlie asked, trying to hide his sarcasm.

"Yeah. You?"

"Nothing but. Hard not to rest when you don't have a personal life." Charlie put his latte and *pain au chocolat* down on his desk hard enough to spill some coffee. He didn't care. "I've booked you for a ten o'clock meeting this morning with a woman who misplaced her husband. If you haven't found it yet, I pulled together a report on what she said and what I could find out about the couple on the internet. It's on your desk."

"Thanks," Declan said. "I'll look that over now."

"I didn't book your meeting first thing this morning because I thought you might have planned a workout session."

"No… I think I'll skip that for today."

"Yeah. I guess you probably had a good workout last night."

Declan just looked at him, then headed back to his office and closed the door.

Charlie immediately regretted what he had said. He wanted to apologise, but thought he should give Declan his space, so instead he wrote him a note.

Sorry for the bitchy comment. No excuse for that. Didn't sleep well – C.

He slipped it under the door, then returned to his desk. A few moments later, a note slid back under the door.

You worry too much – D.

He read it three times, interpreting it differently each time. In the end he decided to read it positively.

When he sat down, he spotted Luke's card on his desk from the day before. He'd thought about it— Declan and Luke. They had seemed to hit it off yesterday. He'd thought about it all night. They seemed to have this...*thing* between them. Charlie wished there'd been a *thing* between him and Declan... A thing that wasn't one-way.

Was it any surprise that Declan was drawn to that cop? Good God, they were a couple of well-matched bookends. They could roll around for hours and not damage each other. Charlie'd be crushed under the weight of either of them... If only he had the chance. He'd taken enjoyment in cancelling their lunch.

In spite of himself, Charlie was fixated on the image of Declan lying on top of him. He tried to remove the image from his brain by studying notes on previous cases while Declan remained in his office. The thought of Declan being mad at Charlie sent shards of glass through his heart. He would have to find a way to make it up to him.

At the appointed time, the street door opened, and there were footsteps on the stairs. A woman who Charlie pegged at being in her fifties entered the office. Charlie stood.

"Mrs Mann? I'm Mr Hunt's assistant, Charlie Watts." He extended his hand, which she took.

"Oh. Like the drummer," she said, mildly distracted.

"Yeah…just a little bit younger, but not so dead," he replied, then realised the impropriety of the *dead* remark when the woman's husband was missing. He moved on. "Would you care for a coffee?"

"No. I've been living on it for the last few days and I think my stomach's ready to move out."

Charlie nodded. "If you'll follow me, please." He led her to Declan's office, knocked and entered.

Declan had Charlie's notes spread out across his desk. He looked up at Charlie and smiled. "Great work on these notes."

A warm feeling flooded Charlie's body. He smiled and announced, "Mrs Katherine Mann to see you."

Declan stood as she entered. "Mrs Mann — may I call you Katherine?" Declan asked as he took her hand.

"Please. I've been Mrs Manned to death by the police since I reported Ian missing."

"Please, Katherine, have a seat. Can we get you anything, coffee, tea, something stronger?"

"I shouldn't…but Scotch, if you have any."

"Scotch it is," Declan said, and poured two glasses, one for her and one for himself.

"Charlie, would you mind sitting in and taking notes?"

"Uh…sure," he said. He had never realised that he would be expected to take dictation. He ran back to his desk, quickly finding a pad and pen. He returned to Declan's office and took a chair in the corner.

Declan began, "So, tell me what you can about your husband's disappearance."

"It's really quite simple. He went out to have drinks with some friends six nights ago — "

"That was Thursday night?" Declan interrupted.

"Yes. Thursday night. He's been getting together with these friends for the last few years. He went out, and never came back."

"Was that common—staying out all night?"

She stared at the floor.

"Not *un*-common," she said, then took a sip of her drink. "But he'd always text or call if he wasn't coming home."

"And you've obviously tried to contact him with no success?"

"When I called, I just got his voicemail. None of my texts have been returned."

Declan continued, "When did you contact the police?"

"After I got a hold of Sheldon, who told me that Ian left the party late Thursday night."

"And Sheldon is?" Charlie asked.

Declan kept an eye on him, curious how much he would ask, and hoped he would know how far he could go.

"Oh—Sheldon Prescott. He's a friend of Ian's who usually hosts these get-togethers. He has a big house in Mountain River Estates."

"Nice area," Declan commented.

"He's the vice-president of a bank."

"Do you know which one?" Charlie asked.

"One that makes lots of money," she answered, smiling for the first time.

Declan continued, "I assume your husband's car was no longer at Mr Prescott's?"

"That's right."

"And there's been no trace of it, since?"

She nodded, shifted in her chair and took another drink.

Declan paused. "Are you all right to continue?"

"Yes," she replied.

"You said that you contacted Mr Prescott. It was Saturday morning, was it?"

She nodded again.

"How did he react to the news that Ian hadn't returned home?" Declan asked.

"He was almost...panicked."

Charlie let out a soft "Hmm," and continued taking notes.

"Did you call anyone else before calling the police?" Declan enquired.

Her eyes welled up. "The hospitals."

"Do you remember which ones?" Charlie asked.

"Foothills, Lougheed, Rockyview General and South Health."

"Thank you," Charlie replied, and gave her a soft smile.

Declan sat forward in his chair, bringing him closer to Katherine. "I need to ask you some personal questions regarding your husband."

Before Declan could continue, she replied, "He wasn't taking any medications, his health was good and he certainly wasn't suicidal. Never has been." She added, almost as an afterthought, "And he wasn't involved with gangs, drugs or the sex trade."

Declan smiled. "The police have obviously already asked these questions. How was your relationship with Ian?"

Katherine finished her Scotch and said, "May I have another?"

Declan refilled her drink and noted that she was fiddling with her wedding band. As he handed her back her glass he said, "I was asking about your relationship."

Katherine took a moment before she answered. "It was...unusual."

Charlie looked up from his notes, then glanced at Declan.

"Meaning?" Declan asked.

"We loved each other. We were each other's best friends. We rarely spent more than twenty-four hours apart."

"So, you didn't have a fight?"

"No."

"Then why are you here, Katherine? It seems to me that the police are the best people to handle the case."

"Well, they would be, except for the fact that when I told them we had an open relationship..."

"Oh..." Declan responded.

Katherine shifted in her chair and scowled. "The one officer got this obnoxious little smirk on his face. He said that it would be best if they left it for another day or so. He said that maybe Ian and his 'friend'—he actually used air quotes around friend—he said they probably just went away for a while—took a trip."

She took a large swig of her drink.

"I told them that Ian would never do anything like that. We had rules that we followed. He said that men followed their cocks before rules every time. He even suggested that Ian might have run off with another man."

"Pretty crude," Charlie judged.

"That describes the cop perfectly."

"And you don't believe Ian could have run off with someone?" Declan asked.

Katherine emptied her glass, then looked at Declan. "My husband had many secrets. I was told that you were a detective that was open-minded when it came to more unusual cases and knew how to keep things quiet."

"I am," Declan responded.

"Me too," Charlie added.

Katherine paused. "Ian wasn't really driven by sexual desire. But, as a photographer, he had an eye for beauty. He was drawn to people who had that, 'something special'. He said that's what attracted him to me in the first place. And God knows I found Ian incredibly attractive.

She set her empty glass on the desk and adjusted the gold chain around her neck.

"Over the past few years, my husband has occasionally been exploring his feminine side by dressing as a woman, and the night he disappeared, he was at a party with other like-minded individuals."

Declan processed this new information. "Do you think it had anything to do with his disappearance?"

Katherine said, "I don't know, but I suspect if the police start to dig too deeply, they'll find out, and it might influence how seriously they take the case. I mean, if they were concerned about an open relationship…" She left the sentence unfinished.

Declan said, "So you're sure Ian wasn't seeing anyone, perhaps from the party?"

"I don't think so," Katherine said. "One thing I do know is that secrecy is of the utmost importance."

"Why's that?" Charlie interjected.

"Ian never told me who attended Sheldon's parties, but I got the idea that some of the attendees were in prominent public positions and wanted their privacy respected."

Charlie nodded. "Makes sense."

Katherine turned back to Declan. "After I spoke to the police, I phoned Sheldon and he gave me your number. Apparently you helped a friend of his on a somewhat delicate case a few years ago. He said that you were one of the few people in this town who could be trusted. He also gave me permission to give you his name and number."

She opened her purse, extracted a piece of paper and slid it across the desk to Declan. He looked at it and passed it on to Charlie.

"Is it safe to assume that you didn't give this particular piece of information to the police?" Declan asked.

Katherine looked at him and said, "To Sergeant Men-Think-With-Their-Cocks? Of course not. Would you? I will not leave my husband open to ridicule from that brainless oaf. I realised perhaps the police wouldn't be much help and telling them might make things worse."

"I would have done the same as you," Declan offered, thinking, *There are many spouses who would not have remained so cool.* "You mentioned that you were in an open relationship. Are you currently seeing someone else?"

Katherine got up and moved towards the window. "Do we have to talk about that? I know it has nothing to do with Ian's disappearance."

Declan remained at his desk. "I think that it's always best to come clean with everything from the start. It saves us from wasting time following the wrong leads, and prevents anything from coming out that you want kept quiet. Remember — we'll be working for *you*."

She returned to her seat and bit her lower lip. "If my relationship comes out, it will be very embarrassing for everyone involved."

"Affairs often are, but it just might help us find Ian."

She sighed. "His name is Michael Taylor. He's the son of our friends Deirdre and Simon."

"And is it safe to assume that the two of you were together the night that Ian disappeared?"

"I had dinner with the Taylors, and Michael drove me home after."

"And he'd be able to attest to that?"

"If I asked him to."

"Would he be able to attest to it without your asking?" Charlie added.

She turned to Charlie. "Of course. I just meant he probably wouldn't say anything unless he knew I told you first."

Charlie cocked his head to one side. "You didn't drive yourself to the dinner party?"

"I don't drive. I Uber when I need to go somewhere, if Ian can't drive me."

"Thank you," Charlie replied, scribbling more notes on his pad.

Katherine looked at Declan and asked, "Do you have enough to go on?"

Declan said, "Just a few more questions. Outside of your personal circle, what do you know about your husband's business dealings?"

She frowned. "He used to invest in real estate, but now he's down to a single building. I don't think I'll be of any help there. We never really talked too much about his business. I think he felt it was a bit...boring." She turned her head towards Charlie. "It was far from the glamorous lives we led in London. Here, work always felt like, well, work. He'd sooner talk to you about the Axemen."

"The Axemen?" Declan asked.

"A hockey team up north in Airdrie," Charlie answered, while still making notes in his book. "A Triple-A team, aren't they?" Charlie asked Katherine.

"Yes," she said with surprise in her voice. "Ian bought the team ten or so years back. He felt it was the best way to show how Canadian he'd become."

"Did he spend much time with the team?" Charlie continued.

"He made sure he went to all of their games. Ian took their publicity shots—he was an excellent photographer. He hadn't done much of that since we moved here. Sad, really. That's what he loved more than anything in life. Way back in the old days, that is."

Katherine went silent. Declan paused then said, "Well, why don't we start with what we have here for the moment? At the same time, we'll try and find out what the police are doing. They probably won't move on anything until either the car is found...or your husband is."

The reality of that statement set in, and the colour left her face. "You think he's dead, don't you?"

"I don't know, but we'll do our best to find out the truth."

Katherine looked like she might faint.

"Let me get you some water," Charlie said. He jumped to his feet and quickly headed to the kitchenette.

He really does care about people, Declan thought.

Charlie came back in with a tall glass of water as Katherine cried into a tissue. "So, you will look into this for me?"

"I'll have Charlie provide you with the contract as soon as we're done here."

After several minutes of being consoled, Katherine had signed the agreement with Declan Hunt

Investigations, which Charlie took to the file room. As she prepared to leave, Declan asked one more question.

"The policeman who questioned you on Saturday — his name wasn't McKeckran, was it?"

"Yes. I think that was his name. Is that important?"

"No. Just curious. We'll be in touch tomorrow, unless we hear of something any sooner."

Charlie returned as Declan shook her hand, and Katherine Mann walked out of the office.

Declan put his hands in his pockets and shrugged his shoulders. "Huh. That's interesting."

"What is?" Charlie asked.

Declan stared at the office door. "I think this is the same case that Luke's working on."

* * * *

Katherine exited the office and got into the back of the Uber she had ordered. As the car pulled away from the curb, she reached for her phone and tapped in a number. After three rings, a smooth, deep voice answered.

"How did it go?"

"I had to tell them about you," she said.

"So soon?"

"I had no choice. It's best to control the release of information rather than react to it."

"But it was just to the detective, right?"

"And his assistant. Anyway, he'll be giving you a call to confirm a few things. Don't let him talk you into anything other than what we discussed. And watch out for his little friend. I don't think he's as innocent as he acts."

Chapter Twelve

"How'd you like to do some more research?" Declan asked.

"Sure," Charlie said.

"Check out all the social media sites and find out anything you can about Ian Mann—his friends, anyone who's said anything bad about him. And look into the Axemen. Same thing. Let's see if there's any dirt out there."

"Will do."

Declan looked at Charlie. "I'm heading to the deli. Want something?"

"Sure. I'll have whatever you're having." Charlie reached into his pocket for his wallet.

"My treat," Declan said, then headed out the door.

Charlie got to work. He started with Facebook. A search showed that Ian didn't appear to have an account, at least under his own name, but a few entries hash-tagged *#ianmann* did pull up a number of interesting posts.

The door opened and Declan dropped a bag off on his desk. "Here you go."

Charlie smiled. "Thanks."

Declan headed into his office.

As Charlie wolfed down his pastrami on rye, he copied the Facebook posts into a file and moved on to Twitter and Instagram.

Charlie worked through the afternoon, copying everything else of interest into a file which he sent to the printer. When he glanced at the clock, it was after five. He grabbed his report and headed into Declan's office.

Declan was on the computer. Charlie rapped on the door jam. "It seems that Ian Mann was not loved by everyone."

"Oh?" Declan slid his chair back and indicated that Charlie should sit down.

"There were a number of posts critical of him for making a profit on real estate sales on the backs of suffering oil companies during the financial collapse."

"Some people have long memories."

"What was more interesting were posts from people from the hockey community who were out for him."

"Interesting."

Charlie continued. "On Twitter I came across a number of tweets concerning the possible sale of the team to a banker from Toronto. Some of the sponsors were starting to question where their money was going and some of the parents felt that Ian, as the owner, might not have been putting all of the player fees back into the team."

"They think he was embezzling?"

"Some people said he was selling before the books could be audited."

Declan's eyes lit up. "Well…I think you've done a very good day's work. Let me take you out to celebrate."

As Declan and Charlie went to lock up the office, Charlie said, "Let me show you how your security system works."

Declan let out a sigh.

Charlie began, "The code is six-seven-seven-two. If you look at the letters on the keypad, that spells out 'MrsB'. So if you punch in the code followed by the 'Stay' button the only thing that will happen is you'll hear three short beeps when someone comes through the street-level door. You won't hear it up in your apartment, though. It's not that loud. If you put in the same code and press 'Away', that arms the main office door up here. If the alarm isn't deactivated by the code within thirty seconds of the door being opened, a siren will sound and the alarm company will be notified. You'll definitely hear that upstairs. Wanna try it?""

"Maybe after we get back. Now, Let's get going. We'll take my vehicle."

"Where is it?"

"Mickey dropped it off behind the building yesterday. There it is."

Charlie looked around for a sexy car. Maybe an Audi, or a Lexus. Something a hot private investigator would drive. "Where?"

"You're standing in front of it."

Charlie stared for a moment. His mouth fell open in disbelief. It was a white Toyota Sienna minivan.

"You have got to be kidding. *This* is your car?"

"What were you expecting—an Aston Martin?"

"Well, yeah!"

"Look, this blends in, it's got great visibility over other vehicles and its manoeuvrability and pick-up are incredible. And it gets great gas mileage."

"It's a minivan! Who are you—James Bond's mother?"

"It's the perfect surveillance vehicle, now get in."

"And you have the nerve to criticise my car Francine," Charlie muttered as he climbed into the passenger seat.

"No offence, but Francine has shitty pick-up and wouldn't hold half the equipment I need."

"Does this have a name?" Charlie asked. He hoped it was something he could mock.

"The van," Declan said, smiling as he punched the accelerator, throwing Charlie back into his seat.

A few minutes later they entered Bar-None. Declan waved at Mickey. Charlie followed close behind, like the caboose of the world's shortest train. He also waved, but one of those child-like waves where the fingers did all of the work while the palm remained stationary.

Declan chose the table. It was in the rear, out of hearing range of the few denizens who inhabited the place.

Mickey arrived moments after they landed in their seats. "What'll you two have?"

"It's a moment of celebration, Mickey," Declan announced. "Charlie's been through a trial by fire these last few days and passed with flying colours. I'll have the Declan Special."

"And you?" Mickey asked Charlie.

"I'll have what he's having," he answered naïvely.

Mickey smiled and turned to Declan. "He has no idea, does he?"

Declan laughed. "He's a man now, Mickey. Time he drank like one."

Mickey returned to the bar.

Declan smiled at Charlie and asked, "So…come here often?"

Charlie was on a high. He was sitting across from the most beautiful man in the bar, who had hired him into one of the coolest, sexiest businesses he could think of, and he had no idea how to carry on a conversation with him.

"Uh…actually, I come here a lot. Well, not exactly a lot. Okay, I've only been here a few times…"

"Oh." Declan was still smiling.

Mickey swung by and dropped off the drinks.

"Thanks," Charlie said, picked up his glass and took a swig.

Charlie had never swallowed liquid fire before, but suspected that this was what it felt like. For once in his life, his instinct for self-preservation woke from its near-permanent slumber and he didn't spit up all over Declan and the table.

"So, is this a regular thing, going out for drinks after a tough spell of work?" Charlie wheezed out.

"Mrs B would have approved," Declan said. "Here's to Mrs B and her health."

"To Mrs B!"

They sat for a moment in silence.

"Things have been a little crazy," Charlie said.

"It's not usually like that. Just so you know, sometimes I have to work weekends, but for you it's a Monday to Friday job."

"Good to know."

"That is, unless I need you for some undercover work."

Charlie's mind immediately interpreted that as *under the covers* work.

"While I think about it, can I have your cell number? Just in case I need you," said Declan.

"Sure. Give me your phone."

Declan unlocked it and passed it over to Charlie who entered it and flagged it as a favourite.

Declan took a sip of his drink, then asked, "So, tell me about yourself. I don't know anything about you other than what was in your application."

"Well, I'm twenty-four years old and I live with my parents, who lead very unexciting lives. My dad sells insurance and my mom teaches grade three children how not to stuff things in their ears and up their noses."

Declan laughed.

Charlie's brain registered the question, *Why am I telling him the truth?*

"I have two close friends, and one's my grandmother. I've never had a real boyfriend and I haven't come out to my parents, which is pretty pathetic — I mean, what is this, the 1970s? — and I obviously have no self-esteem or fear of humiliating myself in front of someone who is basically an absolute stranger."

Declan took another sip of his drink. "We really have to work on the whole self-esteem thing. What I've seen of you so far is an attractive young guy who really cares about people. Someone who can remain calm in a crisis, and is a natural at putting people at ease. You also have the patience to read manuals — something I have no aptitude for at all. You have all the skills I am lacking. I think we'll make a great pair."

"Well..."

"And you handled the interview with Katherine Mann beautifully."

"I hope I didn't talk too much?" Charlie asked.

"Not at all. You made everything seem like normal conversation. You're a natural. Now — speaking of the Mann case — "

Charlie interrupted, "You said Stud-Cop and the Asshole are working on it?"

"Stud-Cop?" Declan laughed.

"Well, with that killer smile, and that basket… Don't tell me you didn't notice."

"We've really got to find you a boyfriend."

* * * *

Charlie picked through the remnants of a nacho plate. Declan stared into his empty glass. He was quite drunk, which made sense, given that he'd matched each of Charlie's drinks with several of his own.

"Last weekend was the anniversary of her death," he said to the glass, not making eye contact with Charlie.

"Your mother's."

"How did you know?"

"Gwen told me. She said it was probably tough coming so close to Mrs B's heart attack."

"What else did she say?"

"Nothing."

Charlie got quiet and stopped moving, one remaining nacho chip suspended between his thumb and forefinger.

"Did your mother die of a heart attack?" Charlie asked.

"No. She was coming to pick me up from school and she was going to drive us away to start over again someplace else. Any place else. She must have fallen asleep…trying to get to me."

"What were you running away from?"

"My father."

There were tears in Declan's eyes. He cleared his throat. "I think I've had enough. Don't forget to Uber home, okay?"

"Sure… Do you want some company?"

Declan looked at him and smiled. "I'm fine." He stared at Charlie for a moment. "I don't deserve you, Charlie Watts."

"Declan?"

"Don't worry. I'll still be around tomorrow."

"Promise?"

"I promise," he said before leaning down and giving Charlie a kiss on the head.

Declan paid the bill at the bar and dropped his car keys in Mickey's hand.

"Be good to yourself tonight, Dec," he said as Declan left the bar.

The conversation earlier in the night had left him feeling unsettled and upset. Declan sat on a park bench, pulled out his phone and texted Luke.

After five minutes, there was no response. Declan considered his options. He wasn't ready to go home yet. He got up and walked. At the street corner, he instinctively turned right. His feet carried him along a familiar route, a path that ended at the doors to The Greek.

Chapter Thirteen

Charlie sat in the Black Bean Eatery across from Carrie. It was the place where they'd cried over bad dates, where Charlie had come out and where Carrie had made her decision about an unexpected pregnancy.

Charlie was still a bit drunk. He'd given up trying to keep up with Declan after the first few drinks.

Carrie looked at Charlie and said, "Well, I think you should tell him how you feel, then quit."

"What would *you* know?"

"What I *know* is you have done nothing but talk about the guy for the last two hours."

"But I think he kinda needs me." Charlie's phone went off. He checked the screen. "Oh my God. It's him! What should I do?"

The phone continued to ring.

"Charlie, if you aren't going to answer, I will," Carrie blurted out.

"Okay, okay," he said. Charlie took a deep breath and took the call. "Hello," he said, hesitantly.

"May I speak to Charlie, please?"

"Uh, speaking."

"Hey, Charlie. My name's Mateo. I'm calling for Declan. He asked me to call you." The voice was gentle, with a slight Hispanic accent.

"Look, Mateo, if Declan is trying to set you up with me, tell him thank you—I'm sure you're a really nice person, but—"

"No. That is not the reason I am calling. Declan is a little too drunk to leave here, and we were hoping that you could come and get him. He told me to look you up on his phone and call you."

"Oh, he did, did he?"

"Yes. I'll text you the address. See you soon. Bye-bye."

Mateo disconnected and a moment later Charlie's phone chirped with a text.

"Declan wants me to pick him up because he's too drunk to find his own way home. If he thinks he can just call me at any hour, just because he needs my help..." Charlie muttered.

"You're going to go get him, aren't you?"

"Of course I am! He *needs* me."

* * * *

The address was a few blocks east at some place called The Greek. *The Greek what?* he asked himself. His question was soon answered. *No way. I can't go in there! What if it gets raided and I get arrested? What would my parents think?*

A hot young blond guy came out of the building. He was wearing an old hockey jersey cut off above the navel and a tight pair of jeans. He paused for a moment to check Charlie out. He cracked the gum he was chewing and blew a bubble, then said, "Are you heading in?"

"Uh…" Charlie muttered, then checked to see if anyone was watching.

"'Cause if you are, I might just have to go back in there," he said, before reaching up and rubbing the back of his hand against Charlie's chest.

Charlie took a deep breath, mustered all of his self-control and said, "Just heading in for work."

"I've never seen you before. I'll look for you next time," the blond said before sauntering away.

Charlie walked cautiously up a flight of stairs, where he found what looked like a ticket booth with red velvet curtains on either side. A handsome Latino man sat behind the glass. He was reading a book. This struck Charlie as odd for a place like this. The book didn't even seem to have any pictures.

Charlie cleared his throat. "Ah, excuse me."

"Yes?" The man closed his book. Charlie noticed the title — *Nietzsche on Truth and Philosophy*. A man exited from behind the red curtain. He wore full cowboy regalia. What wasn't covered in clothes was covered in sweat.

"Ah…" Charlie couldn't focus.

"You must be here for Declan. I'm Mateo," said the man in the booth.

Mateo hung a 'Be Back Soon' sign on his glass window. It bore an image of a muscular male back, used in place of the second word. *Very Nietzsche*, Charlie thought.

Mateo led Charlie behind the red curtain into a world he had only fantasised about. Men of all shapes and sizes wandered down hallways, in all states of undress. Pulsing techno-beat music thrummed in the background. This world seemed to have an unspoken language — a quick glance for "no thank you," a lingering gaze for "I want you." Charlie picked up the language quickly. It was primal. One handsome, well-toned man — Charlie guessed he was in his fifties — locked eyes on him. Charlie stopped in his tracks, held in a trance. The man's hair was silver, his metallic-grey beard was a well-trimmed half-inch in length and his eyes, steel blue. Charlie felt himself being drawn towards him.

"Charlie," a voice said. "No shopping unless you pay. Come." Mateo took Charlie's hand and led him down the hallway.

As they approached a dark-red door, Charlie could make out the sound of a voice he recognised. Mateo opened the door and there was Declan, fully clothed, slumped in a chair and mumbling to a tightly T-shirted burly man. The man looked up at Charlie and smiled.

"I think you're going to need help with this one. At least until you get him to the street," he said as he threw a beefy arm under one of Declan's arms and around his back.

"Okay, my friend, up you go," he said as he lifted Declan onto his feet. Declan's head pivoted around until it faced Charlie.

"Charlie! My dear, dear, dear, dear friend. They found you." Declan's face lit up with a liquid smile. He spun his head towards the burly man and whispered, as if revealing a great secret, "This is my friend Charlie. He's waaaaay smarter than me."

"And hopefully a good deal more sober," the other man replied, then laughed. "Come on, my friend. Let me get you downstairs where your best friend Charlie can get you home."

Declan didn't walk down the stairs as much as he was carried, then was placed in the back of the Uber which Charlie had managed to order on their way down.

The driver took one look at Charlie and said, "He pukes back there and it'll be a hundred-and-fifty-dollar charge."

"If he pukes back here, you'll have to make it three hundred, 'cause I'll be joining him," Charlie added, only half-joking.

"This is my friend Charlie," Declan loudly announced to the driver. "He helps me when I need it."

"Lucky Charlie," the driver commented, with only a hint of sarcasm.

Declan lolled his head onto Charlie's shoulder, snuggling into it like it was a pillow. "You saved me," he whispered.

For a hefty tip, the driver helped Charlie extract Declan from the back of his, thankfully, un-puked-in car. It was only then that Charlie realised that what the muscular man at The Greek had managed to do going downstairs, Charlie was going to have to do going upstairs to the office.

He stood outside the street-level door, wedging Declan against the wall with his shoulder.

"Declan," he shouted, which got some response. "Wake up!" He slapped him lightly across the face. "Oh, please wake up." He slapped him a little harder.

Declan gave out a giggle. "You little bitch."

"What did you call me?" Charlie yelled, then slapped him as hard as he could. That seemed to do the trick.

"Hey," Declan slurred out. "You hit me!"

"Call me bitch one more time and you'll see just how hard I can slap! Now, wake up." Charlie pulled away from him, and Declan stumbled away from the wall. He balanced himself by throwing both arms around Charlie's neck.

"Okay," Charlie said, "this is a good start."

Charlie managed to get his key out of his pocket and open the door. If he was going to make this work, he was going to have to take control.

"Okay, you with me?"

"Yeah," Declan said as more of a breath than a word.

"One step at a time. Got it?"

"Hey, you're really cute close up. You know that?"

"Great. Let's go."

Charlie had no idea how long it took to manipulate Declan's mass of muscle, bone and booze up two flights of stairs, but it felt like hours.

He manoeuvred Declan towards the bed where he planned on leaving him. Charlie turned his gaze towards his boss and found him staring back.

"Thank you for being my Prince Charming," Declan whispered. Then he kissed Charlie lightly on the lips and crumpled into a heap on the bed.

Charlie rearranged Declan's body into what he thought was a more comfortable position, and was headed towards the stairs when he heard rustling from the bed. He turned to see the beautiful man struggling as he tried to remove his top. He had gotten himself trapped. Declan collapsed back onto the bed, a tangle of man and shirt.

"Here. Let me help." Charlie pulled the shirt back down over his torso, then unbuttoned it. He pulled it open then slid the sleeves down his arms. He soon had Declan lying shirtless on his back. Charlie noticed the blue-black bruises covering his ribcage. He caressed them. *Who did this to you?*

Charlie watched as Declan's muscled chest rose and fell with each breath. His washboard stomach pulsated with the rhythm of his heart.

Declan began to fuss, pulling at his pants.

"What the hell," Charlie muttered. He reached down and undid Declan's belt, followed by the button. Charlie's hands shook as he contemplated unzipping the fly. He took a deep breath and unzipped his pants.

"Okay, I'm just going to pull off your pants now." He felt like a doctor describing a physical exam in as much detail as possible in order to de-sexualise the process.

Removing a pair of pants over a well-developed set of buttocks was far more difficult that Charlie had imagined, given that he was attempting to avoid touching Declan's body and keep from removing his underwear.

Declan lay there, stripped of all clothes, other than his tight briefs. Charlie stood there taking it all in. *He kissed me.*

He scanned Declan's body. He wanted to remember every inch of it. He noted how well-endowed Declan was. Charlie's whole body trembled at the sight. There was a magnetic attraction that seemed to draw his hand towards the sleeping man's crotch. He felt the heat emanating from Declan as his hand floated an inch above it. He thought of all the lucky men who had been able to caress what was just below Charlie's hand.

The paralysis that kept his hand hovering was broken when he heard a sound. It pulsated and filled the room. He was frightened that it was so loud it would wake the sleeping giant. Charlie realised it was the sound of his own breathing.

He rushed downstairs and glanced at the clock on the wall across from his desk. It was 2:10 in the morning. He thought of calling for an Uber, but...what if Declan needed him? He *was* pretty drunk...so he texted his parents that he was working through the night on a case, then curled up on the couch in the reception room and closed his eyes.

Chapter Fourteen

Declan stood in the kitchenette, frothing milk for a latte. He deftly poured the heated milk into the espresso, even making a leaf pattern on the surface.

He made himself an Americano and carried them both into the reception area.

Charlie lay on the couch, twisted like a corpse. His hair seemed to point in ten directions at once. His mouth was open, and a trickle of drool ran across his cheek.

The clock read eight-thirty a.m.

"Good morning, princess," Declan chirped.

"Umph," Charlie mumbled as he twisted his head towards the sound. He absentmindedly wiped the slobber from his face, while gradually righting himself. "Ow." He cringed, then rubbed his neck and smacked his lips as if trying to get them to make a coherent word.

"Here," Declan said, passing him a latte. "This might help."

"Thanks," Charlie said as he took the cup and sipped.

Declan stood there, perfectly coiffed and dressed in a pristine white shirt and khakis.

"How...?" Charlie said, as he pointed to Declan's hair, then shirt and pants.

"Years of practice. Now, pull yourself together. You can use the shower upstairs. Give me your shirt and I'll iron it while you're getting cleaned up. Your pants will be fine."

"What's the rush?"

"I have more questions I want to ask Katherine Mann. I texted her this morning and set up a meeting at her place at nine-thirty. After that, we're going to meet with Sheldon Prescott."

* * * *

Charlie locked himself in the bathroom. He'd refused to undress in Declan's presence. There was no way Charlie was going to let Declan see him without his shirt on — especially in light of what he had seen the night before. If he took all of the muscles in his body and bundled them together, they still wouldn't amount to one of Declan's pecs. Charlie was a skinny torso balanced on top of a big ass and too-thick thighs. It was a sight he kept to himself.

"The iron's hot," Declan called out.

Charlie wrapped one towel around his waist, then a second around his shoulders. He opened the door a crack and quickly handed out his shirt before closing the door.

Charlie looked around the bathroom. It was nothing fancy. A toilet, sink and large shower. For a guy who lived on his own, Declan kept it pretty clean — thank God. Charlie couldn't stand mouldy showers.

He turned the tap and when the water ran hot, he dropped his armour of towels and stepped in. The soap and washcloth were already wet from Declan's earlier shower. Charlie held the cloth to his nose and inhaled. It had been up against Declan. He rubbed it all over his own body, scrubbing slowly with the cloth, eventually wrapping it around his now-erect penis and jerking off until he came. He thought about rinsing the cloth clean, then changed his mind. He hung it up where he'd found it and hoped that Declan wouldn't wonder why he had taken so long.

After his shower, Charlie found his neatly pressed shirt on the bed. He dressed and made his way downstairs to Declan's office.

"Here. Let's have a look at you." Declan looked Charlie up and down. "You clean up nice. You'll do the company proud. Now, grab a notebook and pen and let's go."

Declan handed him a medium-sized plastic suitcase.

"Superhero costumes?" Charlie joked.

"Camera equipment. You'll have to learn how to use it eventually."

"Cool." Charlie loved tech.

It was a half-hour drive from the office to the Mann house. Charlie chose to ride in the back seat of the van so that he could play with the camera equipment. Declan was lucky that he liked having his picture taken, because Charlie took dozens of them, close-ups of various body parts — ears were of particular interest — and profile shots, after Charlie had shifted into the front passenger seat.

"I'm pretending you're a body found at a crime scene."

"Charming."

Charlie continued shooting, playing with shutter speed and aperture settings. He was a quick study when it came to anything with a battery and circuit boards.

Katherine Mann's house was in Mount Royal, one of Calgary's wealthiest neighbourhoods. It was a two-storey Georgian-style estate home, located only a few houses down from the Swedish Consulate.

They pulled into the driveway, got out of the van and Declan rang the bell. After a few seconds, Katherine opened the door. Gone were her designer clothes, meticulously groomed hair and impeccably applied makeup. Instead, she wore a loose-fitting tracksuit and looked like she hadn't slept in days. Katherine said nothing, but stepped aside and ushered them in.

The three sat in the comfortable living room. Without asking, she brought in a French press, three mugs, creamer and a sugar bowl.

"I assume you'll join me. It's the only thing keeping me running."

"Please," Charlie said. "May I pour?"

"Thanks. You're a doll," she said, before settling into a deep comfortable chair. She pulled her legs up, and tucked them beneath her.

"Milk and sugar?" Charlie asked.

"I'd better have milk. And a lot of it. My stomach is probably bleeding by now," she replied.

Charlie set her cup on the side table nearest her. He poured cups for himself and Declan.

"Is it safe to assume that you've heard nothing from Ian?" Declan asked.

"Nothing."

"Have you contacted anyone — relatives, business partners or friends — to see if they've had any news?"

"There are no relatives," she said. "I've messaged most of our friends with no luck. As for business contacts... I...I haven't had the energy to do that yet. It's a tricky thing, business. You have to be so careful about what people find out, and when."

Declan leaned forward. "Why would you say that? Has Ian been involved in any contentious business dealings lately?"

Katherine paused for a moment as she looked at the table. "I forgot the scones." She got up and headed out of the room.

Declan and Charlie waited for a few minutes before Charlie called out, "Mrs Mann, may I be of some assistance? Mrs Mann?" He made eye contact with Declan, and they both got up at the same time.

They found her in the kitchen, staring at a large ceramic bowl filled with what appeared to be dough. The counter was cluttered with a bag of flour, boxes of baking soda and salt, a bowl of currants and the remains of a pound of butter. She was shaking her head.

"I could swear I baked these this morning," she said, talking towards the counter before looking up at the two men. "I bake when I'm stressed and... I must have gained two pounds over the past few days. I even left the oven on. I'm losing my fucking mind!"

"I'll tell you what..." Charlie said, looking around. "Why don't we head back to the living room and you can bake them later? We're not going to be that long, anyway."

Katherine nodded and led the other two back into the living room. Once they were all seated, Declan said, "I was asking about any business dealings that might have gone bad?"

She thought for a moment. "I know that a development group was trying to buy his property downtown, but Ian had his own plans for the building."

"Do you know the name of the company?"

She paused. "Ian never told me."

"Did your husband seem particularly worried about this other company?" Declan pushed.

Katherine paused, then said, "Not particularly worried, although he was distracted. He was distracted a lot these last few months. I was pushing him to get back into photography. That's where he was happiest."

Declan noticed Charlie staring at a wall covered in a series of framed portraits of a beautiful young woman.

"Are these all by your husband?" Charlie asked. He walked over to examine the photos. "They're all of you, aren't they?"

"From a long, long time ago," Katherine replied, smiling. She joined him.

Charlie looked at her. "They're remarkable. And, you said he gave up photography?"

"For quite a while, but he was very excited about a new series he'd just started working on. Ian had been shooting a young man this time. He showed me the proofs. Very eighties Bowie, if you know what I mean. Probably the best work he's ever done."

Declan interjected. "Does Ian keep business documents here, in the house?"

"He has an office upstairs."

"I'd like to have a look around up there, if that's all right with you."

"I don't think Ian would like that. He doesn't even like me going in there."

"There may be something in the office that could help us find him," Charlie said.

Katherine looked conflicted, then nodded her head and said, "If you think it will help."

Declan shifted in his seat. "Before we do that, I'd like to ask you more about your relationship with…Matthew, is it?"

"Michael."

"Michael," he corrected himself, knowing full well that it was Michael Taylor. He had just wanted to confirm that her story hadn't changed.

"There's not much to say. I've known Michael since he was born. I know that sounds a bit disturbing, but he went away to St Andrew's College boarding school when he was ten and I didn't see him again until he came back when he was twenty."

"That's a bit late to be graduating high school, isn't it?"

"After he finished, he travelled through Europe for a few years. Deirdre and Simon held a party for him after his return. Sort of a make-up party for missing his eighteenth."

"And you hit it off," Declan pressed.

"It's not quite as cheap as it sounds. I wasn't just trying to shag him because he was an attractive, muscular young man. Michael's very mature. He can converse as easily about fine art as he can about sports."

"And how did Ian feel about Michael?"

"He liked him. Quite a bit. One thing they both had in common was a love of hockey. If you got the two of them talking about that, you might as well leave the room."

"Did Ian know about your affair?"

Katherine paused for a moment, and when she spoke, she seemed to be choosing her words carefully. "You should understand, the open relationship — it was Ian's idea. He did it for me. He wanted me to be happy. But Ian and I had rules. We weren't supposed to sleep with anyone in our circle of friends or acquaintances, and we weren't allowed to bring them home."

Declan pressed, "So you broke the rules."

"Yes."

"Did you ever bring Michael home?"

"Never. On a few occasions we met at Deirdre and Simon's house when they were away on vacation. Other times, at a hotel."

"And you never suspected that Ian knew about this relationship?"

"No."

"And you had no inclination that Ian was seeing anyone else?"

"No."

The doorbell chimed.

Katherine opened the door while Declan and Charlie stayed in the other room. Declan could see the entrance through a reflection in a mirror. Outside stood Luke Fraser and Sergeant McKeckran.

"Mrs Mann, may we come in?" Luke asked.

The police entered the hallway.

Declan heard Luke say, "I'm Constable Fraser. We have some bad news. I'm sorry to have to tell you this, but we think we have found your husband's body."

Katherine sank onto a small padded bench beside the door.

"Do you have someone you would like us to call? A friend or relative?" Luke asked. Declan noticed that Luke was doing all of the talking. McKeckran had remained silent until Declan entered the hall from the living room.

"Hunt? What the fuck are you doing here?" McKeckran said.

"Mr Hunt is a friend of mine!" Katherine snapped back.

Declan knelt by Katherine and took her shoulders in his hands. "Katherine. The officers are going to ask you to go with them. They're going to need you to formally identify Ian's body. Isn't that right, officer?" he said, directing the question to Luke.

"He's right, Mrs Mann. Would you like Mr Hunt to come with you?"

"No. I think I'd like to call my friend, Deirdre," she said.

Declan said, "I'm very sorry, Katherine. We'll leave you with the police, but call me if you need anything."

Declan walked back to the living room to retrieve Charlie. Katherine followed him and grabbed his arm. "I need you to find out what happened. I don't trust them," she whispered, looking back at the police. Declan nodded to her and indicated to Charlie that they should leave.

Charlie gave Katherine a brief hug and said, "We'll figure out what happened to your husband. I promise you."

Chapter Fifteen

The room was comfortable, not cold and sterile as she'd expected. Katherine took in little of it. She was too numb.

She didn't remember the ride in. The two police officers who had come to the door drove her to the Office of the Chief Medical Examiner. Deirdre and Simon were there waiting for her.

"Oh...my dear," Deirdre said, putting her arms around Katherine.

Simon put his hand on her shoulder. "We're here for you, Kat."

"If you will all follow me," Luke said. They entered the one-storey brown brick building, walked past the reception desk, down a few nondescript corridors and through a door marked 'Viewing'.

"Can I get anyone anything?" Luke asked. "Water, tea or coffee?"

"Water would be nice," Simon said.

Katherine just sat there and said nothing.

An older man entered the room. He whispered to the two officers, then turned to the visitors.

"Mrs Mann," Luke gestured, "this is Dr Willart, the coroner."

The coroner began, "Mrs Mann, I know that this is a very difficult time, but if I could ask you a few questions to start with."

Katherine nodded. Deirdre took Katherine's hand in hers.

"Did your husband have any identifying marks? Scars, tattoos, birthmarks?"

"No," she started, then paused. "His eyes. They were different colours."

"What colours would they be?"

Katherine didn't respond for a moment. "Uh…one's blue. The other…greeny-grey."

"Do you recall what colour his right eye is?"

Katherine began to cry and looked toward Deirdre. "I can't remember! Deirdre, I can't remember. I can't even picture it right now." She buried her face in her hands.

Simon's face crinkled into a frown as he asked the coroner, "Why the right eye?"

Deirdre shot him a sharp look. "Simon! You're not being helpful."

"I was just asking—"

"Not…now!" Deirdre said in a loud whisper.

The coroner replied, "I was just hoping to confirm which eye was which colour." He looked at Katherine. "At times like this, memory can easily get…muddled."

Luke interjected, "Mrs Mann, can you think of any reason why your husband might have been along the shores of the Elbow River on the night he disappeared?"

"No."

"So, he wasn't one to go fishing, or...swimming?"

"No. Are you saying he drowned?"

Dr Willart took a breath before continuing. "Mrs Mann, your husband was found in the river. More to the point, he was naked. Constable Fraser was simply trying to determine if he was the type to go for a swim."

"In the river? Why would he..."

"Mrs Mann, I'm going to show you a video image of the man we believe is your husband. Are you ready to see it and tell me if you recognise him?"

Katherine nodded and held tightly onto Deirdre's hand. A screen lit up with an overhead image of a man's face and neck. Below that was draped in a sheet. The left side of his face was covered in a cloth. Katherine looked at the image. The face looked so...colourless. And slack. She couldn't make out the hair. Ian's always fell across his face. This face was bare. Was this Ian?

"I will now show you a profile angle," Dr Willart informed her.

The camera view instantly changed to a side view. The ear looked like Ian's but...

"Is his ear pierced? I can't see it," Katherine asked.

"It is."

"And the other ear?"

Dr Willart answered, "Yes, they're both pierced."

Katherine continued to examine the face. It looked like an amateur artist's rendering of Ian. Everything was there, only not quite right.

"Mrs Mann?" Dr Willart prompted. "Is this your husband?"

"Yes... I think. It looks like it...may have been him. Maybe. It looks...different. His eyes?" Katherine asked.

Dr Willart referred to his notes. "The left eye was grey-green, his right, light blue. One final question — do you wear a particular make and shade of lipstick?"

"What?"

"We found traces of lipstick on your husband's lips. I need to know if it was yours, or, perhaps…"

Sergeant McKeckran snorted and coughed.

"Officer," Dr Willart snapped, "do you need a glass of water?"

Katherine hated the man that coughed. And the hate gave her enough clarity to remember and say, "Tom Ford's Fucking Fabulous Lip Color."

"And what shade do you wear?"

"It only comes in red." She knew it was the only lipstick Ian wore, but she didn't say *that* out loud.

After the viewing was over, Luke escorted them back to the parking lot. Katherine had agreed to Deirdre's request to drive her home.

Before getting in the car, Simon turned to Luke. "What's the next step?"

"For us? We'll find the location where this all happened. We'll start where Mr Mann's body was found, and work upstream."

Katherine turned to the constable and asked, "What happened to him?"

Luke replied, "They're still not sure. The results of the post-mortem will shed some light on that."

"Oh," she said.

"Don't you worry. We'll figure out what happened to your husband. I promise you."

Katherine frowned. That was the second time today she'd heard the same sentence, and she wasn't convinced that the promise would truly be kept.

Chapter Sixteen

After Declan and Charlie left Katherine's, they headed towards Sheldon Prescott's home. They drove west, past the towering ski jumps and serpentine bobsleigh tracks built on the former Paskapoo Ski Hill for the 1988 Olympic Winter Games. Fifteen minutes later, they turned towards Mountain River Estates, an area known for large mansions with impressive views of the nearby Rocky Mountains.

As they made their way down the drive to Sheldon Prescott's house, they were met by a closed gate set into a tall brick wall that surrounded the property.

"Holy... This place must be worth a fortune. It makes Katherine's place look small," Charlie said.

Declan nodded as he buzzed the intercom.

"Can I help you?" a scratchy voice said over the speaker.

"It's Declan Hunt. I'm a friend of Katherine Mann. I have an appointment with Sheldon Prescott."

The gates swung open and they proceeded up the long drive to the house.

"Should I bring the camera with me?" Charlie asked.

"Yeah. We probably won't need it inside, but I'm hoping we'll be allowed to do a search of the grounds."

Declan did a quick scan of the nearby property, noting the presence of several CCTV cameras. He also took in the placement of trees and bushes which might offer cover to someone who wanted to remain unseen.

As they left the van, the front door of the house opened and a heavy-set man in his mid-sixties stepped out onto the stone portico. He was dressed in casual slacks and a colourful print shirt. His hair was obviously dyed jet black and his teeth were a little too white. *He tries to look young, but the face-lift and hair plugs are a bit too obvious*, Declan mused.

"Mr Prescott? I'm Declan Hunt, and this is my assistant Charlie Watts."

"Ah. Like the drummer," Sheldon quipped.

"Yeah." Charlie feigned a weak laugh. "Just like the drummer."

"As you know, we're here about Ian Mann. Can we come in and talk?"

"Please," Sheldon answered, motioning for them to enter. He looked uncomfortable.

Sheldon ushered them into a sitting room to the left of the entrance hall, which was the size of Declan's entire apartment. An orange tabby cat lay on a couch by the window. Sheldon swatted at it. "Scat!"

It wandered away, unfussed.

They sat on what Declan thought of as 'old-lady' furniture — frilly, but very comfortable.

"I hope you don't mind, but I've asked another of Ian's friends to join us," Sheldon started.

"Of course," Declan said.

"Robert," Sheldon called out. "Robert! The detectives are here." Sheldon stood and walked back toward the hall, yelling, "Rob—"

"No need to yell. I'm old, but I'm not deaf," called another voice.

Around the corner from the hall an older man in a wheelchair appeared. He sported a well-fitting grey jacket with matching pants and a powder-blue shirt open at the neck. Unlike Sheldon, it was clear he wasn't trying to hide his age. His hair was thinning and grey. He wore thick-rimmed glasses and his moustache was unevenly trimmed. He had an air of unkempt nobility.

Declan and Charlie stood. Sheldon waved a hand toward them. "Robert, this is Declan Hunt and his assistant, Charles Watts."

"Please, call me Charlie," Charlie added.

"And I'm Robert Williams, Ian's oldest, and I do mean oldest friend."

"I'm so pleased that you could join us, Mr Williams," Declan said.

"Please, call me Robert," he said, grasping Declan's hand in both of his. "As we are dealing with such an intimate situation, I feel that we should all be on a first-name basis. Please, no need to stand on my account."

Everyone sat.

Declan began, "First of all, we want to assure you that everything disclosed today will be held in the strictest of confidence."

As he spoke, Declan could see Sheldon checking them both out. He had no idea if his sexual preference was for males but he hoped that Sheldon would be attracted to one of them. Sexual desire for an interviewer almost always resulted in an interviewee being more helpful.

Robert had positioned himself next to Charlie, staring longingly at the young man.

Sheldon broke the silence. "Katherine's a dear friend. I hope I can help, although…I'm sure you can understand that there are some things I may not be at liberty to discuss."

"Likewise," Robert added.

"Of course," Declan said. "Is it all right with you if Charlie takes notes?"

"Please, go ahead," Sheldon said to Charlie.

Charlie had stuffed his pad and pen into the outer pouch of the camera bag. When he retrieved them, Sheldon became visibly nervous. "May I ask what's in that case?"

"Just some camera equipment, sir," Charlie replied. "Nothing is recording. I'll remove the batteries if that will make you feel more comfortable," he offered, then did so.

Good boy, Charlie, Declan thought.

"Thank you. I know it may seem a bit paranoid…"

"No. Not at all," Declan responded.

"It's important that you feel comfortable," Charlie added. "You've invited us into your home. You should always feel safe here."

Declan saw Sheldon start to relax. Charlie had worked his wonders.

"Now, if you could tell me about what happened the night of Thursday, the seventh of July."

The tabby cat returned to the room. It paid no attention to Declan or Charlie, and hopped up on the couch where Sheldon sat. It nuzzled up to him and flopped into his lap. Sheldon began to absentmindedly stroke it.

"There isn't much to tell," he began. "Ian arrived a little later than usual." He addressed his words to the cat, looking at neither Declan nor Charlie.

"Do you remember what time he got here?" Declan asked.

"He usually arrived just after seven. He liked to get here before anyone else. Ian liked to transform, as he called it, before any of the others arrived. He used to say it helped to set the tone for the evening. Our guests all had different tastes. Some dressed simply, some liked to wear next-to-nothing, but Ian always changed into something truly elegant—"

"He was definitely here before I arrived, which would have been about eight," Robert interrupted. "I was running behind schedule. My driver was late in picking me up. Ian was just putting on his finishing touches before he helped me get ready. He always helped me. I'm not as flexible as I once was. There was a time I would never have allowed that. The *reveal* is part of the fun, like in a magic act."

"Did Ian seem...distracted by anything?" Declan asked.

"Not that I remember," Sheldon answered. "He rarely brought any problems to our soirées. They're a place to escape our troubles. If anyone started to complain about things, Ian was the first to tell them to leave their problems at the doorstep. The night was for pretty people doing pretty things."

Robert interrupted, "That's not exactly true. Don't you remember?"

"Remember what?" Sheldon asked.

"Ian was all fussed about a property of his that someone wanted to buy. Ian needed the money, or so he said, but he had an emotional attachment to the building that was standing in the way." Robert redirected his focus to Declan. "The interesting thing about being in a wheelchair is that people often forget you're there. You become a piece of furniture, and no one bothers to hold their tongue when they perceive you as nothing more than an ottoman next to them."

"Oh, Robert, you're always overreacting."

"Sheldon, if you didn't want me to tell them what I heard, why did you invite me?"

Sheldon sat back, looking mildly annoyed. He began to stroke the cat with more vigour.

Declan intervened. "Did Ian say anything else?"

Robert replied, "He was strangely upset by the whole thing. Imagine, anyone being attached to *any* building in this town. I did ask if he was being strong-armed into doing something and he immediately changed the subject, flattering me on my dress and the new wig I'd bought."

He turned to Charlie. "It was a beautiful shag cut, *a là* 1970s Jane Fonda, not that her name would necessarily mean anything to you. You are so young… It would look fabulous on you, though. You have the figure for it."

Charlie smiled.

"Ian said he should take my picture," Robert continued. "You know, do a real photo shoot. He was always talking about how much he missed being a photographer."

Robert turned his attention to Charlie. "You know, he was *the* go-to photographer when he was still in London," he said, putting his hand on Charlie's knee.

As Robert spoke, Declan kept an eye on Sheldon, who gave the impression of someone used to the limelight who was being upstaged. He stroked the cat even harder. The cat gave Sheldon a swat with its clawed paw.

"Ow. You little bitch," he snapped, pushing it off his lap onto the floor. A small trickle of blood ran down his hand. Sheldon pulled a handkerchief out of his pocket and held it to the wound. "You feed and care for the children, and this is how they show their gratitude."

The cat wandered over to Charlie and hopped up beside him, where it settled in, staring at Sheldon.

Declan decided to refocus the conversation. "Were the usual guests all here that night?"

"All but one," Sheldon said, excited to be back into the conversation. "He was off with his wife in Cancún."

"So, how many guests did you have?"

"I don't know… There would have been me, Ian and Robert…" He started counting on his fingers, then continued in silence until he reached, "Twelve. Yes, twelve guests."

Declan continued his questioning. "Did anything out of the ordinary happen? Any arguments break out, especially involving Ian?"

"No. It was one big happy party," Sheldon said.

"It was a delightful evening," Robert added.

"And what time did Ian leave?" Declan asked.

Sheldon pondered the question for a moment before answering. "Well, he was usually the first in and first out. It would have been about…one in the morning."

"That's the last we saw of him before he disappeared," Robert added.

"Do you think something's happened to him?" Declan asked.

Robert was the first to answer. "Of course I do. There is no possible way that he would leave without saying goodbye to Katherine. He loved that woman. They had a good marriage, albeit unusual by most people's standards, and I'm sure there was no one else in his life. He would have said something to me about that. He told me everything."

"I have a delicate question to ask. You and he seemed to be…close," Declan commented.

"Are you asking if we were lovers?" Robert asked.

Sheldon snorted.

"I suppose I am," Declan said.

Robert smiled. "I should have been so lucky. But, no. I did love him, but it was unrequited. We were just destined to be good friends."

Robert, once again turned to Charlie. "Life seems to be full of amorous rejection. Be prepared for it, my young friend. But accept that it will happen and that, no matter how much the rejection hurts, you will survive, just like Gloria Gaynor says."

Declan saw Charlie's puzzled look and continued the interview. "Do you know if he was seeing *anyone* outside his marriage?"

"I don't think so," Sheldon said.

"Is there anything else that you can add that might clear up his disappearance?"

"Nothing that I can think of. He was a beautiful person, inside and out. I can't see why anyone would want to hurt him," Sheldon said.

Robert looked at Declan. "I hope I was able to help, even in a small way. Ian was very important to me…"

Robert's eyes began to fill with tears. Charlie put his hand on his shoulder, which Robert took in his and kissed.

"Well then, I guess we should be off." Declan got up to go. Charlie remained seated.

"Mr Prescott?" Charlie added.

"Yes?" Sheldon responded.

"I don't think your cat wants me to go."

The cat, now sitting in Charlie's lap, had its front claws deeply embedded in Charlie's leg—ten small spots of blood coloured the fabric of his pants.

"Oh my God! I am so sorry," Sheldon cried out. "Let go of him, you little cunt!" he screeched. The cat detached herself from Charlie's leg, plopped herself down on the floor and swayed out of the room.

"That cat is my ex-wife's. She got most of my money and I got the house and that holy terror. Send me the bill for a new pair of pants. I'll deduct it from her alimony."

"Oh, you poor dear boy," Robert offered, stroking Charlie's hand.

"Thank you for your concern, Robert. I'm fine," Charlie said as he stood and stuffed his notepad back into the camera bag.

As they made their way to the front door, Declan turned back to Sheldon. "I noticed that you have CCTV cameras covering the area. Were they functioning the night of the party?"

"As far as I know," Sheldon replied.

"Would you still have the video from that night?"

"The security company is supposed to keep it for a week. If I call them today, it should be just in time."

"Would you be able to get them to send me video files from that evening? From, say six p.m. until two a.m.?"

"I'll see what I can do."

"Thank you. I'd really appreciate it. And thank you both for taking the time to talk to us."

"I hope you find Ian. He was a good friend," Sheldon said.

"We'll do our best," Declan said, then shook Sheldon's hand.

"One more thing. Do you remember where Ian parked that night?" Declan asked.

"He always parked down by the tall spruce tree near the end of the drive. He said it made for an easier getaway."

"If it's okay with you, we'd like to just look around the area where the cars were parked," Declan added.

"Be my guest."

"Thank you, Mr Prescott, Mr Williams," Charlie added, giving them a crooked smile and shaking their hands.

As they walked back towards the car, Declan said, "You made quite an impression on Mr Williams."

"I didn't lead him on, did I? I just wanted to get the most out of the interview."

"You did well."

"I noticed that when you were interviewing Sheldon and Robert, you didn't mention that they'd found Ian's body."

"Sometimes the hope of saving someone is a stronger motivating force than that of dealing with something that can't be reversed."

They stopped to check out the area where Ian Mann had parked. Charlie put the batteries back in the camera. Declan had Charlie photograph the location and nearby gardens from different angles.

"Is there anything in particular we should be looking for?" Charlie asked.

"I'm just trying to get a feel for the last place Ian was known to be." Declan wandered the area by the tall spruce, looking around. In the detritus under the tree, he found a gum wrapper. He asked Charlie for the camera bag. From one of its pockets he pulled a small Ziploc bag which he flicked the wrapper into with the aid of a twig.

"You never know," he said to Charlie. "It might be useful."

He headed back to the van, Charlie in tow. As they drove towards the gate, Declan pulled over. "One more thing."

Declan hopped out of the van.

"Where are you going?" Charlie asked.

"Stay put. I'll be right back."

Declan walked over to the property line on the side of the gate that Ian had parked on. He worked his way along the wall, carefully studying the ground. Ten feet in, well sheltered from prying eyes, he spotted what he was looking for—a deep set of shoe prints. He placed one of his own feet next to them, careful not to put any pressure on the soil and leave a print of his own. The prints were just about the same size as his shoe—a ten. He snapped a shot of the markings on his phone, with his own as scale. Afterwards, he looked up at the wall. *Eight feet high, maybe more. The guy must've been pretty fit.*

He made his way back to the vehicle carefully.

When he reached the van he said, "The thing we really want is that CCTV video. That'll be gold, if we get it."

* * * *

Declan and Charlie drove back towards the office.

"Don't you ever get hungry?" Charlie asked.

"Why? Are you hungry?"

"Aren't you?"

"A detective can go a day without food. It's like camels and water."

"But I'm an office assistant. Speaking of which, do I get a contract or something?"

"I'll look through the files and find what I had drawn up for Mrs B. We can start with that until we know how long you're staying."

"That sounds good."

They drove on in silence for a few more minutes.

"I'm getting dizzy with hunger."

"Hold on. I have a place in mind."

Declan pulled into a restaurant parking lot. It was a breakfast place and the lot was fairly empty.

"Breakfast for lunch okay for you?" Declan asked.

"Perfect. My body has no idea what time it is."

Declan moved to the booth farthest from the door, and sat facing the rest of the patrons. Charlie plunked himself across from him and browsed the menu on the paper placemat. What he craved was eggs Benedict, but he quickly discovered why the restaurant was called 'No Poaching'. They appeared to prepare eggs any way but.

A waitress approached the table. She wore a black skirt, white blouse, pink apron and a baseball cap. Her name tag said "Doreen".

"Coffees?" she asked, leaning in and smiling at Declan.

"You bet. Thanks," he replied, and gave her a heart-melting smile. "And I'll have the egg-white omelette, please. Doreen."

The waitress finished writing up his order and continued to stare at Declan.

Charlie interrupted her reverie, "And I'll have the eggs over easy with peameal bacon, rye toast...and home fries."

She jotted down Charlie's order and walked away without looking at him.

Charlie looked at him. "Do you have that effect on everyone?"

Declan grinned. "Yup. So, let's look at what we've got. A man has been found dead. He disappeared after leaving a secret party — one that, if it became publicly known, could potentially have done him, and others, a lot of harm, both socially and in business. His wife's been having a secret affair on him, although they had an open relationship —"

Charlie interrupted, "An open relationship where she broke the established rules. So the boyfriend is also a suspect."

"Very good. What else, in terms of relationships?"

Charlie continued, "Robert had a crush on Ian, but Ian didn't feel the same way about him. But if it was a case of jealousy, he'd more than likely kill the other person before he'd kill Ian. And, really, I don't think it would be easy for him to dispose of a body while he's in a wheelchair, unless he was working with someone else."

Declan nodded his head in agreement. "We also know that Ian was involved in a business deal that was causing him stress. Maybe you could find out what land holdings Ian Mann had, both past and present. There might be something online. Or you might have to go down to City Hall and check the land records. If we could find out if anyone has been buying up properties around one of his, we might have ourselves another suspect."

"I'll see what I can find," Charlie said.

The waitress dropped off the coffees. "Here you go," she said, winking at Declan.

Charlie grimaced.

Declan's phone pinged with an incoming text. He glanced down at it.

"Oh-oh."

"What is it?" Charlie asked.

"It's from Luke."

Charlie's upper lip twitched ever so slightly.

"Seems he wants to have a bit of a chat," Declan said, while texting a return message. "Apparently he was surprised to see us at Katherine's."

"How 'bout that?"

"I told him to swing by the office after his shift. Let's see what he has to say."

The waitress dropped off their food. She leaned in towards Declan and asked, "Is there anything else I can get you?"

Charlie quickly replied, "No. We're fine, thanks. And you can bring us the bill."

Chapter Seventeen

It had been a long day. Charlie flopped himself down at his desk. Declan had retired to the couch.

"If I haven't mentioned it already, keep track of all of your hours. Even last night when you got me home from The Greek," Declan said. "You don't officially have any bookkeeping experience, do you?"

"No, but I found Mrs B's spreadsheets. I can use them as templates."

"Perfect. Just let me know how much I owe you each week, and I'll transfer you the money."

They both sat in silence, staring into nothing until Declan said, "I hope I didn't do anything...awkward last night."

"No. You were a perfect, drunken gentleman."

Declan laughed, primarily out of relief. In his hazy memory he remembered wanting to do something. "How the hell did you get me upstairs?" he asked Charlie.

"Oh, you helped, but don't be surprised to find impressions of my bony shoulder on your ass."

"It's late. Why don't you head home? Your folks'll be wondering what you've been up to."

"And that's a question I don't think I'll be answering."

Declan smiled then said, "You're a wise man, Charlie Watts."

* * * *

As Charlie drove home, he realised that, aside from his brief text, he hadn't spoken to his parents in two days. They were probably worried, although not worried enough to text or call him. Charlie pulled up in front of his parents' house. His mind whirled from the events of the past few days — saving Mr Attwal, finding out that he'd be staying on longer due to Mrs B's heart attack, the disappearance of Ian Mann... Then there was Declan.

He remembered watching him flail about like a child, trying to undress himself. He thought of Declan lying there, nearly naked. He could still see that massive chest rising and falling with each breath. He remembered running his fingers along his abs, like they were the keys of a piano. And...he remembered holding his hand over Declan's crotch. He could still feel the heat rising from the bulge in his briefs. *I wish I'd touched it. It was probably the only time I'll get a chance. Stupid, stupid, stupid! And now this Luke guy has slept with him. Declan will never be attracted to me — but he kissed me... He said I was cute.*

It was all too much. Charlie got out of the car.

He walked to the front door of the house then opened it. The sound of the television came from his grandmother's room. She was watching a rerun of *Coronation Street*. Charlie poked his nose in.

He pointed at the TV. "Ken Barlow sell his house yet?" he asked, in reference to one of the show's characters.

"Not yet. They'll stretch that scintillating storyline for the rest of the season," Gran answered, then smiled.

Their eyes connected for a moment, and her smile withered. "What's wrong, love? I haven't seen you in a few days."

Charlie plopped himself down on the floor beside her, and leaned his head on the arm of her recliner. "It's my new job. I'm working for a detective."

"That's good, isn't it?"

"I think he's my Constable Winslow...but I don't think he sees me."

Charlie's grandmother ruffled his hair. "Ah. Have you said anything to him about it?"

"No."

"Well, give it time. Do something that will make him notice you."

"I get him coffee, and I got the office security system up and running."

"No one is going to fall in love with someone because they know how to file."

"Look, I'm new at this...romance thing. I don't know what the hell I'm doing."

"That's obvious. We'll just have to make sure he doesn't find that out," she said. "You have to assess your strengths. You're smart. You're cute as a button—"

"You're my grandmother. You have to say stuff like that."

"You're kind and considerate, and you have the greatest smile I have ever seen. In the end, the best advice I can give is—just be the best you that you can be, and you'll be just fine."

Charlie shifted on the floor and looked at his grandmother. "How do I know who I am?"

"Only you can figure that out."

Charlie raised himself onto his knees and gave her a hug. "Thanks, Gran."

"I'm here for you whenever you need confusing advice."

Charlie headed down to his room in the basement. He flopped onto his bed and stared up at the ceiling... *Tomorrow, I'll make him notice me.*

* * * *

Declan's phone chirped. It was a text from Luke.

Can I come over? We should talk.

Declan responded.

I'm home now. I'll leave the doors open.

This was going to be an interesting meeting.

Be there in ten, Luke replied.

In exactly ten minutes, Declan heard someone coming up the stairs. Luke walked in. He was dressed in a well-fitting pale blue shirt and tight Levi's 501s. He carried a gym bag.

All prepped for fun, Declan thought.

"Hey there," Declan said. "Good to see you again."

"Likewise."

"Can I...get you a drink?" Declan offered.

"That'd be nice." Luke dropped his gym bag on the floor. "I didn't notice how nice this place was last time I was here. You must be doing well."

Declan passed him a tumbler of Scotch. "I get by. One case at a time."

"You own, or rent?"

"Rent. The owner runs the pastry shop downstairs."

Declan sat on the edge of the desk. Luke moved in a little closer. "I should stop in there sometime."

"You hardly seem the type to indulge in sweets," Declan commented, touching Luke's waist, where he found no trace of fat.

"Just for coffee." Luke stared at him in awkward silence. "So...the Mann case. I've got to admit, it was a bit of a surprise to find you there."

"Yeah... Katherine approached me yesterday. She was afraid one of the cops that interviewed her wasn't going to give her a fair shake. I wondered if it might have been the case you told me about the other day, but didn't know for sure until she mentioned McKeckran by name."

"Technically, we shouldn't talk about the case," Luke said as he moved in closer.

Declan shook his head. "We're not on opposite sides. We're both trying to find out what happened to this woman's husband, only you're shackled to a bigoted senior partner and working within the law."

"And you're not?"

"No. My partner isn't the least bit bigoted." Declan smiled.

"You know what I mean."

Luke moved in a little closer. "What if we agree to help each other out," Luke said. "I tell you everything I know about what's going on, if you do the same."

"You'll show me yours if I show you mine?" Declan laughed.

"I'm serious," Luke said. "I could get into a lot of trouble if they ever found out I was talking to you —"

"Then why take the chance?" he said, but Luke said nothing. Declan continued, "Unless if I give you something you can use, it'll make you look better to the brass."

"I never said that."

"But you were thinking it. You'd be a fool not to."

Luke stared at him. "They'll be treating this as a homicide. The bones on the left side of his head were badly fractured and there was a lot of tissue damage. The coroner thinks it was done with an irregular, heavy object, like a rock."

"The damage couldn't have been caused by a fall, could it?"

"Possibly. The question is — how did his body wind up floating in the Elbow River?"

"Where on the Elbow?" Declan asked.

"On the eastern edge of the Glencoe Golf and Country Club."

That's...downstream from Sheldon Prescott's neighbourhood.

"Your turn," Luke said.

Declan began, "The night he disappeared, Ian Mann was attending a house party that involved individuals that certain police officers might be prejudiced against. They'll eventually find out about it, but not from me."

Declan could see Luke processing this new information.

"The lipstick on his face — it wasn't Katherine's, was it?" Luke asked.

Declan just stared.

"I can see why you don't want that to come out. I take it that you've been to the party house?" Luke asked.

"I have," Declan answered.

"And I don't suppose you'd be willing to tell me where it is?"

"Not if I want to maintain any credibility with my clients." Declan walked over to the cabinet containing the safe and brought out two objects. "But I did find this gum wrapper in the garden near where Ian parked his car. I also found this." He passed him a copy of the footprint photo. "I discovered the prints in the dirt by the security wall surrounding the property. That's my foot for scale. A size ten and the impressions were deep, like someone had jumped from the top of the wall."

"May I?" Luke said, taking the evidence. "If I could figure out some way to run the wrapper through forensics for DNA or prints without letting the boss know, would you be interested in the results?"

Declan said, "Sure. Anything for the hottest cop on the Calgary Police force."

"Anything?" Luke asked as he began to kiss Declan's neck.

"I take it that you didn't just come over to interrogate me?" Declan asked.

"Would I have brought along a change of clothes if that was the case?"

Declan smiled and said, "I think we'd better take this upstairs."

Chapter Eighteen

Declan was jarred awake by a loud beeping sound.

"Don't worry," Luke said. "I set my phone alarm so I don't miss roll-call. I've always had this thing about being on time." Luke leapt out of bed, pulled his uniform shirt out of his gym bag and started to put it on.

As Declan watched Luke get dressed, he said, "Were you one of those kids who always wanted to be a cop?"

"Nah."

"Parental pressure?"

"No. My own stupid choice." Luke laughed. "Dad wanted me to follow him into politics. I was an only child, and that's what was expected."

"So. The son of a politician, huh?"

"Not just any politician. Calvin Luther Fraser."

"No way? 'Old Stetson' — he's your father?" Declan was shocked.

"I never should have told you."

Declan grabbed Luke and pulled him back into bed. "Are you kidding? Points to me. I just slept with the son of, what is it, fourth-generation Conservative Party royalty!" Declan tickled Luke's ribs. Luke giggled like a kid. "You choosing to be a cop... That must have been tough on him. It's the end of a political dynasty. That's got to be a kicker for an old-time right-winger like him," Declan said.

"What's really important to him is that I'm happy. That's what we all want for the people we love, isn't it? To be happy?" Luke asked.

"Not my dad," Declan said.

"He must've been proud of you when you signed up for the force."

Declan frowned. "The words 'pride' and 'my dad' don't go together. He basically told me that I'd be joining up right after high school. He thought it'd toughen up his faggot son and I wanted nothing more than to prove that being gay didn't mean I wasn't a man. In training, I pushed myself harder than any of the other cadets. I was the top of my class in everything. Even then, my dad never showed any sign that he was proud of me. I was always a fag to him."

"Did he say that to you?"

"He didn't have to. I could tell." Declan got out of bed, went over to the sink and got himself a drink of water.

Luke sat up on the edge of the bed. "When you got fired—what happened? I asked around but no one would talk about it in detail."

Declan turned around. "After I graduated, I was involved in a domestic dispute call. A guy had beaten up his wife. She was a mess. I flashed back to the fights my folks used to have—not physical, like this one, but just as abusive. I wanted to kill the guy, but my partner could see how it was affecting me and got me out of the way before I did something I'd regret.

"When we got back to the station I went to shower off the stress. There were a bunch of guys in the change room. This one cop, Hays, looked at me and said, 'I've heard the rumours, and there's no way I'm showerin' with a queer! Use the ladies' showers, you fuckin' little cocksucker.'

"I remember flying across the room. A few swift punches left Hays on the floor with three broken ribs, a fractured jaw and a concussion. I walked away with my dignity and a pink slip. I found out later that my dad had saved me from a criminal assault charge by telling Hays that he would let everyone know that he was beaten up by a fag in a shower room if he dared to talk about the incident again. That was the extent of my dad's loving instinct."

"Wow. That's rough."

Declan moved back to the bed and sat down. "So, Constable Fraser, does your dad know what you like to do in your spare time?"

Luke got up and continued to dress. "Not the particulars. Yes, he knows I'm gay but I'd rather not talk about that right now. Look, I gotta go."

"Did I say something wrong?"

"No. I've got to get to work. See you sometime later today?" Luke asked.

"Sure."

"I'm off at four. I'll text you my address in case you want to drop by."

He gave Declan one more quick kiss, finished getting dressed and headed towards the stairs.

* * * *

Charlie got up early and snuck out to avoid having to deal with the questions his parents would undoubtedly ask him. He arrived outside Gwen's shop and tried the door. *Still locked.*

Charlie knocked at the window and Gwen appeared. She waved and made her way around the counter to the café door which she unlocked.

"What gets you up so early?" she asked, ushering him in and locking the door behind him.

"I have a baking emergency," he said with enthusiasm.

"Well, we can't have that, can we? What'll it be?"

Charlie's eyes scanned the display case. "I...don't know," he said, dejected. He turned to her. "What does Declan like best?"

"I know just what you need." She went behind the counter and assembled a box, which she started to fill. "Two *pains au chocolat* – "

"What are those?" Charlie asked, pointing to little pastry balls coated in chocolate, stacked two high, with a little collar of piped cream in-between.

"Those, my hungry little friend, are *religieuses* – *choux* buns filled with pastry cream, topped with a chocolate *ganache* and decorated with a little collar of piped whipped cream. They're supposed to look like little nuns."

"You had me at pastry cream. He likes them?"

"He'll deny it, and he'll curse you for every ounce of weight he puts on, but, yes. He'd choose them over oxygen any day."

Charlie took his box of treats up to the office. When he entered, he noticed that Declan had not armed the security system. He might have forgotten the code. Charlie made a mental note to remind him. He left the pastries on his desk and went into the kitchenette to prepare the morning coffee. Declan would be down in a few minutes.

As he finished pressing the ground espresso beans into the portafilter, the door to Declan's office opened. Through the partially opened kitchenette door, Charlie saw a person. It was not Declan. His first thought was that someone had broken into the office. Then, from the safety of the dimly lit kitchenette he recognised the intruder. It was Luke Fraser. He'd spent the night. Again.

Charlie's heart hit the floor.

"Wait," Declan called out from the inner office. "The alarm'll be on."

Declan ran past Charlie's hiding place. It was the first time Charlie had caught a glimpse of Declan fully naked. He was...glorious. Charlie didn't think his heart could fall any further, yet somehow, it did.

Declan said, "Shit, I forgot to turn this thing on. Charlie'd kill me if he found out."

There was silence. Charlie crept to the crack in the door, and peered through. The two were kissing deeply.

After the kiss finished, Luke turned and left the office. Declan sighed loudly, walked back to his office and went up the stairs to his apartment.

Charlie stood in the dark and started to cry. *Pull yourself together, Charlie. Act like a professional.*

He made his way to the office washroom where he rinsed his face. In the mirror, he could see that his eyes were bloodshot. He would blame it on allergies.

Just then a large crash rang out through the office. It was leg-day for Declan.

Charlie needed to step out.

He made sure to leave a large note on his desk — one even Declan wouldn't miss.

Gone to Gwen's.

He locked both the office and street doors and re-entered the aromatic refuge of *Les Trois Magots*.

"Back so soon?" Gwen asked.

"I guess it's hard to stay away, and I forgot to get coffees."

Gwen stared at him.

"What's wrong?" she asked.

Charlie shrugged his shoulders. "Nothing."

"Then why are your eyes red?" she said as she came around the corner of the counter.

"Allergies," he said to the floor.

Gwen put her hand under his chin and raised his head until he was looking her in the eyes. "You know, you can always talk to me if you're having problems," she said.

"I'm good."

Gwen patted him on the shoulder. "All right. How about a latte?"

Charlie smiled. "Please. And an Americano for Declan."

"You got it."

He thanked her for the coffees, then left the store, pushing the door open with his back. He was surprised to find an attractive young man trying unsuccessfully to open the street-level office door. The man was well-built and stood a little taller than Charlie. He wore an immaculately tailored light-grey suit and expensive Italian leather shoes.

"May I help you?" Charlie asked.

The man seemed a little flustered. "Uh... do you work here?" he said, pointing to the locked door.

"I most certainly do."

"Are you Declan Hunt?"

Charlie laughed. The young man seemed hurt. His face flushed. "Oh, don't worry. If you saw him you'd understand. Do you have an appointment?"

"No. No I don't. I'm sorry—I knew he wanted to speak to me. I was in the area and thought I could get this over with."

Get it over with?

"Come on up. I'll see if he's free."

Charlie's hands were full. "Would you mind..." Charlie said, handing him one of the coffees. Charlie unlocked the door, opened it and asked the nervous young man to follow. At the top of the stairs, he unlocked the office door and held it open.

"After you," Charlie said, plucking the coffee cup from the fellow's hand as he passed. If he wanted one, he'd have to put up with one that Charlie had made. He might have been young and cute, but that coffee was for Declan.

"So, may I have your name?"

"Michael Taylor."

The name more than rang a bell.

"If you'd please take a seat, I'll be right back." Charlie walked quickly to Declan's office, which was empty. He looked at the green door behind the desk. He walked up to it and knocked.

He opened the door and called up, "Declan? You decent?"

There was no response.

He snuck up the stairs, hoping to catch his boss in a compromising situation. There was no one there...

When the door to the bathroom opened, Charlie jumped. Back-lit by the light pouring from the window stood Declan, just out of the shower. The way he held the towel covered the one thing Charlie wanted to see more of.

"Yes?" the detective asked.

Charlie quickly composed himself. "Sorry to barge in, but Michael Taylor is downstairs and would like to see you."

"Well, this is interesting. I'll be right down." Declan spun around and his towel dropped. Charlie took in the glory of the Greek sculpture that stood before him, sliding into his underwear.

When Charlie left Declan's office, he was certain that Michael would hear his hammering heart. "Mr Hunt will be right with you."

"Thank you."

Charlie watched the man absentmindedly rubbing his index fingers with his thumbs as he stared at the wall ahead of him.

Declan emerged from his office. "Mr Taylor? Thank you for waiting. Please, come and have a seat in my office." Declan indicated the way.

Michael stood, straightened his jacket and headed in. Charlie followed. Declan met him halfway.

"This guy looks pretty tense," Declan whispered. "I think he might be more cooperative if this wasn't two against one."

"Yeah. Something's got him wound up. Oh, I got us some coffees," Charlie said, picking up one of the cups from Gwen's. "Do you want yours now?"

"You are a life-saver…" he said, taking the cup with one hand, and rubbing Charlie's shoulder with the other, "but…" He chewed on his bottom lip, then over his shoulder yelled out, "Michael, would you like a latte?"

"Sure," Michael yelled back.

Declan got a sheepish grin on his face.

"Take it," Charlie said.

"My hero." Declan took the coffees into his office, then closed the door.

* * * *

Michael sat in the chair by the window. He had dark brown hair cut in a low fade, and a strong chin with a cleft. His eyes were grey and capped with thick brows. Declan could see why Katherine would find him attractive. He sensed Michael was nervous. Declan handed him the latte.

"Thanks," Michael said.

"Thank you for coming to meet me. I was going to give you a call and arrange to get together."

"I was coming down into the area so I thought I'd save you the trouble."

"What brings you to this part of town?" Declan asked, hoping to lighten the mood.

"I like to go to Dead Cat Records. It's just around the corner."

"The jazz place?" Declan asked.

"I'm into Ornette Coleman."

"Coleman's great. I'm partial to later stuff by Pharoah Saunders and Charles Mingus."

"Those two are pretty awesome."

Michael changed the subject and shifted in his seat. "Katherine said you wanted to talk. About Ian, and...other stuff."

Declan had a feeling that whatever Michael was about to say would have been rehearsed.

Michael told him the same story of reconnecting with her when he had returned from Europe, being dazzled by her European attitudes, to say nothing of her beauty. He professed his love for her and his lack of concern with regard to their age difference.

When Michael had finished his story, Declan said, "I understand your parents are unaware of this relationship?"

The tone of Michael's voice changed from nervous to one of superiority.

"My parents are blind to anything they don't want to know about. I suspect they've never given it a thought."

"How do you think they'd react if they found out?" Declan asked.

"Who's going to tell them — you?" Michael said.

"No."

"Then the chance of them finding out is virtually nil."

As his arrogance increased, Declan found Michael less and less attractive. "Tell me," Declan asked, redirecting the conversation, "what do you do?"

"Other than listen to jazz music? I'm in graduate studies. Business management with an interest in corporate real estate."

"Not law, like your father?"

"Father made it perfectly clear from an early age that he felt that I wasn't cut out for 'the law', as he pretentiously calls it."

"But business... Are you cut out for that?"

"I happen to be very good at it," Michael snapped back.

This was the state of mind Declan had hoped for. "So, how did you get interested in business?" Declan asked.

"I took two years off after high school. My parents agreed to let me tour Europe. I met a man—Pierre Lavigne—a vintner. I saw in his eyes the joy of running your own business. After that, I spent my time there travelling and talking to businessmen from every industry—fashion, computers, hospitality, real estate—and the successful ones all had the same look in their eyes. That trip changed my life. I just needed to gain some credibility, hence the degree in business."

Declan nodded. There was passion there—no doubt about it. "Now, if we could talk about the death of Ian Mann."

Michael hesitated. "Okay."

"To clarify," Declan added, "you don't think Ian knew about your affair with Katherine?"

"No. I always felt, when it came to Katherine's personal sex life, Ian didn't care."

"What makes you say that?"

Michael paused, as if to review his mental notes. "He just never seemed to show any jealousy when other men paid attention to Katherine, even when they were younger and far better looking than him."

"Did you ever talk business with Ian?"

"Not really. He may have been a player a while back, but he inherited everything he had. He didn't build his business up from scratch. I saw him as more of a manager, and not really an effective one. Since the crash, he's down to a single property."

Michael stopped talking. Declan wondered if he'd decided that dissing a dead man made him look bad.

Then Michael continued. "We did spend a lot of time talking about his hockey team."

"The Axemen."

"Yeah. He loved that team. He felt it made him a real Canadian. He treated it like it was an NHL franchise that he'd bought into, which of course it wasn't," Michael said with a patronising sneer.

"So, did you ever hear of anyone who would want him dead?"

"Ian didn't have an enemy in the world, as far as I knew."

Apparently there was someone.

Declan smiled, then stood.

"Thank you so much for stopping by. I really appreciate it. Can I get your number in case I have any other questions?"

Michael passed him a business card with his name, number and a customised realtor logo, then they shook hands and Michael departed.

Declan stayed in the reception room after Michael had gone. He stood there until the three beeps from the alarm system let him know that Michael had left the building, then turned to Charlie.

"He's hiding something. I can just taste it."

Charlie said, "Did you notice his feet? They looked to be around a size ten."

Declan replied, "It isn't an uncommon shoe size." Declan crossed his arms. "You know what's bothering me? What kind of guy refers to his lover by her full first name?"

"What do you mean?" Charlie asked.

"He always referred to her as Katherine. Never Kath, or Kat, or anything like that. What's he up to? And why did he come here unannounced? He really seemed to want to ensure that his rehearsed story was heard. I'm going out for a minute."

Declan ran down the stairs, turned out onto the street and saw Michael halfway down the block. He rushed after him, hoping he wouldn't be seen, but Michael never looked back. Michael reached for his phone and Declan was close enough to make out his voice.

"Katherine... That went well. I don't think he's as smart as you think. He believed everything I said... Look, I've gotta go. We'll talk more later." He ended the call and put the phone back into his jacket, then took something out of his pants' pocket. As Michael rounded the corner, Declan saw him slide a stick of gum into his mouth then slip the wrapper back into his pocket.

Chapter Nineteen

Charlie sighed, headed into the kitchenette to prepare a quick caffeine fix, then returned to his desk. He took his first sip of coffee and felt the immediate rush as it entered his system. Outside, a loud rumble shook the windows. There was a brief revving of an engine, then silence.

I bet Gwen put a quick end to that.

The alarm beeped, warning that someone was entering the building.

What now?

Charlie heard the slow plod of footsteps up the stairs as he took another sip of coffee. The door opened.

"Mr Attwal!" Charlie said with surprise.

"Mr Watts. It is so good to see you again, my friend."

They shook hands. Mr Attwal's left hand was still bandaged. Charlie tried not to stare.

"Yes. I am afraid that will not be growing back. But the doctors feel that they can do a good job of constructing me a new ear, although for now you cannot see the damage under my *pagri*," Mr Attwal said, touching his turban.

"Please, have a seat. I'm afraid Declan's out right now. Can I get you a tea or coffee?"

"Oh, no. Do not go worrying yourself. I will only be here for a minute. I wanted to give you both a gift. A small way of saying thank you for the great gift you gave me."

"Honestly, Mr Attwal, I know I speak for both of us when I say that a gift is not expected."

"That is very kind, but it is something that would give me great pleasure to do." The accountant reached into his pocket and pulled out a tiny box, and handed it to Charlie. "Now, I must be going. My son is downstairs waiting for me. I have to get busy and find some new clients. I lost the Monarch account when I lost this," he said, raising his left hand, "and I just found out that another client of mine has been found in a river. Maybe I should hire Mr Hunt to find me some more clients, eh?" He laughed, shook Charlie's hand again and left, calling out, "Until we meet again my friend."

What an interesting man.

Charlie reflected on what Mr Attwal had said. It gave him an idea. He went to his computer and did a quick search. "Perfect." He continued to look through folders and files.

Ten minutes later, Charlie took a sip of his coffee and looked at the box that Mr Attwal had left. He opened it. Inside was a note.

A real detective needs a real detective's ride. Your car is an embarrassment. Your gift awaits you on the street.

Beneath the note was an envelope containing a set of car keys.

Charlie walked over to the window and looked down. Sitting at the curb was undoubtedly the source of the noise he'd heard earlier — the cherry-red, 1970 Dodge Challenger from Abel's Wrecking Yard. Declan was standing beside it. Charlie ran down the stairs.

"It's gorgeous." Charlie said. "Mr Attwal gave it to us!"

"I guess the police are done with it," Declan replied.

"The car looks great. He must have paid someone to clean it up."

"Too bad, 'cause I have absolutely no use for a car like this."

"What?" Charlie cried out. "But it's…perfect. It's so…red. And shiny."

"Exactly. It's too noticeable for me to drive."

Charlie turned to Declan, disappointed that he didn't want the car. Declan held the keys out to him. "But it might be good to have a second car for you to use. Just in case Francine isn't up to the job."

Charlie couldn't believe what he was hearing.

"Come on upstairs. I'll get the paperwork started on the insurance," Declan said.

Charlie had a company car! How amazing was that? And not only a company car, but a company *muscle* car. Soon Declan was on the phone arranging for the vehicle to be covered by the company insurance.

Declan poked his head out of the office. "The car is good to go by tomorrow. Why don't you drive Francine home tonight and Uber in tomorrow. For now, I'll let you pull the new one around back and we'll leave it there for the night."

"Sure thing. Will do. Now, there's something I discovered while you were out. I was so excited about the car I almost forgot to mention it. When Mr Attwal was here, he joked that he was in the market for some more clients. He specifically mentioned losing the Monarch account, then he said that one of his other clients was" — he paused for effect — "found in a river."

"What?"

Charlie added, "So, I went to the files that we removed from Mr Attwal's laptop, and sure enough, there was a folder named Mann."

"You are a genius! Wait — I thought we sent those files to Mr Attwal?"

"Those were copies. I still had the files on the cloud server, which, I guess I was supposed to have deleted..." Charlie nervously admitted.

"Again — genius!"

"I was able to pull up all of his financials. I also found a list of properties once owned by Ian Mann. Most were smaller buildings which he sold off long ago. But there is one building — the Consolidated Canada Fertiliser Building. Whatever it is now, it's costing him a bundle in taxes and other fees."

"What else do you know about the building?"

"I looked it up online," Charlie said. "It's four storeys and a quarter of a million square feet. It takes up almost an entire city block."

"I wonder who owns the remainder of the block?" Declan stared out the window for a moment. "How much do you really know about accounting?"

"Nothing," Charlie replied.

"Well then, I think it's time to hire a new accountant. Do you happen to know any that are looking for clients?"

"Yeah. I have one in mind."

Declan grinned. "I'm going to visit Mr Attwal. In the meantime, call up Sheldon Prescott. See how the CCTV footage is coming and, while you have him on the phone, ask him if Ian ever mentioned the Consolidated Canada Fertiliser Building. And see if you can get a number for Robert Williams. He said he was Ian's best friend. Ask him if Ian ever said anything to him specifically about that building."

Charlie wrote it all down, then scanned through the contact list on his phone as Declan waved goodbye, and left the office.

Charlie dialled the number. Someone picked up the phone on the other end.

"Hello? Sheldon Prescott speaking."

"Mr Prescott," Charlie said in his cheeriest voice. "Charlie Watts here, from Declan Hunt Investigations. I hope I'm not interrupting anything?"

"No. Not at all."

"I'm calling about the security footage. It would be great to have a look at it as soon as possible."

"No problem, my boy. I just had an email from the security company. They were about to erase the files, but I caught them in time. They said they can do a digital file transfer directly to you, but the fellow I talked to needs clearance, and his boss is away until Monday."

"I'll look for them on Monday then."

"While I have you on the phone, may I ask one more question about the night of the party?"

"Of course. Go ahead."

"When Ian was talking about the property he was being pressured to sell, did he mention the Consolidated Canada Fertiliser Building?"

"Yes, I believe that was the property," Sheldon replied. "He said it was once the jewel in his real estate crown. From the sounds of it, the crown is looking a little shabby these days."

"Thanks so much for the information. I look forward to seeing the CCTV footage."

Before Charlie hung up, he got Sheldon to give him Robert William's telephone number. He called Robert and confirmed what Sheldon had said regarding the building. He had little extra to add, other than to say that if Charlie had other questions, Robert would welcome him with open arms.

Charlie thanked him and disconnected. The phone rang immediately after he hung up. He knew the number.

"Hey, Declan. Sheldon Prescott's security firm should be transferring the video files to us on Monday, and he and Robert have confirmed that the fertiliser building was the property of interest. I'm just going to start looking into who the potential buyer might be."

"Can you do that online?"

"I'll see what I can find out."

"Great," Declan said. "Call me if you need anything. I just wanted to let you know that when I'm finished up with Mr Attwal, I have a meeting with Luke."

"Oh." Charlie couldn't help but sound dejected. *I wonder if the meeting is clothing-optional... Snap out of it!*

"Thanks for letting me know," Charlie said. He hung up the phone and busied himself searching for more information on the building. Another half hour on the computer proved futile. Then an idea hit him. He would simply ask.

He did a Google Street View search of the area around the factory. Prescott was right. It was a dump. The images showed it as a rundown, four-storey brick structure that took up three-quarters of the block. The rest of the block was occupied by smaller buildings of an even older vintage which wrapped around two sides of the factory. These seemed to be mainly independent clothing stores, a record shop, a cheque-cashing operation and, what Charlie was mostly interested in, a good number of vacant buildings.

Charlie checked himself out in the washroom mirror. He looked presentable enough to pose as a... What would his cover be? This was exciting. He'd never pretended to be anything other than himself. He could be a designer, or a painter — they would need a studio space. That might work, but what if someone asked questions like "Oh, you must know..." Then it came to him...

Charlie locked up. On his way down to the parking area behind the building, he took a minute to admire the red Challenger, rubbing his hand on the hood. He'd have to move her later. He made his way to the parking lot and hopped into Francine. Reliable Francine. Just like him.

Charlie turned the key. She made a weak sputtering sound, but didn't start. "Don't worry, girl. I'm not giving up on you," he said, stroking the dashboard. He wished Declan felt like that about him. But why pick the reliable car when he could go with Luke, the shiny new red one?

Francine continued to moan and sputter. It was clear that the car was not going to start.

"Fuck it!" He slammed his hand on the dashboard. "Sorry, girl," he said.

Charlie ran back to the office and picked up the keys. In a flash he was standing beside the Red Beast — that would be its name. Beast for short. Red for when he needed to get personal. He slipped into the driver's seat and slid the key into the ignition. He hesitated before turning the key, but when he did, the four-hundred-and-forty-cubic-inch V-8 roared to life. He'd never wielded this kind of power before, and it scared and thrilled him at the same time. It was then that he realised that the Red Beast had a standard transmission. Charlie hadn't touched a standard since he'd learned to drive eight years ago, but he wasn't about to let that stop him. He had the power, and with no hills between him and where he was headed, five kilometres of road to remember how to shift.

Chapter Twenty

Attwal Accounting Services occupied a storefront in a strip mall in the northwest part of the city. On one side was an electronics repair shop, on the other, a take-out gyros restaurant.

Declan walked through the front door and was greeted by an older woman in a brightly coloured sari.

"May I help you?" she asked.

"Yes. My name is Declan Hunt. I have an appointment with Mr Attwal."

She gave him a stern look and a slight sneer crept across her upper lip. She stood and walked around the corner.

"Palvinder," she called out, then in a lowered voice, but just enough that Declan could still hear, "there is a man out there. He probably doesn't have much money, and I don't like the look of him. He says he has an appointment."

Palvinder Attwal came around the corner, followed by his receptionist. He beamed. "Mr Hunt," he cried out, as he grasped Declan's hands in his. "Mother, this is Declan Hunt, the man who was good enough to save my life."

"But not good enough to save your ear and finger." She didn't even try to hide her contempt.

"I only wish I could have found him earlier. I accept full blame for that," Declan said.

"Bah," the accountant said. "What is a finger good for but to point accusations, and an ear but to hear lies? Now," he said to Declan, leading him towards his office, "come and tell me what is on your mind. Mother — *chai* and *kaju katli*."

They sat down and Palvinder asked, "Now, my friend, what can I do for you?"

"First off, I want to thank you for the wonderful gift you gave us. My partner, Charlie, was speechless."

"It was the least I could do for what you did for me. And that little car of yours...it is a bit of an embarrassment. I can't have my hero driving around in that little shit-box. So after the police had finished with the red beauty, I convinced the wrecking yard fellow to sell it to me in exchange for a bit of help with his taxes. He was so pleased that he did the cleaning and detail work on the car for nothing!"

"Speaking of work, you mentioned to Charlie that you were in the market for a new client."

"Yes," Mr Attwal answered.

"As it so happens, I'm in the market for an accountant."

"Then it must be me! No discounts, of course, for saving my life. This is a business deal."

"Of course. I wouldn't expect it."

"Mother!" the accountant called out.

She entered carrying a tray with two ornate tea cups filled with *chai* and a small plate covered in triangular-shaped sweets. She set them down with a clatter and said, "I'm working on the contract right now. Don't rush me."

She quickly departed.

Declan smiled. "I'm going to like working with you, Mr Attwal."

"Palvinder, please."

"And please call me Declan. Now, I understand that one of your clients was Ian Mann."

The accountant crossed his arms. "I'm not sure how you found out, but yes, he *was* one of my clients."

"His wife hired me to find out what happened to him."

"Interesting." Palvinder nodded. "I thought the city had police to do that?"

Declan shrugged. "Sometimes it helps to have someone who is...free of blinders to look into a case."

"And sometimes it is just easier to handle things on your own, without the constraints of the outside world."

"Exactly," Declan agreed.

"So," Palvinder continued, "do you have any clues as to what happened to Ian?"

"Other than that he was murdered?"

Palvinder took a sip of his tea. "That is unfortunate."

"It seems that he was involved in an unwanted attempt to get him to sell one of his properties. Do you know anything about that?" Declan asked.

"As his former accountant, all I can say is that I was encouraging him to offload unnecessary assets to a developer, a view he didn't share."

Declan leaned in. "You wouldn't happen to know who that developer was?"

Palvinder picked up a sweet which he nibbled. "You are asking me to divulge private information of a valued client."

"Yes."

"Confidentiality is a sacred trust. An accountant is like a priest. You wouldn't expect a priest to repeat what a man said in confession, would you?"

"It depends on whether it would help to solve a murder," Declan replied.

Palvinder pondered that for a moment and took another sip of tea. "Well—it's a good thing I'm not a priest. That, and the fact that the developer is no longer a client of mine. It was Monarch Development."

Declan nodded. "And we know how far they'll go to get what they want."

"Precisely." Palvinder offered Declan the plate of sweets and the detective picked up a single piece and tried it. A cashew flavour flooded his mouth.

"This is delicious." Declan smiled as he continued, "Do you have the name of the person you were dealing with?"

Palvinder stared Declan in the eyes. "The Monarch account was highly unusual. All the transactions were done online and the first people I met from the company were my kidnappers, but I do not think they were in charge. That is all I know."

Palvinder's mother entered the office and handed Declan an envelope. She stared at him for a few moments. He smiled and said, "Thank you for the delicious *chai* and *kaju katli*."

She looked at him, her lips pursed, and without comment left the room.

"You must forgive her. A mother's love for her son is undying, and she was upset that I got hurt. Now, back to your accounting needs, have a look at the documents she gave you and, if you agree, sign them where indicated and courier them back to me."

"Thank you, Palvinder. I feel like I'm in good hands."

They shook hands and, as the accountant escorted him to the front of the office, a little girl came through the front door. She wore a backpack emblazoned with a ladybug. She smiled at Declan, who recognised her as the courier who had delivered Palvinder's laptop earlier in the week.

Palvinder walked Declan out to his van, looked at it and said, "Well, it's a bit better than the thing you rescued me in."

"This one's for surveillance. The car you gave me — that will have its own special uses."

Palvinder nodded. "I hope you find the men behind Monarch, but be very careful. I sense what they did to me was mild compared to what they are truly capable of."

Declan thanked Mr Attwal and got into his van. He wondered if indeed Monarch had killed Ian Mann and, if so, why?

Declan had decided that a quick change of clothes was in order before he paid Luke a visit. He called Charlie with the news about Monarch. The phone rang, then went to voicemail. He decided not to leave a message. He'd just tell him when he saw him later.

Declan parked in front of the office, and waved at Gwen as he walked by her shop. He only half-noticed that she was serving a customer. He mounted the stairs to the second floor. The sun shone through the windows, bathing everything in a warm yellow glow. He paused at Charlie's desk. He'd been lucky to find

Charlie. He had fit in instantly and picked things up quickly. It was hard to believe that he'd been with the firm for less than a week. And what a week it had been.

His stream of thoughts was broken by the chirp of an incoming text. He reached for his phone—but it wasn't his. The sound came from Charlie's phone, which lay on his desk.

"Charlie?" he called out.

He must have already headed out to check on the properties.

Declan went into the kitchenette and peeked out of the window that overlooked the parking lot behind the building. *Odd*, he thought. *Francine's still there...but the Challenger's gone*. He'd have to have a talk with Charlie about driving the car before he had the insurance paperwork.

The door alarm beeped, and he heard footsteps running up the stairs. The office door opened.

"I bet I know what you forgot," Declan called out from the kitchenette as he walked into the office, but the person in front of him wasn't Charlie.

"What the fuck do you think you're playing at?" a man yelled.

Sam Hunt stood in front of Declan in full dress uniform, a block of a man who oozed authority, his eyes blazing. Declan had to fight hard not to raise his arms, fists clenched—not in a boxing pose, but one with arms and fists held close to his chest like a shield to protect him against his father's rage.

Declan's therapist had told him that beneath everyone there lurked a child-version of themselves waiting to come to the surface during times of stress. It could be set free by any number of triggers—a smell, a sound, a person. For Declan, it was the angry side of his father.

He did what the therapist had told him to do — think of things that brought him back into the present — into his adult self. The first image that came to mind was Charlie and his quirky, crooked smile. A deep breath and the thought of Charlie snapped him into the present. The whole process, from recognition of the problem to the implementation of the practiced coping mechanism, took no more than a few seconds.

"Hey, Dad. Let me guess — you've been talking to Gerry McKeckran."

"Talking? That idiot came up to me at the Commissioner's Lunch and started ranting about my son interfering with a police investigation. In front of everybody! My son wouldn't be crazy enough to do something as butt-stupid as that, would he?"

"No, of course not. Unless it was my case to start with."

"This is no joke. Police trumps civilian every time. Your PI licence isn't going to protect you. Now, drop it and go back to peeping through windows or whatever the hell it is that you do!"

Sam turned and marched out, but not before he yelled, "I'm not going to be there to bail you out again."

Chapter Twenty-One

Charlie made it to the factory block with only two embarrassing moments. The first was when he approached a red light and put one foot on the clutch and the other on the accelerator rather than the brake. The Red Beast drifted into the intersection, making enough noise to put a Saturn V moon rocket to shame. The second was when he had to abandon a parallel parking space as a group of teens looked on laughing.

Eventually, Charlie found a nice, unobstructed spot on a side street. He collected himself, reviewed his cover story then headed out on his first undercover mission.

The factory was easy to find. Its ground-floor windows and doors were boarded up, festooned with notices warning trespassers that they were not welcome, and that the building contained hazardous materials.

Why would anyone want this building?

Charlie popped into the nearest shop to the old factory. It was a vintage clothing store called Old Rags to Riches. A young dude, dressed in clothes made of macramé, sat at the cash desk. His eyes were closed as he dozed in the late-day sun. Charlie cleared his throat and the dude's eyes rocketed open.

"Oh. Hi!" he mumbled. "Please tell me you haven't been standing there long."

"Don't worry," Charlie said. "I just came in."

"Thank God. One day I actually slept through a robbery. They cleaned out the till and I didn't even notice."

"Business hasn't been too brisk?"

"Business hasn't *been*," he answered.

"Sorry to hear that."

"No sorrier than me. I opened the store here because I thought this location was up and coming."

"Isn't it?"

"Well, if it was, it came and went while I was asleep." He laughed. "What can I help you with?"

Charlie could think of a number of things this attractive, albeit strangely dressed young man could help him with. He spotted the man's name tag. "Well, Dylan, my name's Scott Lazar, but my friends call me Scootch." He extended his hand. Dylan just stared at him. "I'm looking at renting a space in the area for my business. I'm in computer games."

"Well, you'll have some competition. Sonic Masters across the street's cornered the market in the area."

"I'll be opening a new development studio. I actually create the games."

"Oh. That's cool. Anything I've heard of?"

Charlie wasn't prepared for this. "Yes…uh… *Zombie Manifesto* is one. *Call of…V-valour* is our best seller," Charlie stuttered.

"I've played that one, dude. You invented it?"

"You bet. Every…dead zombie and troll. Now, about the properties around here. There seem to be a lot of empty buildings. Is there a reason for that? Something I should know about?"

"Nah," Dylan said, shrugging. "The company that holds my lease is just looking at renovating some of the older stores. At least that's what I've been told."

"And who's that?"

"Monar—I mean…I'm not supposed to say."

"Why not?"

Dylan looked around, and in a hushed voice said, "Apparently there's a bit of a real estate battle going on. The owner's trying to calm things down to keep our rents low. There's a rumour that if they get the big building, it will be developed into something that will bring us a lot of business." Dylan lowered his voice further. "But they're worried the competition is sending in spies to find out what we're paying, so we've been warned not to say anything to people asking questions."

Charlie nodded and whispered back, "I'm just interested in finding a space. If you can't talk about it, maybe you could give me a name and a number I could call to make my own enquiries? Maybe you'd even get a referral fee."

It was clear that Dylan was working out his options.

"Tell you what—if you leave me your number, I'll make sure to pass it on. I could use one of those referral fees," he said as he grabbed a pen and piece of paper, then stared at Charlie, waiting.

"Right. Perfect. My name's Scott Lazar. That's L — A − Z − A − R."

"Like the light beam, right?"

Charlie wasn't so sure that Dylan's business was ever going to be a great success. "Yeah. Like the light beam."

"Cool. And your number?"

"Here." Charlie took the paper and wrote down a number, passing it to Dylan before realising the number he had made up had only nine digits instead of ten.

Dylan didn't seem to notice. He looked at the paper and said, "Cool. I'll let them know."

Charlie wondered if Dylan's napping was a sign of a more serious medical issue. "Great. Anyway, Dylan, I'll let you get back to work. Have a great day!"

"Same to you."

Charlie waved and left the store. He looked back through the window as he walked by, expecting he'd see Dylan asleep in his chair. Instead, he was chatting away on the phone, gesticulating wildly and looking at Charlie through the window.

Three shop doors down, Charlie entered All Things Go Round, a used record store.

A pretty blonde woman with cobalt blue lipstick and bright pink eyeshadow sat behind the counter. Music played loudly in the otherwise unoccupied store.

"Great song," Charlie shouted.

"What?" the woman responded.

Pointing to the speaker, Charlie yelled louder, "Great song," but by then she'd had time to twist the volume control down, so his voice rang out through the store, overwhelming Simon and Garfunkel's *Bridge Over Troubled Water*.

"They're one of my favourite groups," she said.

Charlie walked over to the counter and leaned on it. In his most seductive voice, he introduced himself. "My name's Scott. Scott Lazar. Can I ask you a question?"

Chapter Twenty-Two

Declan made his way to Luke's apartment. He pondered the Monarch puzzle. If he'd only been able to get the name of the person in charge.

After being buzzed into the building, he took the elevator up to the fifteenth floor. *This place is posh.* Declan knocked on the door, which opened, revealing Luke's million-dollar smile. Declan's heart skipped a beat.

"I'll be back in just a sec. I'm on the phone in the other room. Make yourself at home."

Declan walked in and sat on the couch. From the other room he could hear Luke's muffled voice. He couldn't make out what was being said, but the tone of the conversation sounded heated. Declan looked around. Luke was doing quite well for himself. Through the window of the corner unit, Declan could clearly make out the Calgary Tower, the Bow River and the midway rides on the Stampede grounds. Then his gaze was drawn to the coffee table, and a stack of mail. The top envelope was stamped 'Final Notice'.

"I thought you'd never get here," Luke said, coming back into the room. "Sorry about that. It was my dad." He sat on the couch, grabbed Declan by the shoulders and pulled him in for a quick kiss.

Declan smiled. "Nice place. When I was a constable, I was lucky to afford a basement one-bedroom apartment. Looks like you've got, what, a two-bedroom, with a den and view of the mountains? Something you want to tell me?"

"My folks bought it for me, and the fancy couch we're sitting on is courtesy of a long shot on a horse that paid off."

"Do you always win?"

"Sometimes I win, sometimes I lose, but let's not talk about that." Luke kissed Declan's neck. "So, anything new on the case?"

Declan pushed Luke away. "Not so fast, officer. I don't give up information that easily. What's in it for me?"

"You should know by now, I don't make deals," Luke said.

"Then you're going to have to make me talk."

"Well then, I'll have to take you to the interrogation room." Luke took Declan's arm and dragged him down the hallway. As he pushed him onto the bed, Luke hauled off Declan's T-shirt. He teased Declan's nipples with his teeth before sliding down towards his stomach, taking his time exploring Declan's navel with his tongue.

Luke said, "So, are you gonna talk?"

"You gotta do better than that."

Luke yanked at the waistband of Declan's 501s and the fly-buttons burst open.

"Mmm. Commando. That'll save me time."

Luke wrapped his lips around Declan's hardening cock and started to suck. Declan felt Luke's teeth gently sinking into his flesh.

"Easy there. I've only got one of those."

Luke pulled back, making a popping sound as he released Declan's shaft, then ran his tongue along its length towards his balls. He sucked on one, then the other before pushing Declan's legs back. He paused and said, "By the time I finish this, you won't remember your own name," then he plunged his tongue into Declan's ass.

Declan moaned. His eyes rolled back into his head as Luke penetrated him repeatedly with his tongue. He knew when this was finished that he'd tell Luke anything he wanted to know.

* * * *

Charlie exited the third shop on the strip with no new information. The clerk in the wine store had been downright rude even after he'd bought a nice bottle of merlot.

He turned left to try his luck at another store and walked right into a wall. It was less of a wall than a large slab of a man built like a brick wall. Charlie was so startled that he gasped and dropped his bottle, which smashed on the pavement.

"Mind telling me what you're doin' here?" Brick Wall asked, poking Charlie in the shoulder.

"I was just buying a bottle of…oh, I'm so, so, sorry. I got it all over your pants. It was an accident. I'll pay for your dry cleaning."

"Why are you bothering these fine, upstanding business owners with lots of questions?"

With every word, Brick Wall moved Charlie farther away from the store and closer to a parked van.

"I was just asking—I was just looking to rent a space. I make games," he stuttered out. At this point, Charlie saw another guy who had been hidden from Charlie's view by the bulk of the angry man.

The smaller of the two men said, "Wait a minute. I know dat guy. He works for that detective, Hunt."

Charlie recognised the second man as the one who had come by the office to pick up Mr Attwal's laptop and finger.

"Is that so?" said Brick Wall. "So, you're snooping around for Hunt?"

"No, no. I make computer games—"

The next thing Charlie knew he was flying backwards and slamming into the side of the van.

"Don't lie to me," Brick Wall yelled, "or I'll throw you over this fuckin' van and into traffic!"

He reached for Charlie but had underestimated how far he'd thrown him, and just swatted air.

Charlie took advantage of the situation, rotating away and dodging around the front of the van. Brick Wall tried to follow, but was too large to fit between the two vehicles. Charlie continued his path onto the street then heard the screech of brakes and the squeal of rubber on pavement. He turned his head. The hood of a dark grey car was a foot away from his body.

He jumped as high as he could and made contact with the hood, then hit the roadway.

The last thing he remembered was a voice saying, "Charlie? Charlie, wake up. Wake up."

* * * *

Declan lay on the bed with Luke's head resting on his chest. Both men were spent. Declan said, "That was amazing. You've obviously had lots of practice."

"Not as much as some," Luke said, laughing as he poked Declan in the ribs. "I didn't start 'til I was almost out of university."

"Was that when you came out?" Declan asked.

"Oh, do we have to do this?" Luke replied, laughing as he struggled to get out of Declan's leg hold. "All right. Coming out wasn't as big a deal as I thought it was going to be, given that my family's pretty right-wing. In high school I focused on grades and sports. I loved wrestling and basketball, and I was good at them."

"Of course you were. Especially the wrestling, I bet."

"Asshole." Luke swatted Declan. "Anyway, there was nothing else to do. I grew up in a small town.

"I lived in residence at university where I was corrupted by the sins of alcohol and bar-hopping. By the end of first year I had fallen in love with a member of the intramural volleyball team, a physics major named Jamal. The thought of telling my parents that their son was gay scared the crap out of me. Jamal suggested that I should start by telling them I'd fallen in love with someone who was black, so that when I told them it was a guy, they'd be in such a state of shock, the gay part wouldn't register."

Declan released his leg hold on Luke. "So, how did it go?"

"When I finally got up the nerve to tell my parents, my mother just left the room and said to my father that it was obviously time."

"Time for what?" Declan asked.

"Time for my dad to come out to me."

"No fucking way!"

"Yup," Luke responded. Luke sat up on the edge of the bed. "And Mom knew all along. They'd been best friends since elementary school, and they loved each other. He said if it wasn't for her, her support, her brains and her good judgement, that he wouldn't have accomplished a quarter of what he did.

"He claimed she always knew and, in spite of that, she still agreed to be his wife. He had a solid career, and my mom was happy to help him out as it gave her status. He was just lucky to marry his best friend. I'll always remember what he said — 'sex can be exciting and exhilarating, but it will never last. The key to a long relationship is friendship.' And they did have *some* sex, otherwise I wouldn't be here."

Declan shook his head. "And they kept his secret all this time?"

"Yeah. And I'm hoping you will too. If this were to get out, it would kill my dad."

"I won't say a thing. I promise. Speaking of dads, I had a visit from mine today," Declan said.

"Oh?"

Declan remained silent for a moment.

"Not a pleasant encounter, I assume?" Luke asked

"It never is when it's a visit from the staff sergeant."

"What was the problem?"

"Apparently he was ambushed by McKeckran at the Commissioner's Lunch today. McKeckran made a scene about me meddling in a police investigation and he told my father to warn me that if he caught me doing it again, he'd arrest me on the spot."

"God, that McKeckran is such a self-serving prick," Luke said.

"Speaking of McKeckran, have you got anything new on the Mann case?"

"Just before you got here," Luke started, "I had word that they found where he went into the river. They discovered a blood-covered rock. Whether he fell on it or was hit with it, they're not sure yet. It's in for testing. They also found his car. The trunk contained a suitcase filled with women's clothing. Okay—I've shown you mine, now you show me yours."

Declan said, "The company that was trying to force Ian Mann to sell was called Monarch. I have reason to believe that they're connected to the mob."

"Monarch. Interesting..."

"Have you heard of them?"

Luke's phone rang. He answered, "Yeah?... I understand... I gotta go." Luke put his phone down and started to get dressed.

"Problem?"

"I gotta get into work."

"Okay."

Declan got out of bed and searched for his pants when his cell phone rang. He picked it up. "Hello?"

"Dec, it's Mickey. Look, you'd better get over to the bar, ASAP. I've got Charlie here. He's been in a fight. He was beat up pretty bad before he got hit by a car."

"What the fuck! Is he okay?"

"I checked him over. He's banged up, but I think he'll be fine."

"I'll be right there." Declan disconnected.

"What's happening?" Luke asked.

"Someone's about to regret meeting Charlie."

Chapter Twenty-Three

Charlie woke in a strange, drab room. He was lying on a small cot. There was a grey metal desk at his feet and a filing cabinet to his right. The room was dimly lit. Had he caught him—the massive man who'd thrown him against the side of the van?

"You're safe now," a familiar voice said. "No one's going to hurt you here."

Charlie sat up slowly. His side ached like a son-of-a-bitch. He looked around. Mickey was sitting on a chair.

"You're in my office. At the bar."

The door of the office burst open. "Where is he?" Declan asked.

"He's right there," Mickey said, pointing to the cot in the corner.

Declan hurried to the cot and dropped to his knees. He placed a hand lightly on Charlie's chest.

"Are you okay?" he inquired. Without waiting for a response, he asked Mickey, "Is he all right?"

"I checked him over, and he'll be fine. Bruised as hell, but fine. I've got him on ice packs. It should help reduce the swelling.

"What are the odds? There I was, driving along, minding my own business when I spot Charlie in a fight with two guys. You should have seen him. He was brilliant. First he spun out of the way of this big guy's fist. The guy was built like a fuckin' brick wall. Then he ran into the street right in front of my car. I slammed on the brakes and just at the right second Charlie vaulted up onto my hood and slid right across, landing on his feet, and then he fainted. The little thug who was watching let out a scream — sounded like a five-year-old." Turning to Charlie, he said, "You should take up parkour, Charlie. You're a natural."

"And he'll be okay?" Declan asked again.

"Just fine. Bruised ribs and a scuff to the forehead from when the big guy threw him up against the truck —"

"Big as a brick wall, huh?"

"But other than that, he'll be right as rain."

Charlie was confused. "Are you, like, a doctor?"

"Better than that," Declan answered. "He's a trained Armed Forces medic. He's fixed me up more times than I can count. Now," he said, lowering his face close to Charlie's, "how are you doing?"

Charlie met Declan's gaze. He was determined to be strong…but the relief and fear finally caught up to him and he began to cry. His body shook with sobs.

"I'll be in the bar if you need me for anything," Mickey said, nodding to Declan before leaving the room.

Declan held Charlie in his arms. "Hey, there, it's okay," Declan said. "I'm here and I promise, I won't let anything else happen to you. I want you to know you probably went up against the same guy that kicked the crap out of me last week, and from the sound of it, you handled yourself a lot better than I did."

"I'm so sorry," Charlie choked out between sobs. "I ruined everything... The other guy recognised me. They know I work for you."

"It's okay. It'll all come out soon enough."

"I did find out that the company that owns at least some of those buildings is Monarch," Charlie said.

"Fantastic. There, see, you didn't fail. And you'll have the bruises to show off as your war wounds."

There was a knock at the door and Mickey came back in. "Sorry, I forgot to give you these," he said, holding out Charlie's car keys.

"My keys... How did you —"

"You were talking in your sleep. You kept going on about leaving it behind and pawing at the keys in your pocket. I sent the Kid out to look for it. It's in the back lot beside mine."

"Thank God," Charlie said, flopping back down on the bed. "Ow!"

"I think it's time you got some rest. Come on, let me take you home," Declan said.

"Sure. Thanks." Charlie had hoped Declan would take him back to his apartment, but instead, Declan pulled up in front of Charlie's house.

Charlie asked, "How did you know where I lived?"

Declan smiled, "I'm a detective. That, and the address was on the top of your resumé. Do you need help getting in?"

"No. I'll be fine. Thanks."

As he watched Declan pull away, Charlie smiled. *I took on the guy that beat Declan up, and he said that I handled it better than he did. I can do this job and I really think it's a place I can fit in.* His smile faded as he looked at his cuts and bruises. *How am I gonna explain this to my folks?*

* * * *

Declan returned to the office. He sat at his desk and reviewed the events of the day. One thing stuck in his mind. He had left Charlie vulnerable.

Without thinking, he'd taken it for granted that Charlie could take care of himself. But he couldn't. He had no experience, no training and no time to develop his instincts. Charlie could have died today. One serious punch from Brick Wall could have killed him...and it would have been Declan's fault. He had to do something.

It was a little after nine. Declan picked up the phone and placed a call. After a few rings, it was answered.

"Hello?"

"Palvinder, Declan Hunt here."

"Declan. So nice to hear from you again."

"Sorry for the late call, but something's come up."

"No problem. I never rest. It gets in the way of work. Now — how may I help you?"

"Monarch attacked Charlie this afternoon."

Palvinder gasped. "No. Not Charlie. What happened?"

"He was investigating the area around Ian Mann's factory building."

"You sent your secretary to do your dirty work? Mr Hunt, that is not proper!"

Declan paused and shifted in his chair. "I take full blame for it. No excuses. But I have to make sure it never happens again. I have to keep them away from Charlie. Palvinder... I need names."

"Mr Hunt, I told you before, even if I wanted to, all of the documents were signed with Monarch's digital signature."

"They almost killed Charlie," Declan snapped.

There was silence on the line. Then, in the background Declan heard Palvinder talking to someone in what Declan assumed was Punjabi. He heard a shrill voice talking back. Mr Attwal's voice grew firmer. Then quiet.

"Declan. There was one name on a document. Wait five minutes, then check your email. I'm about to have a leak of corporate information from an untrustworthy employee about someone connected to Monarch."

"Thank you."

"Take good care of Charlie," Palvinder said. "And wish him a swift recovery."

"I promise."

Declan disconnected. In a few minutes, he received an email of two words.

Michael Taylor.

* * * *

Declan called Michael's number and it went straight to voicemail.

He decided to play a hunch and drove as quickly as possible to Katherine Mann's house. As Declan pulled into the drive, he saw that the lights were on.

He rang the doorbell, then hammered on the door when the ring wasn't answered. There was an eye at the peephole, then the door opened. Katherine stood aside and let Declan in.

"I was just going to call you. The police found the car. They found Ian's women's clothing and makeup in the trunk. It was that Sergeant McKeckran who called. He said that Ian had put himself at risk through his degenerate activities. He thinks my husband probably got involved with a bad trick."

Declan said, "I think the cops are on the wrong track. Now, where's Michael?"

"Michael's not here," she said, a bit too loudly.

"Katherine, I know he's working with Monarch Development. I know they're the ones who were trying to buy Ian's factory, which makes him a prime suspect in Ian's murder."

"It's okay, Katherine," a voice said from behind him. "It's time to come clean."

Declan turned around. Michael was coming down the stairs.

"He's smarter than he looks. You were right," Michael said to Katherine.

Declan tensed, ready to fight. Michael just walked by him and flopped down on a couch, looking exhausted.

"This has gone totally to rat shit," Michael said.

"Someone care to explain what the fuck is going on?" Declan asked as he moved closer to Michael.

Michael sighed. "I didn't kill him. I had nothing to do with Ian's death. We were friends."

Declan stood above him. "Last time I checked, friends don't fuck their friend's wife."

"Michael and I aren't lovers," Katherine said as she entered the living room.

Declan stood in silence.

Katherine stared him down, then sat beside Michael and said, "I love Ian as much now as I did when we married. I believed in him and supported him in every decision he made. But I hate living in Calgary. I miss everything about my life in London, and I realised I would die if I had to stay here much longer."

Michael put his hand on Katherine's knee. "Katherine told me she would do anything to get Ian to sell his final property, and I was just starting out in real estate so I thought—if I found a buyer, it could make me enough to set myself up in business, and I could help Katherine out in the process."

Declan sat in a chair across from them. "So, how did Monarch get involved?"

"I started to put out some feelers," Michael said, "and out of the blue, I got an email from Monarch. I'd never heard of them before, but they were offering Ian a good price. They weren't trying to rip him off."

"Who else was involved?"

Michael shrugged. "Just me and my lawyers. Monarch said they would handle all the negotiations."

Declan pressed him. "Do you know who negotiated with Ian?"

"They never told me."

"And Ian had no idea the two of you were connected to the sale?" Declan asked.

Katherine stood up and said, "I couldn't let him know I was trying to get him to sell. He would think it was a betrayal." She moved towards the window and looked out.

Declan thought for a moment. "Now that Ian is dead, who gets the building?"

Katherine said, "I suppose I do."

"And what do you plan to do with it?" Declan asked.

Katherine turned back and looked at Declan. "Once this whole nightmare is over, I guess I'll sell it and go back to London."

Declan was still confused. "So, why did you make up the story of you two being lovers?"

She sighed. "I thought if I told you the truth, you'd think I was involved in Ian's disappearance."

"Are you?" Declan pushed.

"No! If I was, why would I have hired you?" she said as she plopped herself back onto the couch.

"Getting back to the building," Declan continued, "if you sell it, Michael will still see a healthy commission."

Michael clenched his fists. "Yes, but I had nothing to do with Ian's death."

"If I'm gonna believe that, I need a name. Who have you been dealing with?"

"I have no idea," Michael said. Declan could see the frustration on his face. "Everything has always been through emails from Monarch Development."

"Come on," Declan said, "you must have signed some sort of retainer agreement."

"It was a digital signature," Michael said, looking down at his lap. "It was just a series of numbers."

Declan groaned in frustration. "I'm going to need to see a copy of that."

"I'll send it to you when I get home," Michael replied.

"Good," Declan said as he got up to leave. Just before he reached the door, he turned around. "If you want me to find Ian's killer, no more lies."

He got back into his van, drove home and pondered the fact that, even if they were telling the truth, the two of them still had the motive to kill Ian.

Declan climbed the stairs to the office. As he slid the key into the lock of the upper door, something struck him as odd. He knew he had shut the office lights off, but the frosted glass of the door glowed softly. *For fuck's sake. Not tonight. I'm not in the mood for a fight with Brick Wall. I should have set the alarm.*

As quietly as possible, he unlocked the door. He swung it inwards, hoping to catch the intruder unaware. He was so tired that if it turned out to be Brick Wall, he'd just let him beat the crap out of him and get it over with.

Declan sensed no movement in the office area, or squeaks from the floor above. Maybe they'd come and gone, or maybe Declan had just forgotten to shut the lights off. He turned to close the door and saw the intruder. Charlie was curled up on the sofa, sound asleep.

Declan sat across from him. He saw the bandage on his forehead and noticed the bruising on his left bicep, probably from where Monarch's thug had grabbed him when he slammed him into the van.

Charlie's eyelids fluttered open and he took in a sharp breath. Declan watched his face shift from peaceful to worried, then back again in a matter of seconds. He pushed himself up to a sitting position.

Declan stared at him. "I thought I dropped you at home so you could rest."

Charlie fidgeted a bit on the couch. "I had a huge fight with my folks. Dad caught me icing my ribs. He saw all the bruises and… He kinda freaked out."

"So you what—ran away from home?"

"They told me that I had to quit."

Declan paused, then said, "They were worried about you. I've seen some of those bruises. They worried me, too. If Mickey hadn't told me you'd be okay, I would have taken you right to the hospital, which I still might do. You need to take it easy for a few days at least."

Declan moved over and sat beside Charlie. "You scared the shit out of me today, Charlie, and I don't scare easily. I don't want that to ever happen to you again."

"Okay," Charlie said sheepishly.

"Do you need a place to crash?"

"I tried to reach my friend Carrie, but she wasn't answering."

"You can stay here then."

Charlie nodded. "If I could maybe get a blanket and a pillow, I'll just sleep here on the couch."

"No, you're hurt. Come with me. I'm not having you curled up on that thing."

Declan helped him upstairs to his apartment. Charlie stood there, obviously unsure what to do. Declan opened a drawer then took out a clean T-shirt and workout shorts and handed them to him.

"You might be more comfortable in these."

Charlie awkwardly tried to take his shirt off, but he was hampered by his injuries.

"Here. Let me help."

Declan unbuttoned Charlie's shirt and slid it over his slender shoulders. Charlie had a nice build. Not a hair on his chest, and only a slight trail leading from his navel down to the top of his pants. Declan ran the back of his index finger over the worst of the bruises. Charlie inhaled. At first Declan thought it was from pain until he saw the goose flesh rise up on Charlie's arms.

"I'm sorry, but there's not much more I can do for these other than icing. I'll check them in the morning to see if there's any swelling. I can bandage you up if you need it."

He moved to undo Charlie's pants but Charlie stopped him.

"That's okay. I can get those."

Declan suspected that the sizeable swelling under Charlie's pants was not a result of bruising. "Can I at least get your shoes? They can be a little more difficult if you can't bend over."

"Okay."

After taking off Charlie's shoes and socks, he left Charlie on his own and went to brush his teeth. From the bathroom, he called out, "I have a brand-new toothbrush you can have, if you want it."

"Sure," Charlie answered, poking his head into the bathroom.

Declan put some toothpaste on the brush and handed it to him.

"Thanks," he said.

"They look good on you," Declan said, pointing to the gym wear that Charlie now swam in.

Charlie smiled, toothpaste running out of his mouth, which he caught just before it spilled onto his borrowed clothes.

After they finished in the bathroom, Declan helped Charlie into bed. He bent forward and kissed him on the forehead. "Get a good night's sleep, Charlie Watts."

Declan grabbed a blanket and pillow and headed down to the office couch.

Chapter Twenty-Four

Declan woke at seven. He sat up, massaged out the kinks in his neck, then went upstairs to check on Charlie. As he approached, Charlie woke and attempted to get out of bed.

"Ow, ow, ow, ow," Charlie moaned.

"I think it's time for some medication," Declan said in a cheery voice. He went to the bathroom, returning with a glass of water and two painkillers. "Here. Take these."

Charlie obediently followed the instructions.

"Now," Declan said, "did you have any plans for the day?"

"Other than going home and hoping my parents haven't changed the locks? Nothing."

"Are you up for some weekend work?"

"Do I get paid overtime?" Charlie shot him a crooked smile.

"How about your hourly wage plus a free breakfast?"

"That works for me."

Declan smiled. "Good. First, I want you to stand up."

Charlie did as instructed.

"Let's have a look at those bruises." Declan stood in front of him, reached around and gently pulled the T-shirt over his head, then off of his arms. He carefully pressed on Charlie's ribs, watching for any expressions of discomfort. "No pain when I did that?"

"No. It just feels bruised, but not too bad."

Declan took a step back and examined Charlie's torso. The right side of his chest was blotched dark red where bruises were starting to bloom. He stepped forward and touched the back of his hand against Charlie's forehead. "No fever, which is good. When you move your body, does anything hurt on the inside?"

Charlie rotated his upper body and slowly bent his back, and arms. "No. It's just sore muscle." Charlie looked to the floor. "What there is of it."

Declan put his finger under Charlie's chin and lifted his head so he was looking into Charlie's eyes. "You are perfect the way you are. Sure, muscle might give you strength and a little more padding, but it can never improve what's in here," he said, tapping Charlie's head. He lingered a moment before stepping away. "By the way, Mickey saw how you leapt onto the hood of the car, then tucked and rolled. Did you ever take self-defence training?"

Charlie nodded. "Yeah. When I was a kid, I was pretty small. Dad thought it would give me some self-confidence, so I took karate for almost seven years."

"You studied karate? Was that in your resumé?"

"It's rarely a prerequisite for a tech job."

"Well, it's an asset here. When you talk to your dad later, thank him for those lessons. They may have saved a few of your brain cells." Declan turned away. "I'm going to grab a hot shower. When I take you for breakfast, I'll debrief you on what I found out last night."

Declan headed to the bathroom. He stood in the shower, the water as hot as he could take it. He thought about Charlie and the bruises on his body. He thought about Charlie's lean torso and, to his surprise, Declan found himself getting hard. He shook his head. *Remember the golden rule – never sleep with an employee or a client. Besides, I have Luke.* But the thought of Luke and Charlie got him further aroused. He decided to take care of the problem and had just started to come when there was a rap on the door.

Charlie said, "Mind if I come in and brush my teeth?"

Declan was still hard, but the steam on the door would hide the details. "Be my guest," he called out.

Charlie entered the bathroom and brushed his teeth, occasionally turning his head towards the shower stall. Charlie spit out his toothpaste just as Declan turned the shower off.

Declan called out from the shower, "How are you feeling?"

There was silence for a moment, then Charlie said, "The painkillers are kicking in. I think I'll be fine. I'll be downstairs when you're ready."

He heard Charlie leave. "What have I gotten myself into?" Declan said to himself.

* * * *

Twenty minutes later, Charlie and Declan walked into No Poaching. It was packed with the end of the Saturday morning breakfast rush. There was only one table available, and it was piled high with dirty dishes.

"Just grab that table, hun," the waitress told them. Her name tag identified her as Ethel. "I'll clear it as soon as I can."

They sat down. Charlie was still trying hard to forget the silhouette he'd seen in the shower this morning.

"Everything okay? You seem distracted," Declan said.

"No. No. Everything's fine," he answered, avoiding eye contact by pretending to read the menu.

Ethel came back in a flash. She batted her eyelashes at Declan as she dropped off a couple of coffees and said, "I'll start you with these while I clean up." She expertly stacked the dishes that were left behind, leaving some glasses and a folded newspaper.

Declan collected the glasses and put them at the edge of the table. Ethel came back with a tray and a wet cloth. Charlie picked up the paper as she wiped the table down and stacked the glasses on the tray.

"I bet I know what you want," she said, leaning into Declan.

Charlie interjected, "I'll have the special—eggs over easy, rye toast…please."

Declan smirked, then started. "And I'll have—"

"Egg-white omelette," she said, winked then left.

Declan smiled. "You see, Charlie. That's why I come here."

"They do know you're gay, right?" Charlie asked.

Declan shrugged.

Charlie sipped his coffee. "How did your meeting with Mr Attwal go yesterday?"

"You're off the hook. I got the company a new accountant."

"That's a relief," Charlie said.

Declan continued. "And I got him to disclose that Monarch was the developer trying to acquire Ian Mann's building."

Charlie put down his coffee with a clatter. "You already knew? So, I got beaten up yesterday for information that you already had?"

"Charlie, I didn't ask you to go undercover, and if Mr Attwal hadn't revealed that information, your discovery would have been the only source. What you found out corroborates Mr Attwal's statement."

Charlie swirled his coffee in his cup. "At least what I did wasn't a total waste. Did you find out anything else?"

"Plenty. I also found out that the real estate agent working for Monarch is none other than Michael Taylor."

"What?"

"I went to visit him last night. He was hiding out at Katherine's. It turns out their whole affair was a lie."

"Why would they lie about that?" Charlie asked.

"So the Monarch connection wouldn't come out. They were business partners. With Ian dead, Katherine inherits the building and Michael stands to make a tidy profit."

"So that would make them the prime suspects in Ian's murder," Charlie said.

"But we need proof and something's still not sitting right with me. If Katherine was guilty, why would she ask me to investigate the case?" Declan stared out the window.

Charlie didn't want to interrupt Declan's thoughts so he busied himself with looking at the paper. An article in the sports section caught his eye.

"We're missing something. It seems too easy," Declan said. "What else have we been ignoring?"

"Hockey," Charlie said as he dropped the open newspaper in front of Declan. The headline above the article read *The Axemen Lose Their Head!*

Declan picked it up.

"From what it says," Charlie began, "with Ian's death, the potential deal with the buyer from Toronto for the team has fallen through, but a new buyer has stepped onto the ice. A guy named Nick Neves."

"Interesting," Declan said.

"There's more. It looks like he and Ian didn't get along. He was one of the sponsors pushing for an audit of the team's books. And this guy in the photo," Charlie said, pointing to one of two players holding up a trophy, "I know him. I met him coming out of The Greek the night I came to pick you up."

"Are you sure?"

"You don't forget a face like that, especially when it hits on you," Charlie said, rubbing his chest where the guy had caressed him. "And look at the caption — *Terry Fredericks (left) hoists the Governor's Cup, assisted by Justin Neves. (Photo credit: Ian Mann).*"

"And what do you bet that Justin is Nick's son?" Declan said. "This just keeps getting better. You," Declan pointed at Charlie, "have more than earned your breakfast this morning."

Charlie beamed.

Declan's phone went off. He glanced at it. "It's Luke."

Of course it's Luke. Just when it became about me. Charlie frowned.

"Good morning," Declan answered. Charlie stared at the table as Declan listened to Luke.

"He got a hit on the gum wrapper," he whispered to Charlie. "Let me guess, Michael Taylor?" he said to Luke.

Charlie watched the expression on Declan's face change.

"Even more interesting," Declan said to Luke. Declan nodded as he listened to the other end of the conversation. After a few minutes Declan said, "Thanks for this. We'll talk soon."

Declan disconnected. He sat in silence. Charlie couldn't take the suspense any longer. "What did Luke say?"

"They found prints on the wrapper. They belonged to an eighteen-year-old kid with a prior arrest for breaking and entering. It proves the kid was at the scene, but not necessarily on the night of Ian's disappearance. The police aren't interested in following up, but I think we should."

"Why?"

Declan pointed to one of the players in the newspaper picture. "Because the kid was Justin Neves."

Chapter Twenty-Five

Declan and Charlie burst into the office.

"Start looking up everything you can on the Axemen. I need contact info for the team, coaching staff, the guy who cleans up the change room — everyone. I'm especially interested in anything you can get me on Justin Neves. I'll call Katherine and see what she can tell me."

Declan sat at his desk and pulled out a pad of paper and pen. Then he grabbed his phone and punched in Katherine's number. She answered on the third ring.

"Declan? Do you have any news?"

"Katherine, tell me everything you can about the Airdrie Axemen."

Katherine said, "It was the one thing that really excited Ian. There was a big-shot from out east that was looking at buying him out. Ian was considering it, but he knew it wouldn't go over well with the team. Ian needed money to keep the team afloat, which is why I didn't understand his resistance to selling that goddamned factory building."

"Who would I talk to in the organisation who knows about the players?"

"Dave Chalmers. He's the coach. I can give you his contact information."

Declan wrote down the number, thanked her and ended the call.

Charlie walked into Declan's office. "I've pulled together a list of everyone directly involved with the team and facility. Information on the team members was more difficult, since some of them are under eighteen, but I located a bunch of their social media accounts, including those for Justin Neves."

"Those'll come in handy," Declan said, taking the printout.

"I'm heading down to Gwen's. Can I pick you up something?" Charlie asked.

"Americano, please. Extra-large, double shot. And if she tries to send you back with a pastry of some sort, tell her I'll burn the building down."

"Large Americano, no fire. You got it."

Charlie left the office as Declan pulled out his laptop. He had an idea.

* * * *

Ten minutes later, Charlie climbed back up the stairs with two large coffees and two almond cookies. He knew he'd have to eat both himself, but he didn't have the fortitude to say no to Gwen. When he walked into the main office, he heard a strange sound. Coffees in hand, he entered Declan's office to find him streaming a hockey game on the wall-mounted TV.

"Thanks," Declan said, extending his hand without taking his eyes off the screen.

"The Axemen?" Charlie said.

"I located footage of a game. I wanted to get a better sense of the team."

Charlie stood behind Declan watching for a few minutes until he could no longer remain silent. He shouted, "That guy is terrible!"

Declan jumped. "Crap. I didn't know you were still behind me... Which guy is terrible?"

"Neves. I mean, he's okay, but nowhere near up to the rest of the team. His puck handling is mediocre. Here, back it up."

Declan handed him the remote.

"Watch him...there. The way he handled the puck. He lost control over a simple pass to the forward. His right ankle's weak. I can't tell if it's from an injury, or he's just built that way. And there—he can barely skate backwards."

"He looked just fine to me," Declan said.

"Oh, puh-leaz," Charlie said, pointing at the screen. "He gave up after trying for two seconds. Oh shit, and just there. The check. He checks like a three-year-old in the playground."

Declan cocked his head. "Why do you say that?"

"The objective of checking is to unbalance the opposing player. He just about knocked himself over."

"How do you know these things?" Declan asked as he sat on the edge of his desk.

"I've played hockey since I was twelve. It was one thing my dad and I bonded over. I played right up 'til I graduated from university."

Declan smiled. "You played for what—the computer engineering team?"

"No. They sucked. I was brought in as a ringer for the faculty of music's team — the Gustav Maulers. I played defence. I'm used to protecting my man," Charlie said in the deepest voice he could muster.

Declan shook his head. "I thought defencemen are supposed to protect the net?"

"They are. I just thought it sounded more heroic."

"Mr Watts, you continue to amaze me."

Declan looked at him for a moment before asking, "So, Charlie. Do you miss playing hockey?"

"Yeah."

"I hate to ask, but how would you feel about going undercover again?"

* * * *

Declan phoned and arranged a two p.m. meeting with Coach Chalmers at a diner on the edge of Airdrie, just a thirty-minute drive from Calgary. Airdrie was a bedroom community whose prime attractions were the Iron Horse Park Miniature Train, an axe-throwing centre and a farmers' market. There was nothing surprising about that for a city of seventy thousand. What was surprising was that it had an abundance of AAA hockey teams, the Axemen being one of four.

Declan pulled up to the diner and walked in. He immediately recognised Coach Chalmers by his grey mullet and the handlebar moustache he had sported in an online team photo. The coach was already seated at a table near the front and Declan joined him.

"Thanks for agreeing to meet with me," Declan said.

"No problem," Chalmers replied. "I can't tell you how hard-hit the kids were when they heard that Ian was dead."

"Sorry to hear that. How are the people in the office and the coaching staff doing?"

Chalmers shook his head. "Mister, this isn't the NHL. Sure, we have the guys who maintain the building and the ice — they're city employees. Just like the cleaning staff. And the concessions, they're run by contractors. Other than that…it's me, Todd Elmer who's the assistant coach, our travel manager Jan McNab and the owner. Now that Ian's gone, I don't know where the team stands."

"Do you have any idea who might have wanted to kill Ian?"

"Around here? No one! Everybody loved the guy. Since he bought into the Axemen, they've been a winning team. He got them the best equipment, the best publicity — he even got new ice-grooming equipment. Hell, he even badgered the big companies here to kick in for a complete overhaul of the arena." Chalmers raised his empty mug in the direction of the waitress who came over with a second mug and a full pot of coffee. She filled both men's cups.

"Thanks, Maggie," Chalmers said.

Declan waited until Maggie was out of earshot before asking, "What about the rumours that Ian was mismanaging team funds?"

"So, you heard that, did ya? Those rumours were started by Nick Neves, who wanted to get control of the team. He was very much against the possible sale to a Toronto investor."

"What was Nick's connection to the team?" Declan asked.

"He was its lead sponsor. He installed the ventilation system in the new arena, all at his own expense."

"Doesn't his son play for the team?"

"Justin? Yeah, he's with us." Chalmers said.

Declan noted the lack of enthusiasm in the coach's response. "Is he a good player?"

"He's not the best but having him on the team keeps his dad happy and that helps us."

Declan paused. "Is there much money in owning a team like this?"

Chalmers laughed. "For the most part, it's a break-even proposition at best, but a few of our kids have been picked up by the NHL. When that happens, the team owner might see a bit of a...financial reward. Some parents have even offered me a little money to give their kids more ice time when the NHL scouts are in."

"You ever take them up on that?"

"Nope. Won't touch a bribe. I like what I do, and I don't plan on risking that for anything." Chalmers took a long sip of coffee. "What's this all got to do with Ian's death?"

"I'm just gathering as much information as I can."

"Why are *you* doing this, and not the cops?" Chalmers asked.

"They have their own version of what happened to Ian Mann. His wife has a different idea, and she hired me to find out what happened. I'm consulting with the police, though. Coach Chalmers, I'm hoping you can help me get some information about Ian's death."

"Sure. Whatever you need."

"I saw on your website that you've got a summer training camp coming up next week."

"What of it?"

"I want to put one of my people on the ice with your team."

Chalmers snorted. "You think it's that easy? These guys are some of the best players around."

"My assistant will pass for eighteen or nineteen, and he played hockey in university."

Chalmers was silent.

Declan continued, "It may be our best chance at getting a lead on finding out who did this to Ian. And, if we find nothing, it'll clear the team of any involvement."

Chalmers took another sip of coffee. "And you say he can play? If he can't, they'll spot it the minute he steps on the ice."

"Just tell them he's here to try out for the team. Nothing more. You're doing it as a favour for Katherine in memory of Ian. That way, if he can't play as well as I say he can, there's no harm, no foul. Nothing'll reflect badly on you."

Chalmers stared hard at Declan. "Tell him to come for the skills practice Monday afternoon. I'll need him at the arena for three p.m. If he's late, he's out."

Chalmers finished his last swig of coffee and walked out of the diner. Declan picked up the phone.

"Charlie, you're in."

Chapter Twenty-Six

Charlie arrived at his parent's house just as dinner was being served. His grandmother and father were already seated. Charlie's usual place at the table had not been set.

"So, you run out the door last night, but you still come back to eat our food," his mother said, standing at the stove.

He knew the look on her face. She was hurt.

"I'm sorry for last night," Charlie said. "I was upset."

"I don't doubt you were, all banged up like that," his mother replied.

The two at the table remained silent. Gran stared at Charlie. His father stared at the table. Charlie's mother stood with a pot in her hands. "Did you go to the hospital, at least?"

"I was checked over. It's just bruising." *It's just a little white lie.*

She put down the pot and got him some cutlery, setting it at his place beside Gran. It was only then that he felt he could sit down. Gran patted him on his knee and smiled. His father stared at his plate of pasta.

It wasn't until his mother sat with the family that Charlie's father looked up at him. Charlie could see that he was still angry.

"So," his dad said, "where did you stay last night?"

"With a friend."

"If you want to live under this roof, you're gonna follow my rules, do you understand?"

Charlie chewed his lower lip.

"Do you understand?" he yelled and slammed his fist down on the table.

"What are these rules?" Charlie yelled back. "I don't know what they are. I've never seen them. Is there a handbook I should know about?"

"You want to know what the rules are? Fine. Rule number one – give your mother the respect she deserves. Rule number two – quit that damned job of yours and get one you're trained for. Do you have any idea how much money we spent putting you through university, only to have it thrown away by you deciding to play detective when you have no idea what you're doing?"

"For Christ's sake," Charlie shot back. "It's only a short-term contract, and I'm not sure if you noticed, but no one is beating down the door to hire me in spite of my degree."

His mother said, "I think what your father is worried about is that this job might be too dangerous."

"I'm subbing in for a sixty-eight-year-old. How dangerous do you think the job is?"

There was no response from his parents.

Charlie continued, "But I tell you one thing, in the week I've been there, I've felt more useful and achieved more than at any other job I've had, and, if for some reason I was to be offered the job full time, I would take it in a second."

"That's enough," his father snapped.

"For once we agree on something," Charlie said, pushing his chair back and heading towards the basement.

As he left he could hear Gran say, "Leave him be, Ted. He needs some space."

Charlie went to his bedroom and stuffed as many clothes as he could into his backpack. Then he went to the crawl space under the stairs and hauled out his hockey bag. He opened it and saw that everything was there, but from the odour coming from the bag he knew he'd have to freshen some of it up before practice on Monday.

He lugged the heavy bag, three hockey sticks and his backpack to the front door and threw them out onto the porch before he noticed Gran standing in the hall. She looked so small, and her eyes were teary, but there was a smile on her face. He went to her and gave her a big hug.

"'Your time has come, Charlie."

"What do you mean?"

"It's time to get out there and live your own life. You're a man now and you have to make your own decisions, good or bad."

"What if I'm wrong. What if I totally screw up?"

"Then you'll be just like the rest of us. And don't forget, when you walk out the door, it doesn't mean you won't be back here at some time. They already let you come back once. I know it doesn't seem like it now, but you'll be welcomed back with open arms again. They love you. They just have to get used to the fact that you're your own man now."

Charlie threw his arms around her again and gave her another kiss.

He loaded the gear into the trunk of The Red Beast, then plopped into the driver's seat. *What next?*

He pulled out his phone and called Carrie. The phone rang four times. *Please let her pick up.*

On the fifth ring she answered. "Hey, Charlie."

"Where were you last night?" Charlie asked.

"Working late. What's wrong?"

"Do I only call when something's wrong?"

"Lately…yes."

"Can I stay with you for a while?"

"Hmm… Let me think."

"Sorry. You probably have someone with you. Don't worry. I'll—"

She didn't let him finish. "You idiot, even if I did, you take priority. Now, get your ass over here."

Charlie drove over and in fifteen minutes was parked in front of Carrie's house. She greeted Charlie at the door as he waddled up the front steps, unbalanced by the bulky hockey bag and gear.

"Crap. How much stuff do you have?"

"This is it."

Carrie gave Charlie a hand carrying the sports bag up to her second-floor apartment. Once upstairs, she dropped it in the middle of the living room.

"Before you say anything, I'm pouring the wine."

Carrie lit a few candles and turned off the overhead light. The next hour flew by as Charlie filled her in on what had happened over the previous week, and what was going to happen next as they polished off several glasses of wine. Charlie finished by lifting his shirt and showing Carrie the bruises on his chest that were beginning to turn purple.

"Oh my God!" she said. "I know you think Declan's the hottest guy on the planet, but is he worth it? Your folks are right. This job is dangerous."

Charlie frowned. "Your role right now is to support me, not to agree with my parents. That's what a best friend does."

"A best friend tries to stop you from getting killed. Come on. It's late. Let's get you to bed."

As they headed off to Carrie's bedroom Charlie asked, "Can we do some laundry tomorrow?"

"We? Yes, *you* can. And while you're at it, you can do mine as well."

Once the lights were out, they snuggled in bed.

"I like having you over," Carrie said. "Straight guys just don't snuggle as well as you do." After a few minutes of silence Carrie asked, "So, you and the detective... Nothing yet?"

"He gave me a kiss on the forehead last night when he put me to bed. Oh, and a sloppy wet kiss last week when he was drunk, if that counts."

"Does it count with you?"

"Hell yeah," he said, and the two of them broke into giggles.

Chapter Twenty-Seven

Charlie had spent his first full day at Carrie's doing laundry, practising driving his car and taking her out to brunch. Being out of his parents' place had lifted the dark cloud that had hung over him since he'd moved back over a month ago. He knew he couldn't live with Carrie forever, but until he could afford a place on his own, this would be perfect. But that was yesterday. Today his mood was decidedly different.

Charlie hadn't slept well. He was excited about the chance to go undercover and prove himself to Declan. He snuck out of bed, careful not to wake Carrie. Charlie took a quick shower, got dressed in the living room and wolfed down a couple of pieces of cold pizza. Then he grabbed his car and headed off to work. He'd packed all of his clean gear and a few changes of clothes in the trunk the night before.

The trip in went smoothly. The skill of driving standard was coming back to him and he made it to the office just as Gwen was unlocking the door to her café.

"The usual for you?" she asked as she made her way towards the counter.

"You bet." Charlie had a huge grin on his face.

From behind the counter Gwen said, "You seem pretty cheery this morning."

"It's a brand-new week, new adventures await," Charlie said as he propped himself on the back of a chair. "And, I moved in with a friend of mine – "

"Oh?" Gwen said, arching her eyebrows. "Do I sense a hint of romance?"

"Nothing like that," Charlie said. "Carrie and I have been friends forever."

"Well, congratulations anyway."

Gwen finished frothing the milk for his order and passed over a cup and a small bag.

Charlie took his latte and pastry and headed up to the office.

He stopped at the street-level door. His stomach was filled with butterflies. Last time he'd been undercover it hadn't gone so well. Charlie took a deep breath and walked up the stairs.

Declan was sitting at the desk in his office. He stood as Charlie entered. Rather than his usual well-fitting clothes, Declan was wearing worn jeans and a plain work shirt. Charlie, on the other hand, had dressed in a shirt, tie and his newest pair of khakis.

"Should I be more dressed like – " he said, pointing to Declan's clothing.

"No. You're perfect. You're dressed to impress, which is what you're trying to do. I, on the other hand, want to blend in."

"So, you're coming with me?" Charlie asked hopefully.

"Wouldn't have it any other way."

Charlie was relieved. He'd been nervous about taking this on alone.

"Here's the plan," Declan said. "Your job is to go up there and try your hardest to get on the team. You're an eager eighteen-year-old who wants nothing more than to play hockey and make it into the NHL. You've heard players on the Axemen get scouted and go up to the big leagues."

Charlie nodded then asked, "So, what's my cover name?"

"The best name ever. You'll be Charlie Watts," Declan replied with a grin.

"Well, that's no fun."

"You'll be playing yourself, only a little younger. Okay?"

"Okay," Charlie said, uncertain.

Declan moved around the desk. "You'll be fine. All you have to do is go in, do whatever you have to do to make yourself look good and try to make a good impression on Justin. If he was attracted to you outside The Greek, I bet he'll feel the same in the arena, even if he doesn't remember you from before."

Charlie frowned. "What if he does remember me?"

"You say you were there for the same reason he was—a bit of fun." Declan handed Charlie a piece of paper. "Now, I know it's not far from home, but I've booked you into a hotel. Here's your reservation."

Charlie glanced at the paper. "Do I have to stay there?"

"Yes," Declan replied. "That way you can go out with the guys after practice, stay as late as you need to and not worry about sleeping in and missing practice."

"That makes sense."

Declan continued, "I want you to listen for anything they might have to say about Justin or Ian Mann. If something comes up, don't try to remember it, just text me the details. If anybody asks, you're just texting a friend."

Charlie sank into a chair. "What if something goes wrong? I mean really wrong?" Charlie asked.

Declan knelt down beside him. "I'll be watching to make sure nothing bad happens. And if you're spooked, just text me."

"I just don't want to disappoint you."

Declan put his hand on Charlie's leg and leaned in closer. "I don't think that's possible."

Charlie stopped breathing. He wanted the moment to last forever. Declan broke his reverie when he stood and walked out into the reception area. Charlie shook his head and followed.

"So," Declan said in a matter-of-fact tone, "you've got the address of the hotel you're staying at, and you know the plan. Do you need anything else?"

"I'm good. I check into the hotel first, grab some lunch and then get to the arena by two-thirty — early enough to show I'm serious, but not too early to make me look like a pussy."

"I don't recall actually putting it that way."

"I'm channelling my inner eighteen-year-old."

Declan put his hand on Charlie's back and walked him down to the Red Beast.

"Declan?"

"Yeah?"

"Thanks for trusting me with this."

"No problem. So, are you ready?"

"As ready as I'll ever be." Charlie smiled, got into his car then burned rubber as he peeled off down the street.

* * * *

Forty-five minutes later, Charlie pulled into the Airdrie Comfort Inn just off of the highway. He was excited. This was the first time he'd been away on the road by himself.

He discovered that Declan had prepaid the room. After checking in, Charlie unpacked his suitcase and scoped out his accommodation. It was basic with a small fridge, which to Charlie's disappointment didn't contain any tiny bottles of booze.

He stopped in at the restaurant next door for a light pre-practice lunch, then headed out for his undercover mission.

When Charlie pulled into the parking lot of the Alconco Arena, he was surprised to find a dozen cars already parked there.

Shit, if I'm late...

He leapt out, pulled his hockey bag out of the trunk and ran to the front doors. He desperately searched for the change rooms.

"Hey," a voice yelled out from behind him. Charlie spun around and the momentum of the twenty-five-pound bag sent him spinning into the vending machine.

"Dude, if you're that hungry, I'll give you the money. You don't have to smash the machine."

Charlie saw a little guy, maybe five-three, at the end of the hall with his arms crossed. "The name's Todd. I'm Coach Chalmers' assistant."

"Am I late? I was told to be here for three."

"There was a last-minute time change and Coach didn't know how to reach you. Let me take you to the change room and get you settled."

Todd dropped Charlie off and showed him his locker. "Come out onto the ice when you're ready."

Charlie was annoyed with himself. *Great way to make a good first impression.*

Once Charlie was in full gear he made his way onto the ice surface. The team was running passing drills. Todd was talking to someone who had to be the coach. The man skated over.

"You must be Charlie. I'm Coach Chalmers."

"Hey...I'm really sorry—"

"You should've given me your number. I couldn't reach you. We got our time bumped by the arena early this morning. If you're late again, you're out."

"I'll get you my cell number once we're done here."

"Good," Chalmers said, then yelled out to the others on the ice. "Gimme focus, guys. This is Charlie Watts, who still managed to make it here from Calgary sooner than Dawes and Hedges, wherever the hell they are. Over the next few days, he'll be trying out for the team. Try not to be your typical dick-assed selves."

They laughed and skated up in a line, bumping gloved fists with Charlie. The last was Justin Neves, who locked eyes with him and gave him a big smile.

"Okay, Watts. Let's see what you can do," Chalmers said.

Whatever awkwardness Charlie had been feeling disappeared once he started to skate. He joined in the passing drills, then a six-station on-ice course of conditioning exercises involving legs, balance, crunches, backwards dips off the net frame to strengthen the triceps, shuttle sprints and ending with push-ups — never his strong suit.

"Come on, Watts. You do push-ups like a five-year-old," the coach yelled.

Other than the push-ups, he felt he was keeping up with most of the team. Sure, a couple of the muscle-mutts had smoked him, but he wasn't worried. Speed and accuracy were his strengths and he used those skills to good advantage.

"Okay, MacGregor, you're in goal. I want you all to form a line and try to get one past him."

Charlie took the last position. He knew well enough to respect the seniority of the other players. After five attempts, he'd landed four.

At the end of the practice, Coach Chalmers called out, "Good work, guys. Let's wrap it up for the day. I'll see you back here tomorrow morning at eight sharp. Watts, come and see me."

Charlie skated up to the coach.

"Not bad, Watts. Hunt wasn't lying. You can really play. See you tomorrow."

Charlie headed for the dressing room. Most of the players had ditched their gear and were sitting around in their compression jocks and socks, cooling down and laughing about something.

"Hey, Watts, nice work out there," one of the muscle-mutts called out.

"Thanks. It was great to practice with you guys." Charlie made a decision that it was time to put his first theory to the test. "Just in case I make the team, I think you should know that I'm...gay. If that makes you uncomfortable, I can find another place to change."

He stood there waiting for a response. Several of the players looked at the ground.

The team's captain, the largest of the muscle-mutts, got up, then swaggered towards Charlie and stood in front of him. "Then I guess you won't be changing here. I doubt you'll make the team anyway. The visitors' change room is across the hall."

Charlie looked towards Justin to check out his response, but he was focused on packing up his gear.

Charlie took his stuff across the hall and changed back into his street clothes, then bagged up his gear. He decided to text Declan with a report on how things had gone as soon as he got back to the hotel.

When he headed out into the parking lot, a number of the guys were hanging around his car.

"Hey, Watts. Is this yours?"

"Yeah. It was a gift from…my folks."

"Shit. The best mine ever gave me was a new hockey bag."

"No," another yelled out, "the best you got from them was not stuffing you into a rock-filled sack and tossing you into the river!"

The crowd laughed, and the team captain said, "I've got my eye on you, Watts."

Charlie stared him down. The muscle-mutt spit at Charlie's feet and walked away as the rest of the team dispersed to their own cars.

Charlie pulled out his keys, opened the trunk then dropped in his hockey bag. When he closed the lid Justin Neves was standing beside the car.

Charlie jumped. "Shit. You scared me."

Justin smiled. "Yeah, well you scared me back there. Coming out to a room full of strangers like that… It took a lot of balls."

Justin stared at Charlie then said, "I'm gay, too."

Charlie was relieved that Justin didn't seem to recognise him from their brief encounter at The Greek. "That's cool. Does anyone else know?"

"Not really…other than you. And me."

Charlie smiled. "Can I buy you a coffee?"

"Only if you promise to drive me in this beautiful beast," he said, patting the trunk lid.

"You got a deal. Hop in."

"Sweet!"

Charlie was about to pull out of the parking lot when he asked, "Where are we going?"

"Sammy's if you want coffee."

"Or we could grab a beer. I saw a pub next to the Comfort Inn where I'm staying."

"The Comfort Inn it is!"

Charlie drove quickly back to the hotel and they made their way into the bar and sat at a booth.

Justin said, "I'll be back. I just gotta pee."

While Justin went to use the washroom, Charlie texted Declan.

Try-outs were interesting. Out for a beer with Justin. I'll see what I can find out.

Declan texted back a thumbs-up. Then he sent another text.

You really can skate. I was impressed.

You were there?

Charlie wondered where Declan was now. He looked over his shoulder. The bar windows overlooked the parking lot. Along the roadside parking spots he saw it. A white Toyota Sienna van.

Charlie's phone chirped again.

Good luck!

He turned back to catch another glimpse of Declan.

"Whatcha lookin' at?" Justin asked, as he slid back into the booth.

Charlie snapped his head back around. "The beautiful view, of course."

Justin laughed. "Yeah. Airdrie — the Paris of Alberta."

The waitress came by and dropped off a couple of glasses of water. "What would you boys like?"

"An Alley Kat Pale Ale if you've got it," Justin said.

"I do, and you can have it if I can see some ID. From both of you." They both pulled out their driver's licenses. Charlie made sure that Justin couldn't see his, and prayed she didn't mention how old he was.

"And for you?" she asked Charlie.

"The same, thanks. And maybe we could get an order of nachos, if you have them."

"Nachos it is," she said, then left them in privacy.

"So," Justin asked, "what part of Calgary are you from?"

"Brentwood. In the Northwest."

Justin paused for a moment. "Do you have a boyfriend?"

"No," Charlie replied then took a sip of water. "I fell pretty hard for an older guy, but it hasn't worked out."

The waitress dropped off their beers, then left.

"So, how long have you been playing hockey?" Charlie asked.

"My dad had me in skates as soon as I could walk. He taught me how to play on our backyard rink and got me into Atom League when I turned nine."

Charlie smiled. "You don't sound too happy about it."

"Dad lives for hockey." Justin started to play with his cutlery. "I think he's always dreamed of having a son in the NHL. He used to tell his friends that he was raising the next Gretzky."

"No pressure there. It's gotta be tough," Charlie said.

He rolled his eyes. "Tell me about it. Is your dad like that?"

"He always encouraged me, but he never pushed."

"That's probably 'cause you've got talent."

"I wouldn't go that far," Charlie said.

"No—I watched you. You were fluid out there. Some people got it. I don't."

Charlie said, "But you're on the team. They must have seen something in you."

"What they saw was a free ventilation system for the arena. That's what my Dad does. He installed the system for free if I got a spot on the team."

"So if you don't like it, why do you keep it up?"

A fly landed on the table and Justin swatted at it.

"It's part of his dream… Just not mine."

Charlie stared at him. "And what's yours?"

"I haven't found it yet." Justin smiled sadly.

Charlie took a sip of his beer. "So, do you have anyone around here you can at least talk to? Someone gay?"

Justin let out a mocking laugh. "Around here? Not a chance."

Charlie leaned in a bit. "So…where do you go for action then? There's gotta be some horny farm boy around here you could do on the back of his tractor."

Justin had a mouthful of beer which he choked on, then it shot out through his nose. The two burst out laughing.

"I'd be happy to settle for a farm boy. I go into Calgary from time to time. Around here, the only guy that paid attention to me was the team owner."

"What? Wasn't that a bit creepy?"

"No. He's a pretty good-looking guy, for his age. Really sophisticated. At least he was."

The expression on Justin's face changed. He went silent. Charlie had the feeling that Justin had said more than he'd planned to. He stared down at the table.

"You boys want anything else right now? I'm goin' on break," the waitress said as she dropped off the plate of nachos.

"Maybe another couple of beers," Charlie replied.

"You got it," she said, then headed back to the bar. Justin and Charlie sat sipping their beers until the waitress dropped off two more bottles. Justin broke the silence.

"Can I trust you?" Justin asked.

"Yeah. Of course… Did something happen to you?"

Tears were welling up in Justin's eyes. Charlie reached over and touched Justin's hand. Justin pulled away before looking around. It was clear he was checking to see if they were alone but nobody was looking their way.

Justin started slowly. "Ian was a photographer. He said there was something special about me. He thought I'd make a great model."

"He said that to you?"

"Yeah, but he wasn't one of those guys that shoot porn. He showed me what he'd done. His pictures are all over the internet. He was like a huge fashion photographer in England. He took pictures of everybody famous like...ever hear of a guy named Bowie?"

"Yeah. My parents used to listen to him."

"He said I kinda looked like Bowie."

Charlie really looked at Justin's face for the first time. He had such delicate features. Without his masculine haircut, his face was quite androgynous.

"He told me he wanted to restart his career and had an idea for a new exhibition. He asked if I wanted to be a part of it. He wanted me to be his model. Can you imagine? Me—a model? He was the first person to see me as anything other than a future short-order cook. He said this could change my whole life—that I could be famous."

"You know, sometimes people say things just to get what they want."

"It wasn't like that, if that's what you're thinking."

"As long as he didn't make you do anything you didn't want to do," Charlie said. "I don't like the thought of someone doing that."

Justin's expression started to relax. "He never touched me other than to put on a bit of makeup to smooth out the colour of my skin. He took me to a studio in Calgary and shot a bunch of pictures. The first batch were of me in my hockey gear. Then he shot hundreds of just my face."

"How many times did you sit for him?"

"Three or four. He said when he was photographing Princess Di—yeah, I looked up the pictures on the net. He actually took pictures of a princess. He said when he was photographing her, he didn't have much time and he regretted it, because it takes longer to get to know the essence of your model... That's what he said, at least."

Justin stopped speaking for a while. He sat there with his second beer almost finished. Charlie had barely touched his first. Justin looked at his phone. "I should go. I've gotta get home for dinner." He reached into his pocket and pulled out his wallet.

"No," Charlie said. "This one's on me."

"Thanks."

Charlie paid the bill at the bar then walked back to the table. "Hey, I've got all your stuff in my car. Let me give you a ride home."

"You okay to drive?"

Charlie looked at his first half-finished bottle of beer and untouched second. "I'll be fine."

As they walked out to the car, Charlie asked for Justin's phone and typed in his number. "Just in case you want to talk."

Charlie drove Justin home in silence. He suspected that the house that he dropped him at wasn't where he lived. As Charlie drove away, he looked in the rear-view mirror and saw Justin walk further up the block.

After he'd dropped Justin off, Charlie texted Declan.

Justin opening up about Ian. Said he modelled for some photos for him. Seemed emotional about what happened. Gave him my number.

A few moments later a text came in from Declan.

Interesting. Be available for him if he needs you. Do you want to meet and have a talk?

Charlie responded.

No, I'm good.

Soon after a message came back.

Great. Treat yourself to a good dinner. I'll look into the photographs. Then I'll head back to the office. Talk soon.

Charlie headed back to the pub. He was on his own now.

Chapter Twenty-Eight

On the drive home, Declan pulled into a gas station to fill up, then placed a call to Katherine Mann.

"Declan? Is everything okay?"

"I need your help. You mentioned a series of new photographs that Ian took of a young man. Do you have them?"

"Yes... Do they have anything to do with Ian's death?"

"I'm not sure. Can I come by and have a look at them? It won't take long."

"I'll have them ready."

Declan pulled into Katherine's drive forty minutes later. As he approached the door, it opened.

"I've laid them out in the kitchen," Katherine said. "Can I get you a coffee?"

"I'd love one. Thanks."

Declan walked into the kitchen and pored over the pictures. There must have been thirty or forty shots. Individual images of a young man in various states of dress — no nudes — with and without makeup. And not just subtle makeup. Broad character makeup — almost theatrical, accentuating the subject's physical features while, at the same time, eliminating the signs of an identifiable gender. *No. Not eliminating gender, but accentuating both the male and female. Ian was showing the body as a spectrum, not a binary.* The model was definitely Justin.

There were also a few photographs that appeared to be selfies showing both Justin and Ian, dressed in similar makeup. In all of the images, Declan saw joy in their faces.

"They're the best he ever shot," Katherine said.

"Were there any others…with other young men?"

"No. Just these… Is this what got him killed?"

"I don't know yet."

Declan took a swig of coffee, then headed to his van and drove back to the office.

When he got there, he logged into his laptop. He opened his email and noticed a message labelled *Sheldon Prescott CCTV*. He clicked on the message and found a link for downloading the video files. There were six of them. He chose the one labelled *West Driveway Camera — July 8, 6:00 p.m. — 2:00 a.m.*

* * * *

It was eight-thirty when Charlie's cell phone rang. *It's probably Declan*, he thought as he picked it up, then he saw the caller ID — it wasn't Declan.

He answered the call. "Hey, Justin."

"Sorry to call so late."

"No problem. What's up?" Charlie asked.

There was a pause on the other end of the line, then Justin said, "Can we talk?"

"Sure," Charlie replied.

"In person, I mean?"

Charlie tried to play it cool. "Yeah... Where do you want to meet?"

"Can I come to you?" Justin asked.

"Sure. I'm at the Comfort Inn." Charlie paused before saying, "Room two-oh-five."

Justin said, "Thanks. I appreciate it. I've got no one else to talk to. See you soon."

As soon as Justin disconnected, Charlie texted Declan.

Good news. Justin wants to talk. He's coming over to the hotel. I'll let you know what happens.

Charlie set the phone down and noticed a strong odour. He hadn't had a shower since practice, and he needed one. He stripped off his clothes and headed to the bathroom.

He'd just finished drying himself off and thrown on something clean to wear when there was a knock at his door. He opened it and let Justin in.

* * * *

Video from the west driveway camera came to life on Declan's computer. Several times, he saw a shadow of someone moving in the garden. At one point a head was clearly visible from the rear — one with light hair in a man's cut.

Ian came into view wheeling his suitcase to the car. Declan saw motion in the garden again. Out stepped his possible assailant. Ian let go of the suitcase and backed up. The person stepped forward, their features still shadowed by the trees. Declan paused the video. Although he couldn't clearly identify any definite facial features, he could assess the person's physique. It was most certainly a male, about the same height as Ian's six feet and of a moderately muscular build.

He pressed 'Play'. Something in the guy's hand flashed, like polished steel catching the light. *He's got a knife.*

The person with the knife came into view. It was Justin.

Ian and Justin seemed to be in a heated discussion. Justin gesticulated wildly at times. He made advances on Ian, who at first backed away, then moved forward, putting his hand on Justin's shoulder.

Declan continued to watch. To his surprise, Justin left Ian and walked back into the garden. Ian put his suitcase into the trunk, got into his car and drove off.

Ian drove away by himself...

Declan's phone rang. He glanced at the caller ID. It was Luke.

"Hey," Declan answered.

"I was just thinking about you. I'm just around the corner. Mind if I come up?"

"Sure. The door's open."

A few minutes later the door alarm beeped and Luke walked in. "What are you looking at?" Luke asked.

"I got a hold of the CCTV footage from the party house where Ian Mann was last seen. Justin Neves was definitely there on the night Ian disappeared."

"He was at the party?"

"No. He was waiting in the bushes for Ian by his car. He had some sort of confrontation with him. And it looks like he may have had a knife. The interesting thing is, Justin walked away and Ian left the party by himself."

"That doesn't mean he's not involved," Luke warned.

"That's what I'm trying to find out. I sent Charlie in undercover to try out for Justin's hockey team —"

"You did what?"

Declan continued, "He met with Justin this afternoon and discovered a link between him and Ian Mann connected to some photos Ian took."

Luke leaned towards Declan. "This is a murder investigation, and Charlie's got no experience. Just because Justin walked away doesn't mean that he wasn't working with an accomplice...or he might have seen something. It's enough to bring him in for questioning. And Charlie could be in danger."

"Isn't Airdrie out of your jurisdiction?"

"Given what you've told me, my boss'll back me up on this one. I think I should go now."

A text arrived from Charlie.

Good news. Justin wants to talk. He's coming over to the hotel. I'll let you know what happens.

Declan said, "I'm coming with you."

* * * *

"I hope you don't mind. I brought these," Justin said, pulling a couple of beers out of a plastic bag. "They're not the best, but it's what my dad drinks."

"They're great. Thanks," Charlie replied.

Justin opened a beer and sat on the edge of the bed.

"What's wrong?" Charlie asked as he sat beside him.

"There was more to that story I told you about Ian."

Charlie looked at Justin. He seemed more like a scared kid than a young adult.

Justin was silent for a moment, then said, "He brought a lot of makeup to our last photo shoot. He said he wanted to recreate some of the early pictures taken of Bowie. The ones where he was made up almost to look like a clown." Justin took a swig of his beer.

"And you were okay with that?" Charlie asked.

"I didn't think anything of it. You really lose yourself when you're totally made up, like when I used to wear masks at Halloween."

"What do you mean?"

Justin turned to face Charlie. "You're not afraid to be whoever you want to be, even the real you."

Charlie took a sip of beer.

Justin continued, "Ian made himself up, too. I painted this big black star on his face and he covered the rest in white. Then we got into these cool white suits. He turned on some music, then started taking pictures as we both started to dance around. We were killing ourselves laughing. For the first time I didn't care about anything—school, hockey, my dad, nothing—because for that moment I was just *me*."

"That all sounds great." Charlie said.

"It was. Then a couple of days later he showed me the pictures. They looked fantastic. He told me he was so proud of me. He said I was a natural." Justin was getting agitated. He started to rub his thighs with the heels of his hands.

Charlie's phone chirped with an incoming text. Without looking, he silenced it and put it on the nightstand. "What happened, Justin? What did he do?"

Justin took a few deep breaths before saying, "He said he was going to show the pictures to other people. Here. In Airdrie! He wanted to get people's reactions." Justin started to rock back and forth. "I emailed him and asked him not to, but he said he was going to submit them to a big magazine and people around the world would see them!"

"But...that's what you wanted, wasn't it?" Charlie asked.

"I never thought about it. Then all of a sudden it hit me. People would see me. Dressed up like that. They'd all know I was a fag. My dad would find out."

Justin started to cry. Charlie moved closer and put his hand on Justin's knee.

"I kept emailing Ian, telling him that he couldn't do that. I told him people might hurt me if he did. Ian tried to tell me that no one would know it was me, but I knew better. They'd spot me the second they saw the pictures. Then Ian stopped returning my emails."

Justin was choking with sobs. Charlie wrapped his arm around him and Justin leaned into him.

"I knew I had to do something to stop him," Justin said.

"Justin... What did you do?"

"I went to his house but he was just leaving in his car. So I followed him." Justin paused.

"It's okay," Charlie said. "You can tell me."

"He went to one of those mansions in Mountain River Estates. I had to jump a stone wall to get in and I waited by his car until he came out. He was mad that I'd followed him."

"Then what happened?" Charlie probed.

Justin continued, "When I told him he couldn't publish the pictures, he still wouldn't change his mind…so I pulled a knife on him."

Charlie felt Justin's body tense.

"I wasn't planning on doing anything like that," Justin said. "I thought if I scared him enough he'd rip up the pictures!"

Charlie held him by the shoulders and looked him in the eyes. "Justin…did you hurt Ian?"

"No," Justin said. "When I pulled the knife, Ian just looked at me with these really sad eyes. He said he saw how much it was upsetting me. He apologised and said he never wanted to hurt me."

Charlie asked, "Did you believe him?"

"Yes. He said that he'd give me a set of the photos and get rid of the files. And maybe someday, I would look at them and be proud of what I'd done."

"And then what did you do?" Charlie asked.

"I got back into my truck and went home. We were going to meet up the next day, but Ian never showed. Then I heard that he'd disappeared." Justin started shaking.

Charlie wrapped his arms around him, and held him tight. For the first time he noticed how muscular Justin was. He remembered the first time they'd seen each other, outside The Greek—how attractive Justin had looked. How in control he'd acted. And now, here he was, so vulnerable.

"Thanks for being here for me," Justin said.

"Any time."

"I feel like I can really trust you. It figures that if I was ever going to find a real friend, he wouldn't be from this town." Justin stared at Charlie, then leaned in and gave him a gentle kiss on the lips. Then a second, more passionate kiss. Justin undid the top button of Charlie's shirt, then looked at him.

Charlie wasn't sure what to do. He didn't want to blow his cover and he sensed in his gut that Justin had told him the truth. And Justin was so... Charlie nodded that it was okay. Justin pulled open the shirt to reveal the bruises on Charlie's torso.

"Oh, God, what happened to you?" Justin asked.

"Oh...I was hit by a car."

"You were what? You poor guy. Does it hurt much?" Justin caressed Charlie's bruised ribs. Goosebumps rose on Charlie's flesh. He inhaled.

"Sorry," Justin said. "I hope I didn't hurt you."

"No. You didn't."

Justin's eyes gleamed as he stepped away from the bed and began to undress. Charlie sat motionless and watched transfixed. Justin's shoulders were sculpted, as were his chest and toned stomach. He peeled off his tight jeans, revealing that he wore no underwear. His uncut cock and low-hanging balls were like fruit waiting to be picked.

Justin lay on the bed and said, "Your turn."

Charlie removed his shirt, then hesitated a moment before taking off his pants. He was nervous. He stripped away his underwear and lay down beside Justin.

Justin put his head on Charlie's chest. "Does this hurt?" he asked.

"No," Charlie responded.

Justin put his hand on Charlie's chest and began to slide it towards his navel. Justin's cock started to swell against Charlie's thigh. He grazed his lips over Charlie's left earlobe and teased it with his teeth.

"Does this hurt?"

"No," Charlie replied, breathing faster.

Justin took Charlie's cock in his hand. Charlie's heart pounded. Then Justin rolled on top of him. "Does this hurt?" he said.

"No," Charlie whispered.

Justin took Charlie by the wrists and pinned his arms above his head and began to grind his crotch against Charlie's.

"I've never gone this far before." Charlie moaned.

"I'm gonna take good care of you, Charlie Watts. You can trust me."

And Charlie believed him.

Chapter Twenty-Nine

The first thirty minutes of the drive to Airdrie were done in silence. A bad accident on Highway 2 had traffic snarled, and Luke had been forced onto secondary roads, which limited his speed. While Luke focussed on driving, Declan continued to text Charlie with no response.

"Why the fuck isn't he answering?"

Luke ignored the question as he ran a stop sign and at the next intersection took a hard right back onto the main highway. "We're almost there."

"If anything happens to Charlie…"

"Don't worry," Luke said, "we'll be there in plenty of time for his knight in shining armour to save him."

"What do you mean?"

"Oh, come on," Luke teased.

"What?"

"How can you not have seen it? He follows your every move with those big puppy-dog eyes."

Does he? Declan wondered.

Luke shook his head. "He's obviously head-over-heels in love with you, and why not? You are about as gorgeous as they get. On top of that, it's obvious that he doesn't like me. But I guess I'm the competition." Luke took the exit towards the hotel. "Are you sure you're a detective?"

Before Declan had a chance to reply, Luke said, "We're here."

They pulled into the parking lot. Declan jumped out of the car and ran to the hotel front desk. Luke was right behind him.

Luke flashed his badge. "We have a potential hostage situation. You need to give me the key card to room…"

"Two-oh-five," Declan shouted.

The young man behind the counter said nothing but, with shaking hands, passed a key card to Luke. As they reached the door, Declan heard muffled yells. Luke drew his gun, tapped the key card to the reader and shoved the door open with his foot, yelling, "Police. Stay where you are. Put your hands on your head where I can see them. Now!"

Declan followed Luke into the room. Charlie was on the bed naked with Justin straddling him. Both had their hands on their heads.

Before Declan could say anything, Luke shouted, "Justin Neves, I'm authorised to take you in for questioning regarding the death of Ian Mann. Please…disengage yourself from Mr Watts and get dressed."

"Charlie, are you all right?" Declan asked.

"I'm fine!" he yelled as Justin dismounted.

"What's happening?" Justin cried.

Luke pulled him away from the bed and said, "Where are your clothes?"

Justin pointed to a heap on the floor. "Please," Justin sobbed. "I didn't do anything. Charlie, tell them I didn't do anything."

Before Charlie could reply, Luke said, "Declan, search his clothes for a weapon."

Justin looked confused. "Charlie...how do these people know you?" His voice was cracking. No one answered.

Declan checked all of the pockets of Justin's clothes, but found nothing except his wallet, cell phone and a keychain with an Axemen tag. He handed the contents to Luke.

Declan looked at Charlie and said, "Go into the bathroom and get yourself cleaned up."

As soon as Charlie had left, Declan watched Justin get dressed. Then Luke put him in handcuffs. He turned to Declan and said, "I'll take care of Justin. Can you get home by yourself?"

"I can use Charlie's car," Declan replied as Luke roughly escorted Justin out of the room.

Declan waited for Charlie as he finished showering and getting dressed.

When he came out of the bathroom, Charlie packed up his things in silence and followed Declan, who dropped off the key card at the front desk. "Room's paid for," he said, then he led Charlie out into the cool of the night.

"I'll need the keys. I'm driving," he said to Charlie, who seemed to not care. His face was an unreadable mask.

As they drove off Declan said, "Why didn't you answer my texts?"

"I was busy," Charlie said, turning his head away and staring out the window.

They drove on for a few minutes before Declan broke the silence. "I checked into the CCTV footage. I saw Justin there. He had some sort of fight with Ian. He had a knife. I was worried about you."

Charlie muttered, "I already knew about the fight with Ian."

"What do you mean?" Declan asked.

"Justin told me about it," Charlie said. "He just wanted the photographs back. Ian wanted to publish the pictures but Justin was terrified that people would find out he was gay if anyone in town saw them."

"So nobody in town knew he was gay?"

"He hadn't told anyone. Keeping a secret like that can eat away at you. I know — I haven't told my folks yet. But I'm lucky. At least I have friends to talk to about it. Can you imagine what it's like for a guy like Justin? Alone out here... Do you even remember what it was like to come out? He's scared, that's all. You have no idea how bad it can be. You're so confident, I bet it was easy for you."

They drove on in silence for a few minutes. Declan glanced over at Charlie and made a decision. He said, "I'm going to tell you something that very few people know. Coming out wasn't easy for me either, Charlie. I still remember it like it was yesterday."

"When did you come out?" Charlie asked.

"I was in grade ten. I was just getting out of English class. It was held in one of the portables behind the school. Greg Delaney, who was the cutest guy I'd ever seen, came up behind me. We were the last to leave the class. He called out my name.

"He was the kind of guy who normally wouldn't waste his time on a little kid like me and he was at the centre of every one of my fantasies. He asked me if I had a sec. I remember my voice cracking when I said 'Sure.' I knew I'd be late for math class, but who cared? Greg Delaney wanted to talk to me.

"He took me behind the portable and made me swear not to repeat what he was going to say. I remember he put his hand on my shoulder when he asked this. I thought my heart was going to pound out of my chest. I would have sworn on a mountain of Bibles that I would keep his secret if it would have given me a few more minutes with him."

Charlie nodded. "I know what that's like."

Declan continued, "He said he had a wrestling match that afternoon and he told me he couldn't go on like he was. He took my hand and put it on his crotch. He had a full hard-on. He claimed he could only get rid of it if he had his cock in someone's mouth. He begged me to help him out, saying he couldn't go out there like this, and if he didn't wrestle today, he'd be kicked off the team."

"Holy shit," Charlie said.

"Delaney promised to suck me off after the match, which he said he'd win for me. He pushed me down on my knees and shoved my face into his crotch. I can still remember the smell of sweat and denim... And I can still hear a voice yell out 'I told you he was a fag.' I looked up to see a dozen kids standing there, yelling out insults. Delaney was laughing his guts out. He'd set me up."

"That's awful. So what did you do?" Charlie asked.

"I just wanted to run, but my muscles froze and I couldn't move. I just stayed there on my knees until Mr

Johnson, the phys-ed teacher came around the corner. One kid yelled out that I was trying to do things to Delaney. Delaney freaked out. I guess he never thought a teacher would get involved. I remember Delaney yelling, 'Get away from me, you fucking perv,' and he kicked me to the ground."

Charlie shook his head. "Jesus. That's rough."

"It got worse. They called my parents. I got a two-week suspension and a few beatings from my father."

"But you didn't *do* anything."

"It didn't matter," Declan said. "My dad asked me if I was gay, and I couldn't lie to him. We used to get along before the world got pulled out from under my feet. From then on, he blamed everything that went wrong in the family on me being gay."

Charlie put his hand on Declan's leg. "I'm sorry that happened to you."

Declan took his eyes off the road for a second and looked at Charlie. "I think what I learned was it's all about control. If you don't choose your own time and place to come out, someone will take that power away from you. So, maybe I do understand what Justin's going through, but we have to make sure he didn't kill someone to keep his secret. And as for you, Charlie Watts, you choose your time coming out to your parents, but don't leave it so long that it winds up hurting you."

"Well, that time's not right now. I had another fight with them about working with you and I moved in with my friend Carrie."

Declan took the exit off the highway before he said, "Look...I'd understand if you decide that family's more important than this job."

Charlie smiled. "I'd sooner die than give up this job."

"Let's hope it never comes to that. You've already been hit by a car and slept with a possible murderer."

"Please…don't mention that. You could have at least called and warned me you were coming."

"Maybe if you'd answered your texts…"

"Well, I was…"

Declan laughed.

"And I still think you've got it wrong," Charlie said. "I don't think Justin could have hurt Ian. I believe him."

"Let's wait to see what Luke finds out."

Charlie said, "Turn right just up here. Carrie's place is the second one from the corner."

Declan parked the car then helped Charlie pull his belongings out of the trunk. "I'll leave the car with you. I can walk to the office from here. Why don't you take tomorrow morning off and I'll see you in the afternoon. Oh, and I'll let the coach know that you've wrapped things up and won't be in for practice."

As Declan went to leave, Charlie hugged him and didn't let go for a full ten seconds before he said, "Thanks…for everything," then walked into the house.

* * * *

Luke drove towards Calgary while Justin sat handcuffed in the back seat of his car.

"We have CCTV and fingerprint evidence that prove you were at the house where Ian Mann was last seen on Thursday, July seventh. Wanna tell me what happened?" Luke asked.

"I didn't do anything. I just wanted to talk to him. He had something of mine, and I wanted it back."

"What did you want so badly that you pulled a knife on him?"

Luke watched Justin in the rear-view mirror. He was chewing his lower lip. It was like he was deciding on what story to tell. "You can start now, or we can wait'll I get you down to the station and we get your folks involved. Maybe they'd be interested in hearing about your hotel buddy."

"No. Please don't call them. There were some photographs Ian Mann took of me and I wanted them back, that's all."

"Naked photos? Was that what he was into, taking naked shots of teen boys?" Luke asked.

"No. I was just…dressed up, and I thought if anyone else saw them, they'd think maybe I was…gay, or something. I can't have people saying that about me. I'd be dead." Justin stared at the floor as he spoke.

"And you pulled a knife on him?"

"Just to scare him. I wasn't gonna use it. And it worked. He said he was sorry he'd upset me so much, and he promised not to show anyone the pictures. Then he said he'd give them to me."

Luke probed, "What did you do next?"

"I left the way I came."

"How did you know he was going to be at that house?"

"I knew where he lived. I went there to ask for the pictures but when I got there, he was getting into his car. I followed him. I couldn't get in, because the gate closed behind him, so I had to climb a wall. That's the way I got out, too."

"Did you follow him when he left?" Luke asked.

"No." Justin paused. "But I did see something."

Luke tightened his hands on the steering wheel. "What did you see?"

"When Ian left, there was a car just down the street. A guy got out of it and stopped him."

"Did you see what this guy looked like?"

"It was too dark to make out anything clearly. He was a muscular guy. About your size."

"How about the car?"

"I don't know. It was a car, not a truck."

"See if you can remember anything else."

"I got spooked and drove away. I just saw someone stop Ian's car, and then I left. I don't know what happened after that."

Luke glanced at Justin in the rear-view mirror. His eyes were closed. Streaks of tears marked his cheeks. Then Justin opened his eyes. He looked at Luke with a strange expression on his face. "I'd like to make a phone call. I'm allowed that, right? When we get to the station, I'll need my phone."

Luke stared back and said, "No. I don't think so," as he turned off the highway away from the police station, and drove towards a place he'd been one time before — a boarded-up store between a bistro and a condo under construction.

Chapter Thirty

"Well, that must have been embarrassing," Carrie said.

Charlie sat at the table in her kitchen relating the previous day's adventures. He wore her second-best bathrobe and stayed out of her way as she scrambled eggs and made toast.

"I have never been more humiliated in my life. I'd always pictured him seeing me naked under different circumstances."

"The circumstances being *under him*?"

Charlie sighed. "Why is life so cruel?"

"Oh, stop whining and eat these," she said, plunking his plate in front of him. "And don't expect this kind of service every time you're caught in bed with a murderer."

"That's the thing. I don't think he did it."

Charlie scooped up some eggs and shovelled them into his mouth. "God, these are good."

"I'm glad you like them. I'll teach you how to make them for next time."

"I'm sorry. I must be getting in the way. I promise I'll start looking for my own place soon."

"You are not in the way. I kinda like having you around. You're my best friend in the world, and it's nice having someone I trust to cuddle up to at night without worrying about sex. That, and you look ridiculous in that robe, and that makes me laugh."

She reached over and tousled Charlie's hair as his phone rang. Carrie grabbed it off the table. The display said 'Declan'.

"It's your boyfriend calling." she said with a smile.

"Which one?" Charlie teased.

"The older one who isn't in jail," she said, handing him the phone.

Charlie answered the call. "Morning, Declan."

"Hey, Charlie. You all right?" Declan asked.

"Fine. Taking the morning off, as instructed. Have you heard anything from Luke?"

"Nope. He wasn't answering his phone. I left a message on his voicemail but he hasn't gotten back to me. Before I see him, I want to check on something. I'm going to head over to Katherine's to fill her in on what you learned last night. I want to have another look at those pictures. You up for coming along?"

"You bet."

"Good. I'd like to have you there. She seems to relax more when you're around."

"Do you think she knows something she's not telling us?" Charlie asked.

"I don't know. There's something not quite sitting right. What you said about Justin… I'll swing by and pick you up at one."

"See you then," Charlie replied, before putting the phone down. "He thinks I might be right," Charlie said.

"He said that?"

"Well, not in so many words. But he implied it. He's coming over to pick me up so *we* can interrogate a former suspect."

"If it's a former suspect, why are you interrogating them?"

"It's detective stuff. You wouldn't understand," he replied with a mock sense of superiority. Charlie sat back and had another sip of coffee, trying to look serious in the frilly floral bathrobe.

* * * *

At a quarter to one the doorbell rang. Charlie, now dressed for work, ran to the door. "You're here," Charlie said, smiling.

"I hope you don't mind. I'm a little early."

"Not a problem."

Carrie came down from the top of the stairs. "You must be the mysterious Declan that Charlie can't stop going on about."

Charlie shot her a look that said *shut up*.

"That would be me," Declan said. "And you must be the kind friend who took this poor sod in off the street. It's nice to meet you."

Charlie turned to leave but was stopped by Carrie clearing her throat. He turned to see her standing with her arms open wide. Charlie reluctantly went over and gave her a goodbye hug.

Charlie got into Declan's van, and within a half an hour, they were pulling into Katherine's driveway. Charlie was starting to feel comfortable in his role as

Declan's assistant. The butterflies in his stomach were gone.

Katherine greeted them at the door as they mounted the front steps. "I have coffee ready, if you'd like some."

"That would be great. Thank you," Charlie answered.

They sat in the living room and waited for Katherine, who entered carrying a tray of steaming mugs. They each took one, then Katherine asked, "Do you have any news?"

Declan said, "Last night, the police brought in Justin Neves for questioning. Did Ian ever mention his name?"

"Not that I remember."

"He was a player on the Axemen. He was the young man in the photographs."

"And you think he killed Ian?" Katherine asked.

"At this point, the police have him in for questioning," Declan said. "The photographs of him may provide him with motive. Apparently Ian wanted to have them published and Justin was afraid of what that might do to his reputation."

Katherine sighed. "You mean that people might think he was gay, or that he liked to…dress up? People are so narrow-minded."

"I agree. Could we see the photographs again, with that in mind?"

"They're still in the kitchen. I'll go get them."

Charlie was starting to feel the effects of his third cup of coffee of the day. "Mrs Mann, would you mind if I used your washroom?" he said.

"Of course not. Use the one up the stairs, second door on the right."

"Thank you."

Charlie made his way upstairs and easily spotted the bathroom. As he walked down the hall he noticed that all of the doors in the hall were open, except one. *I wonder…*

He could hear voices from downstairs as he crept over to the closed door. The floors were carpeted, and his footsteps made no sound. He cautiously opened the door and walked in. Plaques on the walls commemorating Ian Mann's contributions to various community organisations confirmed that this was Ian's office.

The one thing that struck Charlie was, aside from a computer, a desk lamp and a framed photograph of Katherine, the desk surface was clear of clutter. Other than the commendations on the walls and a bookcase holding a few dozen books on photography, the office was bare. *Did Katherine clean up the place?*

Charlie moved to the desk. The drawers stuck when he tried to open them. He was afraid that if he wasn't careful, one of them would squeak and give his intrusion away. As he wiggled a drawer back and forth to coax it open, the photo of Katherine toppled forward. Charlie reached to catch it, but in the process, his elbow knocked the lamp onto the floor. Charlie froze. If it hadn't been for the carpet, the crash would have given him away. As he went to return the lamp to its place on the desk, he noticed a USB stick which the lamp had hidden.

What do we have here?

Charlie returned the lamp and picture to their proper places, then popped the USB stick into his pocket, left the office and closed the door. He headed to the washroom, and when he was done, he returned to the others downstairs.

"Charlie, come and have a look at these," Declan said, indicating the photos spread out on the coffee table. "How do these fit with what Justin said?"

Charlie leafed through the pictures. "They're pretty much as he described them. Justin looks great in all of them and they both seem to be having a ball in the shots where they're together." Charlie looked up at Declan. "But I can see why he was worried about them getting out. Some small-minded people might look at these and think *fag*."

Declan said, "I think that's exactly what Justin was afraid of, and that would give him motive to do whatever he could to stop them from getting out."

"And what do *you* believe?" Katherine asked Charlie.

"I don't think Justin's got it in him to kill someone. These photos... Could we borrow them? I think if I could see Justin's reactions to them in person, I would know for sure if he was telling the truth."

"Do you really think it could help?" Katherine asked Declan.

"I'm learning that my partner's a good judge of human nature, and I think we should take his intuition seriously," Declan replied.

Katherine put the photos into an envelope and handed it to Charlie.

Declan thanked Katherine and said, "We'll be in touch as soon as we find out more."

As soon as they got back into the van, Charlie said excitedly, "You're not going to believe what I found when I went upstairs. Ian's office was almost empty. It was like someone had cleaned it out. But look what I found hidden under the desk lamp." Charlie pulled out the USB stick.

"You stole that from Ian's office?"

"Well, maybe it contains something that relates to the case…"

"Charlie Watts, I could kiss you. Let's get back to the office and see what you've found."

Declan drove quickly and, as soon as they got through the door, he said, "You check the USB stick, and I'm going to have another look at the CCTV footage and see if the other cameras picked anything else up."

Charlie ran to his desk and pulled the USB stick from his pocket, then waited for his computer to come to life. As soon as he got through the login, he slid the key into the USB port. When the file manager opened, there were two files. One was a still shot showing a man. It was difficult to make out any details as he was back-lit by a window. He seemed to have a muscular build and short-cut hair.

The other file was a Quicktime video. The date stamp on the video was July seventh. The timestamp was 4:05 p.m.

Charlie hit 'Play'.

The video had been taken in a bar. Charlie figured it was the same bar as in the still image. Ian had obviously hit 'Record' then placed it on the table. The phone was pointed at an odd angle, showing mainly the ceiling and the occasional person squeezing by the table.

Charlie listened to the full conversation.

A voice said, "Ian? Thank you for meeting me. You know why I'm here, but before you reject the offer, please just listen to what I have to say."

Ian replied, "I'm listening."

The other voice continued, "These are the facts — your property is sitting vacant and costing you money. Just to remind you, this spreadsheet has the figures for the last ten years highlighting your costs."

"I don't suppose you'd be willing to reveal the name of the thief who provided you with these?"

"Look, Ian, it's a purpose-built chemical production facility — a nitrogen fertiliser plant to be precise — and we all saw what happened with one of those in Beirut —"

"That," Ian interrupted, "was a fully filled, unventilated fertiliser storage barn, and you know it. There hasn't been a scrap of nitrogen phosphate in my building for over fifty years."

"Still, it's in an area that's an up-and-coming part of town," the other man added, "and fears are harder to wash out of people's minds than fertiliser out of a building. That aside, it's an industrial facility that can't easily be converted to any other use given the structural configuration and rumoured lingering chemical contamination. The floors are wood, Ian. It absorbs. If you converted it into condos, who would want to move into it? Besides, the cost of remediation would bankrupt you. Any other guy would bulldoze the property and turn it into a parking lot. The taxes would be a tenth of what you're paying now."

The fellow continued with his pitch. "The company is aware of the sentimental attachment that you have to that building. It's the last remnant of your family's empire, isn't it?"

There was a pause in the conversation, then the man continued, "They're having new plans for the development drawn up as we speak, plans that will maintain the beautiful steel façade of the building —

restore it, actually, to its original state — and, now here's the topper — the company is offering to name the new place the Mann Building in honour of your family. So do we have a deal?"

Ian responded, "I must politely decline. I don't do business with mobsters."

The other man pressed, "I'm going to ask you one more time, and if the answer's the same, I can't say what will happen."

Ian said coolly, "I think this meeting has come to an end."

"You have no idea who you're dealing with here, Mann. A decision like that can get you fucking killed."

Ian replied, "The answer's still no."

There was a loud slam. Charlie figured the man had hit the table with his fist. It was hard enough for the phone to bounce and land at an angle. It was now focused clearly on the face of the other man.

"Oh, shit. Declan!" Charlie yelled.

He ran into Declan's office. "Ian had a meeting with Luke on the day he disappeared," Charlie said. "Ian recorded it and stored it on the USB stick. Luke told him he could get killed."

Declan said, "And that's not all." He rotated his laptop so Charlie could see. It was a dim picture taken from a high angle. It showed the back of a car and a man standing beside it. It was clearly Luke.

"He was there on the street outside Sheldon's house the night Ian disappeared. It's all fucking here in one of the other CCTV files, if I'd bothered to open it. And watch…"

Declan pushed 'Play' and the video continued. The view was partially obstructed. Charlie guessed the camera was mounted high up between the trees that surrounded the property.

Luke was pacing back and forth. A minute later, he stepped out into the road. He looked like he was waving his arms. A car stopped. Charlie couldn't clearly make out the details of the car, or the driver but he could see Luke reaching behind his back and pulling out something tucked into the waist-band of his pants. It looked like a gun. Luke yanked the driver out of the car and locked him in the trunk. The driver was Ian.

"The camera must have been well hidden. I don't think he had any idea he was being filmed," Charlie said.

Declan made no comment.

"Declan?"

"He was playing me all along. Once he found out we were involved, he used me to find out what we knew." Declan started to hammer out a text on his phone.

"Declan, if he's the killer... What happened to Justin?"

"Oh, shit!"

Declan grabbed his phone and placed a call. "Hi. Can you transfer me to the holding cells? Thanks."

Charlie sat there, wanting to talk, but not knowing what to say.

"Holding? Do you have a Justin Neves in custody? Was he ever in custody?"

"Maybe he's in another district?" Charlie whispered.

Declan held up a finger. "Nowhere then... Okay. Thanks."

Declan disconnected. "There's no trace of him anywhere in the system."

Charlie said, "What are we going to do?" He started to shake.

Declan went back to his phone and punched in a number. "It's Declan. I need your help."

"What now?" a voice at the other end of the line snapped.

"I have to know what's happening with the Ian Mann case," Declan said. "A boy's life might be at stake."

"I told you to keep your nose out of police business."

"A boy's gone missing. He could be in trouble."

There was a muttering of voices on the end of the line. Sam Hunt came back on the phone. "McKeckran closed the case. His notes on file show it as death by misadventure. Ian Mann was down by the river, slipped, hit his head on a rock and fell in and drowned."

Declan yelled, "That's bullshit! If the case was closed, why did Constable Luke Fraser pick up Justin Neves from Airdrie last night and take him in for questioning for his role in the murder? And why is the boy not listed as being held in custody?"

"He did what? Wait a second."

There was a brief silence on the other end of the phone. Declan could hear the clacking of a keyboard.

"If it was a busy night, they may have been tied up in holding and haven't gotten around to entering him into the system," Sam said.

A muffled voice on the other end of the call yelled out, "Get down to holding and see if they have anything on a Justin Neves there. Now!"

Declan said, "We've got files that show that Luke had a fight with Ian Mann on the day he disappeared, and footage of Luke kidnapping him that evening. I'll get Charlie to send them to you right now."

Declan wrote an email address on a scrap of paper and Charlie quickly disappeared to the outer office to send the files.

On the other end of the phone, Sam said, "But Fraser was the one who discovered Mann's car up-river from where the body was found."

Declan replied, "He and McKeckran were working the case together. I'll bet I know why McKeckran closed the case down. Luke did this. I know it."

"All right. I'll put out an APB on both Luke and the Neves kid. We'll find them."

"Thanks. Let me know what you find out. In the meantime, I'm going to try to find Luke."

"Declan… Don't do anything stupid. Let us handle this."

"We wouldn't be in this mess in the first place if the police had done their job." Declan slammed the phone down.

Charlie returned to Declan's office. "The two files are on their way," Charlie said. "Where could he have taken Justin?"

Declan paced the room. "Not back to his own place. That would be crazy. Even for him."

"What about friends, relatives or business associates?" Charlie asked.

Declan halted and turned to Charlie. "I think I might know where he is."

"Good. Let's go," Charlie said as he made his way to the door.

"No. You're staying here."

Charlie turned. "You're not the only one responsible for what happened."

"It could get really hairy, and I don't want to have to be rescuing two of you."

"Ever think for once that you might need rescuing?" Charlie yelled. "Who's gonna be there to watch your back?"

Declan recognised a losing battle when he saw one. "Okay, but you'll do exactly as I say." He went to his office safe and pulled out something he suspected might come in handy. "Come on. We'll swing by your place and pick up the Beast. We might need two vehicles."

Declan drove the van back to Carrie's apartment. When they arrived, Charlie got out of the van. "Just follow me in your car, okay?" Declan said.

"Got it." Charlie looked anxious.

"We'll find him," Declan assured him. He hoped he was right.

Chapter Thirty-One

It took fourteen minutes to reach the building in the Mission District. Declan turned onto a side street and stopped the van. Charlie pulled in behind him. Declan jumped out of his vehicle and walked up to the driver's door of the Red Beast.

"Wait here. I'll be right back."

"Sure."

Declan got back into his van and did a circuit of the block, driving past the building he suspected Luke would be in. He spotted Luke's car parked in the alleyway.

After Declan had driven back and parked near the Red Beast, Charlie got out of the vehicle.

"Follow me," Declan said.

He walked Charlie a full block before he halted at an intersection. "See that construction site?" he said, pointing down the block.

"Yeah."

"There's an alleyway between it and the old building to its left."

"Okay."

"I want you to pull up and block the alleyway. I'll seal it off at the other end with the van. Stay in your car until you see me."

"Got it," Charlie said.

Declan moved the van around to the back of the alleyway and pulled in. Charlie had already blocked off the other end. Declan got out and waved towards Charlie, who left his car and ran to him.

There, at the small dumpster where he'd had his first encounter with Brick Wall, Declan gave Charlie his next instructions. "I want you to climb up here and carefully peek inside the window. I'll hoist you up and then brace it so it doesn't roll. Tell me if you can see anyone in there."

"Okay," Charlie whispered. Declan checked to see if anyone was watching, then placed his hands around Charlie's waist and lifted him up onto the lid. Charlie raised his head so he could see through the window and scanned the room. Charlie looked down at Declan and shook his head. Declan signalled for him to come down.

"They're probably in the basement," Declan whispered. "Come on."

He led Charlie to a side door where he tried the handle. It was locked. Charlie tapped him on the shoulder and pointed up. There, in faded peeling paint, was an old sign that read "Monarch Bakery." Declan hadn't spotted that on his previous night-time visit.

"All roads lead to Monarch," he said.

"What now?" Charlie whispered.

Declan pulled out a small case. "They probably haven't updated these locks since that sign was painted." The door had an old wafer-tumbler lock. *This should be a breeze.*

Declan inserted the thin picks into the keyhole, and in less than a minute, was able to rotate the tumbler. He eased open the door, praying it didn't squeak, then stuck his head in. It was, as Charlie had said, empty. But from the basement, he could hear voices, then a muffled scream.

Declan pulled back out of the doorway. "Give me your phone," he said, dialling a number and handing it back to Charlie. "Ask for Staff Sergeant Sam Hunt. If it's not him that answers, tell whoever it is that his son's life is in danger. Give him the address. Tell him I said no sirens. And no matter what you hear, you stay here. We can't take the chance that they'll miss the place. And if for some reason Luke runs out of here, you run the other way, 'cause he'll be pissed."

"All right," Charlie said. Declan saw him press 'Dial', then he headed through the door.

Declan crept to the back of the building then took the stairs to the basement.

He heard a voice from below, "I didn't tell anyone. Please, let me go. I'll go away and you'll never see me again. I promise…"

Declan got to the bottom of the steps and rounded the corner. Luke stood with his back towards him, maybe fifteen feet away. Too far to rush him unnoticed. Beyond him Justin was tied to a chair, his head lowered like he didn't want to see what was going to happen to him next.

"Let him go, Luke," Declan ordered.

Luke spun around, pulling out his gun from his waistband. Declan stood still, his hands raised to show Luke he was unarmed.

"Fuck, Declan... Why are you here? How did you..."

"Put the gun down, Luke. I'm not going to do anything. I just want to talk. That's all." He could see the wild-eyed look of confusion on Luke's face.

"Justin," Declan said, maintaining a calm tone, "are you hurt?"

The boy raised his head. He was terrified. "No. I told him I wasn't going to say anything but..." He broke into quiet sobs.

"Luke, put the gun down. Tell me what's going on."

Luke kept the gun trained on Declan. "It wasn't my fault," Luke said. "I had no choice. I had to help them."

"Help who?"

"You know who," he spit back. "You've seen what they can do."

"You mean Monarch? What do they have on you, Luke?"

Luke lowered the gun slightly. Declan knew from experience that a gun might not be big, but it could get very heavy when a person pointed it at someone they didn't want to kill.

"I owed them money—a lot of it—and I couldn't afford to pay them back. Never go to a loan shark. Not even to pay off a bookie."

"If you owe them money, Luke, maybe I could help."

"A hundred grand? Do you have that? Is business that good?"

"That's a lot."

"No one can help me, Declan. They said they had a way for me to pay off my debts. I just had to meet a guy and convince him to sell his building. So I met with Ian Mann, but he said no. When I told Monarch what had happened, they said I needed to try harder, or they would make things very difficult."

Declan said, "For you?"

Luke scowled. "Not just for me, but for my dad too. They found out his little secret, and mine. They said they would reveal that he was gay and destroy his career. It would kill him. So I did what they said. I'm in way too deep, Declan. And I've got nothing left. They drained me dry and the interest keeps mounting and I keep thinking about my dad."

Declan just had to keep him talking until help arrived. "How long have you been gambling?"

"Since high school. I've always had a thing for horses. It comes from being raised in the country, I guess." He let out a weak laugh. "It got really bad in university. When I got out, I took out a loan against the condo my folks bought me, and now…"

"But, Luke, to kill Ian Mann…"

"I was just supposed to scare the shit out of him. I didn't mean to kill him! It was an accident. He ran and fell and cracked his head open on a rock. He did it to himself."

"But he wasn't dead, Luke. The autopsy showed he drowned."

"I thought he was dead. I panicked. I stripped off his clothes to make it look like he'd gone swimming, then threw the body in the river. And then I found his dresses and wigs in the trunk of his car and I had an idea."

Declan moved in closer. "Why didn't they use one of their thugs? Wouldn't it have been easier?"

Luke replied, "Monarch had me over a barrel and I owed them. By using me they were extending their power into the police. I'm probably not the only cop on the force that they control."

"Is McKeckran involved with Monarch?" Declan asked.

Luke thought about it. "I don't think so, but it was easy to get him to close down the case because he hates queers. Imagine—McKeckran's homophobia almost saved my life. And I would have gotten away with it if it wasn't for him," he said, waving his gun at Justin. "Monarch had someone on the inside who texted me about the party house where Ian went, and Justin saw me there. I didn't know someone else was tracking Mann down." He turned to face the boy. "If you'd only just minded your own fucking business…"

"Luke, you can't hurt the kid."

"I don't want to. That's why I called Monarch. They know how to clean up my messes."

"Oh fuck, I don't have time for this shit," Declan said as he lunged towards Luke.

* * * *

Charlie could hear nothing from the doorway. He kept his eyes peeled for the police. *What's taking them so long?*

He checked his cell phone again. Still only the first text from Declan's father.

On the way. Keep yourself safe.

A crash came from inside the building. Charlie couldn't wait any longer.

He followed the sounds coming from the basement stairs. There was another loud crash. Charlie leapt down the last few steps and into the basement room. Declan had Luke in a headlock on the ground. A shattered table lay beside them. Luke struggled free, kicking Declan's right leg hard, just above the knee. Declan screamed in pain. Charlie spotted the handgun a few feet away. He dove for it and picked it up.

"Everybody freeze or I'll shoot," he yelled. The ball of muscles and fists on the floor stopped rolling. Charlie stood there, gun pointed towards the ceiling, hands shaking. From behind him, a calm voice spoke.

"I'll take that," the person said, plucking the gun out of his hand.

Charlie turned. Four police officers were standing at the foot of the stairs, guns drawn. The oldest one, who now held the gun, said, "You must have been trained by my son. He's not so good at following orders either."

Declan pushed himself up off the floor.

Sam Hunt walked past him towards Luke. "Face down on the ground, Fraser. Hands behind your back."

He handcuffed him, then two other cops lifted him off the ground and searched him.

"Luke Fraser, you're under arrest for the murder of Ian Mann and for the kidnapping of Justin Neves. God knows what else I'll come up with. Take him away."

He turned to Declan. "I got the files you sent me. I'll forward them to Major Crimes."

"I recorded the confession he made a few minutes ago," Declan said, pulling his cell phone out of his pocket. "I'm not sure if it'll stand up in court, but it can't hurt. I'll forward you the file."

Charlie watched as the two faced each other, not saying anything. Declan's father blinked first. He nodded his head and said, "Good work."

Charlie ran to Justin, who sat in his chair, motionless. "I'll get you out of these," he said, fumbling at the zip ties that bound him.

"Here. This might be useful," Declan said, handing a pocket knife to Charlie.

"Just another second," Charlie said, cutting through the bindings. He rubbed Justin's hands and legs, hoping it would restore some feeling to the limbs.

"Who are you?" Justin asked.

"Charlie Watts. Just like I always was," he said with a smile, helping him to stand. Justin had trouble with his balance so Charlie put his arm around him for support.

"Are you with the police?"

"No. I'm just part of your rescue party."

Declan came up to Charlie and Justin. "Justin, they'll take your statement, get you checked out by a doctor and then get you home."

Justin nodded.

"Oh, one other thing," Declan said, walking over to the remains of the broken table. He rifled through the broken wood and came back. "I think everything's here," he said, handing a wallet, a set of keys and a cell phone back to Justin.

"If you need anything, you can call me," Charlie said.

Justin frowned. "I'm not sure I will. I trusted you, and you lied to me."

"I thought you were involved in Ian's murder," Charlie confessed. "I think you should call your folks and tell them that you spent the night at a friend's and apologise for not calling earlier. You might eventually have to tell them what happened."

"Will I have to go to court?"

"I don't know. I'm kinda new to all of this. If you do, stuff will probably come out. Stuff you don't want to. But I promise, I'll get those pictures back to you. After that, what you do is up to you."

Justin's expression was hard to read. He nodded and headed towards the door with the police officer. A few minutes after Justin had left, Charlie heard shouting, followed by the sounds of a fight. Charlie and Declan ran upstairs. The police were putting two men in handcuffs in the alleyway. Charlie grinned at the anger and confusion on the faces of Brick Wall and his accomplice.

Declan turned to Charlie and said, "I think it's time to finish with the police and call it a day. What do you say, Mr Watts?"

Charlie grinned and said, "I love working with you."

"And I love working with you," Declan replied.

Charlie couldn't wipe the smile off his face.

Chapter Thirty-Two

Declan sat at his favourite table in Bar-None. He nursed a vodka and soda as he waited.

The door opened and light flooded into the bar. Charlie walked in and went straight to Mickey, who took his car keys and handed him a beer.

"Good to see you back in here. I thought you must have taken offence at me hitting you with my car."

"It would take a lot more than that to keep me away," Charlie said.

"How about a plate of nachos on the house?"

"Sweet! I gotta start throwing myself in front of cars more often."

"He's in the corner," Mickey said.

Charlie made his way over to Declan.

Declan raised his glass and said, "Tonight we celebrate. Tomorrow, we'll be spending more time with the police. When Luke comes up for trial, it'll be a shit-show. Everybody will be out to protect their own asses, especially the cops. McKeckran just about had the case thrown out."

"What about Katherine and Michael?"

"I think they'll be fine. They weren't directly involved, although Michael will have to distance himself from Monarch if he wants to come out of this with a decent reputation. He was just a real estate agent trying to get a deal, and Katherine thought the sale would convince Ian to go back to England. They did nothing criminally wrong."

"And who is Monarch?" Charlie asked.

"Who knows? I don't think Michael has a clue who's behind it. Even Mr Attwal didn't seem to know. And I doubt Brick Wall will talk. Guys like him don't live to be his age by talking."

"That leaves Luke," Charlie said.

"I'm not sure if he knows anyone higher up than Brick Wall. These organisations survive by working in cells. You only know what you need to."

Charlie nodded. "Speaking of Luke... How are you doing? I mean...the two of you were... I'm sorry, it's none of my business."

"No. It's okay. I gotta admit, it took me by surprise. I keep asking myself if there was something I should have caught. Once he found out we were involved in the case, I was his direct line to any clues we might have discovered that could implicate him. I guess next time I'm attracted to someone, I have to use better judgement."

Declan drained his glass and signalled to Mickey that he wanted a refill. "How about you and Justin? You got pretty close."

Charlie blushed. "It was just something that happened in the heat of the moment. I don't think he trusts me, and my feelings are all mixed up right now." Charlie took a swig of his beer. "Why did Luke have to kidnap Justin? It makes no sense. He knew he wasn't involved in Ian's murder."

"Luke was driven by fear. All of the decisions he made were based in that. He was afraid that Monarch would destroy his father, so he agreed to help them convince Ian to sell. He was afraid that when Justin told him he'd seen someone outside Sheldon's house, that he knew it was Luke. He wasn't thinking when he took Justin to the bakery building. He hoped Brick Wall would be able to get him out of that mess."

Mickey came by and dropped off another round of drinks just as the Kid brought them a plate of nachos.

"So," Declan said. "I had a call from Mrs B just before you got here."

"How's she doing?"

"Still on the mend. She's sounding great, but she did have some bad news."

"Oh?"

"Yeah, it seems she's enjoying herself down there. The weather's perfect, the dollar goes a long way and, from the sounds of it, she has a very attractive orderly who is paying her a lot of attention."

"So, what's the bad news?"

"She tendered her resignation. She said her heart attack showed her that she needs to spend more time enjoying herself, instead of taking care of me. So I guess I'll be looking for a permanent replacement for her. Do you happen to know anybody who would want the position? I mean, you only signed up for three weeks."

Charlie got a serious look on his face. "I can only think of one person who would be crazy enough to want to work for you."

"Do you think they'd say yes?"

"I'm pretty sure he's crazy enough to do that."

They raised their glasses in a toast to Mrs B and to Charlie coming on board full-time. The warmth of the vodka penetrated Declan's body. He was more relaxed than he had been in a long time.

"You know, of all the stories Luke told me, the strangest one involved you."

"Oh?"

"Yeah. He had this strong suspicion that you were attracted to me. Those weren't his exact words, but…"

Charlie blushed. "Now why would you believe a guy like that?" Charlie asked. "Maybe he was just testing you to see if you'd cheat on him if someone expressed any interest?"

"Maybe," Declan said with a smile.

* * * *

They left the bar and walked back to the office. When they got to the door Declan looked at Charlie. "I need to know—was Luke right about you being attracted to me?"

Charlie looked down. "Even if I were attracted to you, which I'm not saying I am, but it would not necessarily be beyond the realm of reason given…your looks… It would be inappropriate since you're my boss, and a relationship, if it were to develop into one, which I'm not saying it would, would not be in the best interests of our…working relationship…"

Before Charlie could finish, Declan leaned in and kissed him. Not a drunken one like before but a deep, passionate kiss. Charlie's body tingled with excitement as arousal took hold of every fibre of his being. He wrapped his arms around Declan, and pressed into him, wishing this moment would last forever. Declan came up for air, but Charlie wasn't finished. He grabbed a hold of Declan and kissed him again.

Declan laughed. "Well, I guess I got my answer." He paused then said, "I'm gonna regret this, but do you want to come upstairs?"

Charlie beamed, then the smile on his face slowly melted.

"What's wrong?" Declan asked.

Charlie backed away. "I want to, but I can't. Not yet. This is too important. I don't want to fuck this up."

Declan nodded his head. "I can wait."

As Charlie walked away Declan called out, "You're an exceptional man, Charlie Watts. I'm lucky to have met you."

Charlie turned back. "I'm the lucky one."

"See you tomorrow then?"

Charlie grinned. "You couldn't keep me away."

Charlie walked home in a daze. His life had changed so much over the past few weeks. He had a job he loved. He was finally away from his parents. And Declan... That was complicated. But there was no rush to figure that out. Charlie realised for the first time in his life he was exactly where he was supposed to be.

Want to see more from this author?
Here's a taster for you to enjoy!

The Declan Hunt Mysteries:
Hoodoo House
Peter E. Fenton

Coming Summer 2024

Excerpt

Mrs Cameron stood at the kitchen sink doing up the last of the dishes from the breakfast biscuits that were baking in the oven. She stared at the boarded-up kitchen window, the result of a strong dust devil that had hit the north side of the house and torn off a section of the roof a week ago. A sheet of plywood shielded it from falling debris from the repair work on the decaying roof of the one-hundred-and five-year-old wood-framed house.

With the light from the outside cut off, the window glass became a dim mirror reflecting the activity and inhabitants of the kitchen. Mrs Cameron looked at her reflection and saw a woman with a jowly countenance and hair that had gone completely white. She hadn't turned full-on apple doll yet, but it was inevitable — unless, of course, death took her first.

When did you become so old?

Her reverie was interrupted.

"What's this symbol called?" Henry asked, holding up a piece of paper and pointing to an indiscernible character. He was surrounded by the remains of his math homework spread all over the table.

"Well, you're gonna have to bring it here. My eyes aren't telescopes."

Henry scooted the chair back, brought her the paper and held it up to her milky blue eyes. She pulled her reading glasses out of the pocket of her apron and held them in front of her, like a jeweller would hold their loupe while examining a rare gem.

"It's a pi," she said.

"I like pie," he said with a smile.

Mrs Cameron raised an eyebrow. "Now how long have you been waiting to tell that joke?"

"It's not so much a joke as witty wordplay," he said, heading back to his chair.

This from a fourteen-year-old, she thought, shaking her head. Henry often seemed wiser than a boy of his age. Although he was only her ward, she thought of him as the child she'd never had.

She patted him on the shoulder. "Now, clear up your mess and set the table. Then you can go and tell Mr Tulle breakfast is ready."

Henry quickly did as he was told.

Mrs Cameron smiled. The kitchen was her domain and nobody in Hoodoo House would dare to question anything she ordered here or, frankly, anywhere else on the property. She was the housekeeper, cook, scullery maid and holder of just about every other staff position. She was as permanent a fixture in the building as the ancient stove or the kitchen's large wooden prep table and she loved every scrap of wood and broken-down fixture in it...almost as much as she loved young Henry.

Writer Malcolm Tulle, however…

An acrid smell hit her nostrils.

"Damn."

She ran towards the oven. A cloud of smoke filled the air as she pulled out the tray of burnt baking.

"You damned fool," she said to herself as she removed the biscuits and placed them on a cooling rack. She could scrape the char off the best ones and they'd be fine. The others she'd save for crumbling up for the chickens, or perhaps the centres could be used for stuffing. Either way, they would end up inside a chicken.

She checked the coffee perking in the pot and dabbed the fat off of the freshly cooked bacon. She turned back towards the kitchen table and was startled to see Henry standing at the door, his eyes wide, his mouth open. It took him a moment to speak.

"There's something wrong with Mr Tulle."

"Well, what's wrong?" she asked.

"He's asleep on his desk and he's lying in his own sick."

Mrs Cameron hurried to the writing room. Henry followed. She went to the desk and examined the prone man. She'd been around long enough to know when something wasn't alive, but to be certain she checked for a pulse. Nothing.

"Henry, leave the room and don't touch anything. And don't come back in here."

She scurried past the boy and headed back to the kitchen where she called the doctor…and the police.

About the Author

Peter E. Fenton's first book, *The Woodcarver's Model* came out in April of 2022 and was a four time nominee in the Goodreads M/M Romance Readers' Choice Awards. His latest novel, *Mann Hunt* will be released in August of 2023 and is the first in the three part *Declan Hunt Mysteries* series.

His previous work was focused on writing for the stage, with award-winning productions of *The Giant's Garden*, *Newfoundland Mary*, and *Bemused*. His newest play, *The Detective Disappears* will tour in Canada in the fall of 2023.

He spent many years working in palaeontology in remote locations including the Canadian Rockies, the Northwest Territories and Nunavut.

Peter lives in Toronto, Canada with his partner of more than twenty years, Scott White. At heart, he is an incredible romantic.

Peter loves to hear from readers. You can find his contact information, website details and author profile page at https://www.firstforromance.com/

PUBLISHING

Sign up for our newsletter and find out about all our romance book releases, eBook sales and promotions, sneak peeks and FREE romance books!